I

WAS

HERE

I
WAS
HERE

BY

Gayle Forman

VIKING
An Imprint of Penguin Group (USA)

VIKING

Published by the Penguin Group
Penguin Group (USA) LLC
375 Hudson Street
New York, New York 10014

USA ◆ Canada ◆ UK ◆ Ireland ◆ Australia ◆ New Zealand ◆ India ◆ South Africa ◆ China

penguin.com
A Penguin Random House Company

First published in the United States of America by Viking,
an imprint of Penguin Group (USA) LLC, 2015

LIBRARY OF CONGRESS CATALOGING-IN-PUBLICATION DATA
Forman, Gayle.
I was here / Gayle Forman.
pages cm
Summary: In an attempt to understand why her best friend committed suicide, eighteen-year-old
Cody Reynolds retraces her dead friend's footsteps and makes some startling discoveries.
ISBN 978-0-451-47537-4
[1. Suicide—Fiction. 2. Grief—Fiction. 3. Best friends—Fiction. 4. Friendship—Fiction.
5. Mystery and detective stories. 6. Washington (State)—Fiction.] I. Title.
PZ7.F75876Iam 2015   [Fic]—dc23   2014011445

Printed in U.S.A.

3   5   7   9   10   8   6   4

Set in Berkeley Oldstyle   Designed by Nancy Brennan

For Suzy Gonzales

x x x

I
WAS
HERE

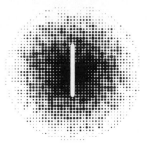

The day after Meg died, I received this letter:

I regret to inform you that I have had to take my own life. This decision has been a long time coming, and was mine alone to make. I know it will cause you pain, and for that I am sorry, but please know that I needed to end my own pain. This has nothing to do with you and everything to do with me. It's not your fault.

Meg

She emailed copies of the letter to her parents and to me, and to the Tacoma police department, along with another note informing them which motel she was at, which room she was in, what poison she had ingested, and how her body should be safely handled. On the pillow at the motel room was another note—instructing the maid to call the police and not touch her body—along with a fifty-dollar tip.

She sent the emails on a time delay. So that she would be long gone by the time we received them.

Of course, I didn't know any of that until later. So when I first read Meg's email on the computer at our town's public library, I thought it had to be some kind of joke. Or a hoax. I called Meg, and when she didn't answer, I called her parents.

"Did you get Meg's email?" I asked them.

"What email?"

There are memorial services. And there are vigils. And then there are prayer circles. It gets hard to keep them straight. At the vigils, you hold candles, but sometimes you do that at the prayer circles. At the memorial services, people talk, though what is there to say?

It was bad enough she had to die. On purpose. But for subjecting me to all of this, I could kill her.

"Cody, are you ready?" Tricia calls.

It is late on a Thursday afternoon, and we are going to the fifth service in the past month. This one is a candlelight vigil. I think.

I emerge from my bedroom. My mother is zipping up the black cocktail dress she picked up from the Goodwill after Meg died. She's been using it as her funeral dress, but I'm sure that once this blows over, it'll go into rotation as a going-out dress. She looks hot in it. Like so many people in town, mourning becomes her.

"Why aren't you dressed?" she asks.

"All my nice clothes are dirty."

"What nice clothes?"

"Fine, all my vaguely funereal clothes are dirty."

"Dirty never stopped you before."

We glare at each other. When I was eight, Tricia announced I was old enough to do my own laundry. I hate doing laundry. You can see where this leads.

"I don't get why we have to go to another one," I say.

"Because the town needs to process."

"Cheese needs to process. The town needs to find another drama to distract itself with."

There are fifteen hundred and seventy-four people in our town, according to the fading sign on the highway. "Fifteen hundred and seventy-three," Meg said when she escaped to college in Tacoma on a full scholarship last fall. "Fifteen hundred and seventy-two when you come to Seattle and we get our apartment together," she'd added.

It remains stuck at fifteen hundred and seventy-three now, and I suspect it'll stay there until someone else is born or dies. Most people don't leave. Even when Tammy Henthoff and Matt Parner left their respective spouses to run off together—the gossip that was the hottest news before Meg—they moved to an RV park on the edge of town.

"Do I have to go?" I'm not sure why I bother to ask her this. Tricia is my mother, but she's not an authority in that way. I know I have to go, and I know why. For Joe and Sue.

They're Meg's parents. Or they were. I keep stumbling over the verb tenses. Do you cease being someone's parents because they died? Because they died on purpose?

Joe and Sue look blasted into heartbreak, the hollows under their eyes so deep, I don't see how they'll ever go away. And it's for them I find my least stinky dress and put it on. I get ready to sing. Again.

Amazing Grace. How Vile the Sound.

I've written a dozen mental eulogies for Meg, imagining all the things I might say about her. Like how when we met in the first week of kindergarten, she made me a picture of us, with both of our names, and some words I didn't understand because unlike Meg, I could not yet read or write. "It says 'best friends,'" she explained. And like all things Meg wanted or predicted, it turned out to be true. I might talk about how I still have that picture. I keep it in a metal toolbox that houses all my most important things, and it is creased from age and multiple viewings.

Or I might talk about how Meg knew things about people that they might not know themselves. She knew the precise number of times in a row everyone generally sneezed; there's a pattern to it, apparently. I was three; Scottie and Sue four, Joe was two, Meg was five. Meg could also remember what you wore for every picture day, every Halloween. She was like the archive of my history. And also the creator of it too, because almost every one of those Halloweens was spent with her, usually in some costume she dreamed up.

Or I might talk about Meg and her obsession with firefly songs. It started in ninth grade, when she picked up a vinyl single by a band called Heavens to Betsy. She dragged me back to her room and played me the scratchy record on that old turntable she'd bought at a church jumble sale for a dollar and rewired herself, with a little help from YouTube instructional videos. *And you will never know how it feels to light up the sky. You will never know how it feels to be a firefly,* Corin Tucker sang in a voice so simultaneously strong and vulnerable that it seemed almost inhuman.

After the Heavens to Betsy discovery, Meg went on a mission to find every good firefly song ever written. In true Meg fashion, within a few weeks she'd amassed an exhaustive list. "Have you ever even *seen* a firefly?" I'd asked her as she worked on her playlist.

I knew she hadn't. Like me, Meg had never been east of the Rockies. "I have time," she'd said, opening her arms, as if to demonstrate just how much life there was out there, waiting for her.

x x x

Joe and Sue asked me to speak at that first service, the big one that should've been held in the Catholic church the Garcias had attended for years, but wasn't, because Father Grady, though a friend of the family, was a rules man. He told the Garcias that Meg had committed a cardinal sin and therefore her soul wouldn't be admitted to heaven, nor her body to the Catholic cemetery.

The last bit was theoretical. It took a while for the police to release her body. Apparently the poison she'd used was rare, though anyone who knew Meg wouldn't be surprised by this. She never wore clothes from chain stores, always listened to bands no one else had heard of. Naturally, she found some obscure poison to swallow.

So the casket everyone sobbed over at that first big service was empty, and there was no burial. I overheard Meg's uncle Xavier tell his girlfriend that maybe it would be better if there never was one. No one knew what to write on the gravestone. "Everything sounds like a reproach," he said.

I tried to write a eulogy for that service. I did. I pulled out the disc Meg had burned of firefly songs for inspiration. The third one up was the Bishop Allen track "Fireflies." I don't know if I had ever really listened to the words before, because when I did now, they were like a smack from her grave: *It says you can still forgive her. And she will forgive you back.*

But I don't know that I can. And I don't know that she did.

I told Joe and Sue that I was sorry, that I couldn't give a eulogy because I couldn't think of anything to say.

It was the first time I ever lied to them.

x x x

Today's service is being held in the Rotary Club, so it's not one of the official religious services, though the speaker appears to be some kind of reverend. I'm not sure where they keep coming from, all these speakers who didn't really know Meg. After it's over, Sue invites me over for yet another reception at the house.

I used to spend so much time at Meg's house that I could tell what kind of mood Sue was in by what I smelled when I walked through the door. Butter meant baking, which meant she was melancholy and needed cheering. Spicy meant she was happy and making hot Mexican food for Joe, even though it hurt her stomach. Popcorn meant that she was in bed, in the dark, not cooking anything, and Meg and Scottie were left to their own devices, which meant a buffet of microwave snack foods. On those days, Joe would joke how lucky we kids were to get to pig out like this as he made his way upstairs to check on Sue. We all played along, but usually, after the second or third microwave corn dog, you kind of wanted to throw up.

I know the Garcias so well that when I called that morning after getting Meg's email, I knew even though it was eleven o'clock on a Saturday that Sue would be still in bed but not sleeping; she said she never did learn to sleep in once her kids stopped waking up early. And Joe would have the coffee brewed and the morning paper spread out over the kitchen table. Scottie would be watching cartoons. Consistency was one of the many things I loved about Meg's house. So different from mine, where the earliest Tricia usually woke was noon, and some days you might find her pouring bowls of cereal, and some days you might not find her at all.

But now there's a different kind of constancy about the Garcia household, one that is far less inviting. Still, when Sue asks me over, much as I'd prefer to refuse the invitation, I don't.

x x x

The crowd of cars outside the house is thinner than it was in the early days, when the whole town came on sympathy calls carrying Pyrex dishes. It was a little hard to take, all those casseroles and the "I'm so sorry for your loss"es that accompanied them. Because elsewhere in town, the gossip was flying. "Didn't surprise me. Girl always hung her freak flag high," I heard people whispering in the Circle K. Meg and I both knew that some people said things like that about her—in our town she was like a rose blooming in the desert; it confused folks—but with her dead, this sentiment no longer felt like a badge of honor.

And it wasn't just Meg they went after. At Tricia's bar, I overheard a couple of townies sniping about Sue. "As a mother, I would know if my daughter was *suicidal*." This coming from the mother of Carrie Tarkington, who had slept with half the school. I was about to ask Mrs. Tarkington if, being all-knowing, she knew *that*. But then her friend replied. "Sue? Are you joking? That woman is floating in space on a good day," and I felt sucker-punched by their cruelty. "How would you feel if you'd just lost your child, you bitches?" I sneered. Tricia had to escort me home.

After today's service, Tricia has to work, so she drops me off at the Garcias'. I let myself in. Joe and Sue hug me tight and for a moment longer than is comfortable. I know that they must take some solace in me being here, but I can hear Sue's silent questions when she looks at me, and I know that all the questions boil down to one: *Did you know?*

I don't know what would be worse. If I did know and didn't tell them. Or the truth, which is that even though Meg was my best friend and I have told her everything there is to tell about me and I'd assumed she'd done the same, I'd had no idea. Not a clue.

This decision has been a long time coming, she wrote in her note. A long time coming? How long is that? Weeks? Months? Years? I have known Meg since kindergarten. We have been best friends, sisters almost, ever since. How long has this decision been coming without her telling me? And more to the point, why didn't she tell me?

× × ×

After about ten minutes of sitting in sad polite silence, Scottie, Meg's ten-year-old brother, comes up to me with their—or now his—dog, Samson, on a leash. "Walkies?" he says, to me as much as to Samson.

I nod and stand up. Scottie seems to be the only one who retains any semblance of his former self, which is maybe because he's young, though he's not that young, and he and Meg were close. When Sue would disappear into one of her moods and Joe would disappear to take care of her, Meg was the one to mother Scottie.

It's late April, but no one has alerted the weather. The wind kicks up fierce and cold, with a mean grit. We walk toward the big empty field that everyone lets their dogs shit in, and Scottie unleashes Samson. He bounds off, jubilant, happy in his canine ignorance.

"How are you holding up, Runtmeyer?" I feel false using the old jocular nickname, and I already know how he's doing. But with Meg no longer playing mother hen and Sue and Joe lost in their grief, someone has to at least ask.

"I'm up to level six on Fiend Finder," he says. He shrugs. "I get to play all I want now."

"A side benefit." And then I clamp my hand over my mouth. My bitter gallows humor is not meant for public consumption.

But Scottie lets out a gruff laugh, way too old for his age. "Yeah. Right." He stops and watches Samson sniff a collie's butt.

On the way home, Samson straining at his leash because he knows food is next, Scottie asks me, "You know what I don't get?"

I think we're still taking about video games, so I'm not prepared for what he says next.

"I don't get why she didn't send me the note too."

"Do you even have an email address?" I ask. Like this was her reason.

He rolls his eyes. "I'm ten, not two. I've had one since third grade. Meg emailed me stuff all the time."

"Oh. Well, she probably, probably wanted to spare you."

For a second, his eyes look just as hollowed out as his parents'. "Yeah, she spared me."

x x x

Back at the house, the guests are leaving. I catch Sue dumping a tuna casserole into the garbage. She gives me a guilty look. When I go to hug her good-bye, she stops me. "Can you stay?" she asks in that voice of hers, so quiet, so different from Meg's garrulous one. Meg's voice that could make anyone do anything, anytime.

"Of course."

She gestures toward the living room, where Joe is sitting on the couch, staring into space, ignoring Samson who is begging at his feet for the expected dinner. In the fading twilight, I look at Joe. Meg took after him, with his dark, Mexican looks. He seems like he's aged a thousand years in the past month.

"Cody," he says. One word. And it's enough to make me cry.

"Hi, Joe."

"Sue wants to talk to you; we both do."

My heart starts to hammer, because I wonder if they're finally going to ask me if I knew anything. I had to answer some cursory questions from the police when all this went down, but they had more to do with how Meg might have procured the poison, and I had no idea about any of that except that if Meg wanted something, she usually found a way to get it.

After Meg died, I went and looked up all the suicide signs online. Meg didn't give me any of her prized possessions. She didn't talk about killing herself. I mean, she used to say things like, "If Ms. Dobson gives us another pop quiz, I am going to shoot myself," but does that count?

Sue sits down next to Joe on the worn couch. They look at each other for half a second, but then it's like that hurts too much. They turn to me. Like I'm Switzerland.

"Cascades's term ends next month," they tell me.

I nod. University of the Cascades is the prestigious private college where Meg got a scholarship. The plan had been for both of us to move to Seattle after high school graduation. We'd been talking about this since eighth grade. Both of us at the University of Washington, sharing a dorm room for the first two years, then living off campus for the duration. But then Meg had gotten this amazing full ride at Cascades, a way better package that what the UW offered. As for me, I'd gotten into the UW but without scholarships of any kind. Tricia had made it pretty clear she couldn't help me. "I finally got *myself* out of debt." So in the end, I turned down the UW and decided to stay in town. My plan was to do two years at community college, then transfer to Seattle to be near Meg.

Joe and Sue sit there quietly. I watch Sue pick at her nails.

The cuticles are a complete mess. Finally, she looks up. "The school has been very kind; they've offered to pack up her room and ship everything to us, but I can't bear a stranger's hands touching her things."

"What about her roommates?" Cascades is tiny and hardly has any dorms. Meg lives—lived—off campus in a house shared with some other students.

"Apparently, they've just locked up her room and left it like that. Her rent's paid through the end of the term, but now we should empty it out and bring everything . . ." Her voice catches.

"Home," Joe finishes for her.

It takes me a second to realize what they want, what they're asking me. And at first I'm relieved because it means I don't have to fess up that I didn't know what Meg was contemplating. That the one time in her life *she* might've needed *me*, I failed her. But then, the weight of what they're asking skids and crashes in my stomach. Which isn't to say I won't do it. I will. Of course I will.

"You want me to pack up her things?" I say.

They nod. I nod back. It's the least I can do.

"After your classes end, of course," Sue says.

Officially, my classes end next month. Unofficially, they did the day I got Meg's email. I've got Fs now. Or incompletes. The distinction hardly seems to matter.

"And if you can get the time off work." This from Joe.

He says it respectfully, as if I have an important job. I clean houses. The people I work for, like everyone in this town, know about Meg, and they've all been very nice, telling me to take all the time I need. But empty hours to contemplate Meg aren't what I need.

"I can go whenever," I say. "Tomorrow if you want."

"She didn't have very much. You can take the car," Joe says. Joe and Sue have one car, and it's like a NASA expedition how they plot out their days so Sue can drop Joe off at work and get Scottie to school and get herself to work and then scoop them all back up again at the end of the day. On weekends, it's more of the same, doing the grocery shopping and all the errands there's no time for during the week. I don't have a car. Occasionally, very occasionally, Tricia lets me use hers.

"Why don't I take the bus? She doesn't have that much. Didn't."

Joe and Sue look relieved. "We'll pay for your bus tickets. You can ship any extra boxes UPS," Joe says.

"And you don't have to bring everything back." Sue pauses. "Just the important things."

I nod. They look so grateful that I have to look away. The trip is nothing: a three-day errand. A day to get there, a day to pack, a day to get home. It's the kind of thing Meg would've offered to do without having to be asked first.

Every so often, I'll read some hopeful article about how Tacoma is gentrifying so much that it's rivaling Seattle. But when my bus pulls in to the deserted downtown, it all feels kind of desperate, like it's trying too hard and failing. Sort of like some of Tricia's friends from the bar, fifty-year-old women who wear miniskirts and platforms and makeup but aren't fooling anyone. *Mutton disguised as lamb* is how the guys in our town describe them.

When Meg left, I promised I'd come visit once a month, but I wound up coming only one time, last October. I'd bought a ticket to Tacoma, but when the bus pulled into Seattle, Meg was waiting at the station. She'd had this idea we'd spend the day roaming Capitol Hill, have dinner at some hole-in-the-wall dumpling place in Chinatown, and go out to see a band play in Belltown—all the things we'd talked about doing when we moved here together. She was so hyped about the plan; I couldn't quite tell if the day was her idea of a sales pitch, or a consolation prize.

Either way, it was a bust. The weather was rainy and cold, whereas back home it had been clear and cold. Another reason not to move to Seattle, I told myself. And none of the places we visited—the vintage clothing shops and comic book stores and coffeehouses—seemed as cool as I'd thought they would be. At least that's what I told Meg.

"Sorry," she said. Not sarcastically, but sincerely, as though Seattle's shortcomings were her fault.

It was a lie, though. Seattle was great. Even with the rotten weather, I'd have loved living here. But I'm sure I'd have loved living in New York or Tahiti or a million other places I'd never get to.

We were meant to go see a band play that night, some people Meg knew, but I begged off, claiming I was tired. We went back to her house in Tacoma. I was supposed to stay most of the next day, but I told her I had a sore throat, and caught an early bus home.

Meg invited me to come again, but I always had reasons why I couldn't: my schedule was busy, bus fare wasn't cheap. Both of which were true, even if they weren't the truth.

x x x

It takes two buses to get from downtown to Cascades' tiny, leafy waterfront campus. Joe had instructed me to go to the administration building to get some papers and a key. Even though Meg had lived off campus, the university runs all student housing. When I explain who I am, they immediately know why I'm here, because I get that look. I hate that look, and I've come to know it well: practiced empathy.

"We're so sorry for your loss," the lady says. She is fat and wearing the drapey kind of clothes that only make her bigger. "We've been holding weekly support groups for those impacted by Megan's death. If you'd care to join us for one, there's another gathering coming up."

Megan? Nobody but her grandparents called her that.

She hands me some literature, a color copy with a big smiling picture of Meg that I don't recognize. On top it says *Lifeline* with hearts dotting the *i*'s. "It's Monday afternoon."

"'Fraid I'll be gone by then."

"Oh, shame." She pauses. "They've been very cathartic for the campus community. People are quite shocked."

Shocked is not the word for it. Shocked is when I finally got Tricia to tell me who my father was, only to find out that up until I was nine, he'd been living not twenty miles away from us. What happened with Meg is something altogether different; it's like waking up one morning and finding out you live on Mars now.

"I'm only here for a night," I tell her.

"Oh, shame," she says again.

"Yes, shame."

She hands me a set of keys and gives me directions to the house and tells me to call if I need anything and I'm out the door before she hands me a card. Or worse, gives me a hug.

At Meg's old house, no one answers when I knock, so I let myself in. Inside it smells of beer and pizza and bongwater, and something else, the ammonia scent of a dirty cat box. There's the sound of jam bands, Phish or Widespread Panic, the kind of bad hippie music, I muse, that would make Meg want to shoot herself. Then I catch myself and remember that she did, in effect, shoot herself.

"Who are you?" A tall and ridiculously pretty girl stands before me. She's wearing a tie-dyed peace sign T-shirt, and she is sneering.

"I'm Cody. Reynolds. I'm here for Meg. For her stuff."

She stiffens. As if Meg, the mention of her, the existence of her, has completely harshed her mellow. I already hate this girl. And when she introduces herself as Tree, I wish Meg were around so we could give each other that imperceptible look we'd developed over the years to register our mutual disdain. *Tree?*

"Are you one of her roommates?" I ask. When she first arrived, Meg sent me long emails about her classes, her professors, her work-study job, and, in some cases, these hilarious character portraits of each roommate, actual charcoal drawings she scanned for me. It was the kind of thing that normally I'd have adored, reveling in her haughtiness, because that's how it had always been: Meg and Me Versus the World. Back home, they referred to us as the Pod. But reading the emails, I had the sense that she was purposefully playing up her roommates' faults to make me feel better, which only made me feel worse. In any case, I didn't recall a Tree.

"I'm friends with Rich," bitchy hippie Tree replies to me. Ahh, Stoner Richard, as Meg called him. I met him last time I was here.

"I'll get on with it," I say.

"You do that," Tree replies. Such open hostility is a shock after a month of people tippy-toeing around me.

Outside Meg's door, I half expect one of those shrines that have popped up in town; whenever I see one, I want to yank the heads off the flowers or throw the candles.

But that's not what I find. There's an album cover pasted on the door: Poison Idea's *Feel the Darkness*. The image is of a guy holding a revolver to his head. *This* is her roommates' idea of a memorial?

Breathing hard, I unlock the door and turn the knob. Inside, it's not what I expect either. Meg was notoriously messy, her bedroom at home full of teetering stacks of books and CDs, drawings, half-completed DIY projects: a lamp she was trying to rewire, a Super 8 film she was trying to edit. Sue said that her roommates had just locked the door and left it as was, but it looks like someone has been in here. The bed is made. And much of her stuff is already neatly folded. There are unassembled boxes under the bed.

It will take two hours to do this at most. Had I known, I would've taken the Garcias' car and done it as a day-trip.

Sue and Joe had offered me money for a motel, but I didn't accept it. I know how little they have, how every spare cent went toward Meg's education, which, even with a full scholarship, still had all kinds of hidden costs. And her death has been a whole other expense. I said I would sleep here. But now that I'm in her room, I can't help thinking of the last time—the only time—I slept here.

Meg and I have shared beds, cots, sleeping bags, without a problem since we were little. But the night of my visit, I'd lain in bed awake next to a soundly sleeping Meg. She was snoring slightly and I kept kicking her, like it was her snoring that was keeping me awake. When we got up Sunday morning, something mean and hard had taken root in my belly, and I felt myself itching for a fight. But the last thing I'd wanted to do was fight with Meg. She hadn't done anything. She was my best friend. So I'd left early. And not because of any sore throat.

I go back downstairs. The music has changed from Phish to something a little more rocking, The Black Keys, I think. Which is better, if a strange turn. There's a group of people sitting on a purple velour couch, divvying up a pizza and a twelve-pack. Tree is with them, so I walk on by, ignoring them, ignoring the smell of pizza that makes my stomach gurgle because I haven't eaten anything except for a Little Debbie snack cake on the bus.

Outside, it's misting. I walk a ways until I get to a stretch of diners. I sit down at one and order a coffee, and when the waitress gives me a dirty look, I get an anytime $2.99 breakfast and figure that this earns me the right to camp here for the night.

After a few hours and four or five refills, she mostly leaves me be. I take out my book, wishing I'd brought some page-turnery thriller. But Mrs. Banks, the town librarian, has me on a Central European author kick these days. She goes through phases like that with me. Has done ever since I was twelve and she spotted me reading a Jackie Collins novel at Tricia's bar where I sometimes had to hang out when Tricia worked. Mrs. Banks asked what else I liked to read, and I rattled off a few titles, mostly paperbacks Tricia had brought home from the break room. "You're quite a reader," Mrs. Banks said, and then she invited me to come to the library the following week. When I did, she got me signed up for a card and loaned me copies of *Jane Eyre* and *Pride and Prejudice*. "When you finish, tell me if you like them, and I'll get you something else."

I read them in three days. I'd liked *Jane Eyre* best, even though I hated Mr. Rochester and wished he'd died in the fire. Mrs. Banks had smiled at that, then handed me *Persuasion* and

Wuthering Heights. I tore through those in a few days. From that point on, I would go into the library at least once a week to see what books she had for me. It seemed amazing that our tiny branch had such an endless stock of books, and it was years later that I'd learned that Mrs. Banks was special-ordering books through interlibrary loan that she thought I'd like.

But tonight the contemplative Milan Kundera she gave me is making my eyelids heavy. Every time they flutter closed, that waitress, as if possessing radar, comes by to refill my coffee even though I haven't touched it since the last refill.

I hold out until about five in the morning and then pay my bill and leave a big tip because I'm not sure if the waitress was being rude by not letting me sleep or if she was keeping me from getting kicked out. I wander around the campus until the library opens at seven, and then I find a quiet corner and fall asleep for a few hours.

When I make my way back to Meg's house, a guy and a girl are drinking coffee on the porch.

"Hey," the guy says. "Cody, right?"

"Yeah."

"Richard," he says.

"Right. We met before," I say. He doesn't seem to remember. He was probably too stoned.

"I'm Alice," the girl says. I remember Meg mentioning a new roommate moving in for the winter term, taking the place of some other girl who transferred out after one semester.

"Where'd you go?" he asks.

"I stayed in a motel," I lie.

"Not the Starline!" Alice asks in alarm.

"What?" It takes me a second to realize that the Starline is *the* motel. Meg's motel. "No, some other dive."

"Would you like some coffee?" Alice asks.

All the coffee I drank last night has turned acidic in my stomach, and though I'm hazy and exhausted, I can't fathom drinking any more. I shake my head.

"Wanna smoke a bowl?" Stoner Richard asks.

"Richard," Alice swats at him. "She has to pack up all that *stuff*. I don't think she wants to be stoned."

"I'd think she'd *wanna* be stoned," Stoner Richard replies.

"I'm good," I say. But the sun is fighting its way out of the thin haze of cloud and it's making everything so bright that I feel dizzy.

"Sit down. Eat something," Alice says. "I'm practicing making bread, and I have a new loaf."

"It's slightly less bricklike than usual," Richard promises.

"It's good." Alice pauses. "If you slather it with lots of butter and honey."

I don't want the bread. I didn't want to get to know these people before, and I certainly don't want to now. But Alice is gone and back with the bread before I know it. The bread is kind of dense and chewy, but she's right; with butter and honey, it's decent.

I finish it up and brush the crumbs from my lap. "Well, I'd better get to it." I start toward the door. "Though someone already did the heavy lifting. Do you know who packed up her stuff like that?"

Stoner Richard and Alice look at each other. "That's how she left the room," Alice says. "She packed it up herself."

"Girl was on top of shit till the bitter end," Richard adds. He looks at me and grimaces. "Sorry."

"Don't be sorry. It saves me work," I say. And my voice sounds so nonchalant, like this is such a load off my plate.

x   x   x

It takes about three hours to pack the rest of her stuff. I pull out holey T-shirts and underwear because why do they need that? I throw away her stacks of music magazines, piled in a corner. I'm not sure what to do about her bed sheets because they still smell like her, and I have no idea if her scent will do to Sue what it's doing to me, which is making me remember Meg in such a real visceral way—sleepovers and dance parties and those talks we would have until three in the morning that would make us feel lousy the next day because we'd slept like hell but also feel good because the talks were like blood transfusions, moments of realness and hope that were pinpricks of light in the dark fabric of small-town life.

I am tempted to inhale those sheets. If I do, maybe it will be enough to erase everything. But you can only hold your breath for so long. Eventually, I'll have to exhale her, and then it'll be like those mornings, when I wake up, forgetting before remembering.

x   x   x

The UPS place is downtown and I'll have to get a taxi, cart the stuff over, ship it, come back for the duffels, and be ready to catch the last bus at seven. Downstairs, Alice and Stoner Richard are where I left them. It's unclear to me if these students at this supposedly well-regarded college ever actually study.

"I'm pretty much done," I tell them. "Just have to close the boxes and I'll be out of here."

"We'll get the cats for you before you go," Stoner Richard offers.

"The cats?"

"Meg's two kittens," Alice says. She looks at me and cocks her head to the side. "She didn't tell you about them?"

I refuse to show any surprise. Or hurt. "I don't know anything about any cats," I say.

"She found these two stray kittens a couple months ago. They were totally emaciated and sick."

"Nasty shit coming out of their eyes," Stoner Richard adds.

"Yes, they had some kind of eye infection. Among other maladies. Meg took them in. She spent a ton of money at the animal hospital on treatments, and then she nursed them back to health. She loved those kittens." She shakes her head. "That's what was the biggest surprise to me. That she'd go through all that trouble for the kittens and then, you know. . . ."

"Yeah, well, Meg worked in mysterious ways," I say. The bitterness is so strong, I swear they must be able to smell it on my breath. "And the cats are of no concern to me."

"But someone has to take them," Alice says. "The house has been looking out for them, but we're not supposed to have pets and we're all leaving for the summer and none of us can take them."

I shrug. "I'm sure you'll think of something."

"Have you seen these kittens?" Alice goes to the side of the house and starts making kissing sounds, and soon enough two tiny fur balls bound into the living room. "This one's Pete," she says, pointing to the mostly gray one with a black splodge on its nose. "And the other one's Repeat."

Pete and Repeat went out in a boat. Pete fell out. Who was saved? Meg's uncle Xavier told us this joke, and we used to torment each other with it. Repeat. Repeat. Repeat.

Alice puts a kitten in my arms, where it immediately starts doing that pawing thing that cats do when they're trying to find milk. But then it gives up and falls asleep, a little ball against my chest. Something tickles inside, an echo from another time when it wasn't all frozen in there.

The cat starts to purr, and I'm screwed. "Is there, like, an animal shelter here?"

"There is, but there are dozens of cats there, and they only keep them for three days before, you know." Alice mimes a knife to the throat.

Pete, or maybe it's Repeat, is still purring in my arms. I can't bring them home. Tricia would have a shitfit. She'd refuse to let them come inside, and then they'd get eaten by coyotes or killed by the cold in no time. I could ask if Sue and Joe wanted them, but I've seen the way Samson goes after cats.

"Seattle has a few no-kill shelters," Stoner Richard says. "I saw an Animal Liberation Front thing about it."

I sigh. "Fine. I'll swing up to Seattle on my way out of town and drop the cats off."

Stoner Richard laughs. "It's not like dry cleaning. You can't just drop them off. You have to make an appointment for, like, an intake or something."

"When have you ever had anything dry-cleaned?" Alice asks him.

Pete/Repeat mewls in my arms. Alice looks at me. "How long is your drive back?"

"Seven hours, plus I have to ship the boxes."

She looks at me and then at Stoner Richard. "It's three now. Maybe you should go up to Seattle and bring the cats to a shelter, and you can leave first thing tomorrow."

"Can't *you* bring the cats to a shelter?" I ask her. "You seem to have it all worked out."

"I have a Women's Studies paper I need to work on."

"What about after you finish?"

She falters for a second. "No. Those cats were Meg's thing. I don't feel right sending them to a shelter."

"Oh, so you'll leave the dirty work to me?" I hear the anger in my voice, and I know that it's not Alice who's left me the dirty work, but when she cringes, I get a grim twist of satisfaction.

"Dude. I'll drive you to Seattle," Stoner Richard says. "We'll get the felines settled, and you can come here and get out of town first thing in the morning." He seems like he wants to be rid of me as much as I want to be rid of him. At least it's mutual.

Seattle pet shelters, it turns out, are harder to get into than the hippest velvet-rope night clubs. The first two are full, and no amount of begging works. The third one has space, but it requires an application and a copy of the cats' vet records. I tell the pierced girl with her hipster no-leather shoes that I'm leaving town, that I have the cats in the car, and she gives me the most snide look in the world and tells me that I should've thought of this before I went and adopted a pet. I almost smack her.

"Wanna smoke that bowl now?" Stoner Richard asks after strike three. It's eight o'clock and the shelters are all closed for the night.

"No."

"You wanna go to a club or something? Blow off steam? Since we're in Seattle?"

I'm exhausted from the night before and I don't want to be here with Stoner Richard and I'm trying to figure out how I'll get vet records when tomorrow is Sunday. I start to beg off but then Richard says: "We can go to one of those hole-in-the-walls that Meg liked to go to. Once in a while she'd deign to let us tag along." He pauses. "She had a whole klatch of friends up here."

I'm momentarily stunned by Richard's use of both *deign* and *klatch*. But the truth is, I do actually want to see these places. I think of the club we were meant to have gone to the weekend I came to visit. All the clubs we were meant to have gone to all the weekends I didn't come to visit. I know how excited Meg was to be amid the music scene, though after the time I visited her, the breathless emails about it all started to taper off and then stopped.

"What about the kittens?" I ask Richard.

"They'll be fine in the car," Richard says. "It's, like, fifty-five degrees tonight. They have food and water." He points to Pete and Repeat, who, having squealed and yowled the entire drive up, are now quietly nestled together in their carrier.

We drive to a club in Fremont by the canal. Before we go in, Richard lights up a small pipe and smokes out the window. "Don't want to give the kitties a contact high," he jokes.

As we pay our covers, he tells me that Meg went here a lot. I nod as if I know this. The place is empty. It smells of stale beer, bleach, and desperation. I leave Richard at the bar and go play pinball by myself. By ten o'clock the room starts filling up, and by eleven the first of the night's bands comes on, a very feedback-heavy outfit whose lead singer growls more than he sings.

After a few okay songs, Stoner Richard finds me. "That's Ben McCallister," he says, pointing to the guitar player/growler.

"Uh-huh," I say. I've never heard of him. It takes a while for the Seattle scene to filter all the way down to Shitburg.

"Did Meg mention him to you?"

"No" is all I say. Though I want to scream at people to stop asking me that. Because I don't know what Meg told me and I ignored, and what Meg didn't tell me. Although one thing I know for damn certain is that she didn't tell me that she was in such intense pain that the only way to take it away was to order a batch of industrial poison and drink it down.

Stoner Richard is going on about Meg being obsessed with the guy, and it's all sort of white noise, because Meg was obsessed with a lot of guitar players in her day and in her way. But then this particular guitar player, this Ben McCallister, he stops to take a pull from his beer, holding the long neck of the bottle between two fingers, his guitar hanging off his lanky hip like it's a limb. And then he turns out toward the crowd and the lights are on him, bright, and I see that his eyes are impossibly blue and he does this thing, like he's shielding his eyes from the sun and looking out into the crowd for someone, but the way he does it, it makes something click.

"Oh, that must be Tragic Guitar Hero," I say.

"Nothing heroic about that guy," Stoner Richard says.

Tragic Guitar Hero. I do remember her writing about him once or twice, which was notable because she hadn't written about any guys. At first it seemed she was into his band and she crushed on him the way that she always crushed on the guys— and the girls—she met in bands.

Tragic Guitar Hero. She'd told me about his band, retro Sonic Youth–Velvet Underground sound, infused with some modern sensibilities. Typical Meg stuff. But she'd also written about his eyes, so blue, she'd thought he wore contacts. I look at them now. They *are* weirdly blue.

And then I remember a line from one of her emails. Meg had

asked, "Do you remember the advice that Tricia gave us back when she started working at the bar?"

Tricia loved to dispense advice, especially when she had an audience as attentive as Meg. But somehow I'd known right away which pointer Meg was talking about. *Never sleep with the bartender, girls,* Tricia had warned us.

"Why? Because everyone does?" Meg had asked. She loved the way Tricia talked to us, as if we were her friends from the bar, as if either of us was sleeping with anyone.

"There's that," Tricia had replied. "But mostly because you stop getting free drinks."

Meg had written that it held true for Tragic Guitar Heroes, too. And I'd been confused because Meg hadn't mentioned being into this guy or going out with him, let alone sleeping with him, something she had never done, except for that one time that we had both decided didn't really count. And surely if Meg had done something as momentous as sleeping with a guy, she'd have told me. I was going to ask her about it when she came home. And then she didn't.

So that's him. That's Tragic Guitar Hero. He seemed so mythic, and usually attaching a name to a mythical creature tames it. But knowing his name, Ben McCallister, doesn't do that.

I watch the band intently now. He does that thing that rockers do, swiping away at his guitar, leaning into it and into the mic and then stopping playing, grasping the mic like he would a lover's neck. It's all an act. But it's a good one. I can imagine his line of groupies. I just can't believe Meg would be one of them.

"We're the Scarps. Silverfish is up next," Ben McCallister says at the end of their short set.

"You about ready to go?" Stoner Richard asks me.

But I'm not ready. I'm wide-awake and furious at Ben Mc-Callister, who, I now understand, screwed my friend, in more ways than one. Did he treat her like some throwaway groupie? Didn't he realize that this was Meg Garcia he was dealing with? You don't throw Meg away.

"Not yet," I tell Richard, and then I'm up out of my seat and over at the bar where Ben McCallister is standing, drinking another beer and talking to a group of people who are telling him what a great set it was. I march up to him, but once I'm standing right behind him, so close I can see the vertebrae in his neck and the tattoo atop his shoulder blade, I have no idea what to say.

But Ben McCallister seems to know what to say to me. Because after a few seconds' chitchat with the other girls, he turns around and looks at me: "I saw you out there."

Up close, Ben McCallister is much prettier than any boy has a right to be. He has what I can only assume are Irish good looks: black hair, skin that on a girl would be called alabaster but on a rocker is just perfectly pasty. Full, red lips. And the eyes. Meg was right. They look like contacts.

"You saw me out where?" I ask.

"Out there." He points to the tables in the club. "I was looking for a friend of mine; he said he'd come, but it's impossible to see anything with the lights." He mimics shielding his eyes against the glare, just as I'd seen him do from the stage. "But then I saw you"—he pauses for a beat—"like maybe *you* were who I was looking for."

Is this what he does? Use this line? Is it so rehearsed that he even plants the little eye shield squint-into-the-crowd thing during the show? I mean, it's a great line. Because if I was in the crowd, then it's like, *Wow, you were looking for me.* And if I wasn't, well, then you said that nice thing and what a sensitive rocker you must be to believe in something like fate.

Is this the line he used on Meg? Did *this* work on Meg? I shudder to think of my friend falling for this crap, but then with Meg far away from home, with glitter dust in her eyes and guitar fumes up her nose, who knows?

He takes my silence for coyness. "What's your name?"

Will my name ring a bell? Did she mention me to him? "Cody," I say.

"Cody, Cody, Cody." He gives my name a test drive. "It's a cowgirl name," he drawls on. "Where you from, Cowgirl Cody?"

"Cowgirl country."

His smile is slow, like he's intentionally rationing it. "I'd like to visit Cowgirl country. Maybe I can come and you can take me for a ride." He gives me a meaningful look, in case I haven't caught the double entendre.

"You'd probably get bucked right off."

Oh, he likes that. He thinks we're flirting, the dickwad. "Would I, now?"

"Yeah. Horses can smell fear."

Something on his face falters for a second. Then: "What makes you think I'm scared?"

"City dicks always are."

"How do you know I'm a city dick?"

"Well, we're in a city. And you're a dick, aren't you?"

A flurry of confusion passes over his face. I can see he's not sure if I'm just a violent flirter, the kind of girl who'd be hot, if a little angry, in bed, or if this has actually passed over into something else. But he arranges his face into the lazy wannabe rockstar slackery smile. "Who exactly have you been talking to, Cowgirl Cody?" His tone is light, but underneath it's laced with something less pleasant.

I make my voice go all breathy, the way Tricia does so well. "Who have I been talking to, Ben McCallister?" I lean in close.

He leans in close too. Like he thinks we might kiss. Like most of the time, it really *is* this easy for him. "You know who I haven't been talking to much?" My voice is pure breath.

"Who?" he says. He's close enough that I can smell the beer.

"Meg Garcia. I haven't talked to Meg Garcia in more than a month. How about you?"

I've heard the term *recoiling* before, but when I see Ben McCallister snap away from me, I understand what it means. Because he jumps back like a snake—recoiling—before it strikes.

"What the fuck?" he asks. The flirting portion of our evening has ended, and Ben's voice is now truly a growl, a wholly different sound from the bullshit thing he sang with.

"Meg Garcia," I repeat. It's hard to look into his eyes now, but in the last month, I've become an expert at hard things. "Know her?"

"Who are you?" His eyes are burning with something, a kind of fury, and they make the irises icy. They don't seem like contacts anymore.

"Or did you just screw her, and screw her over?"

There's a tap on my shoulder. Stoner Richard is behind me. "I've got to be up in the morning," he tells me.

"I'm done here."

It's getting on for midnight and I've had three hours' sleep and have forgotten to eat another meal, and I'm shaky. I manage to walk to the front of the club before I stumble. Richard grabs my arm, and it's then that I make the mistake of turning around to throw one last death-ray at the cocksure, shallow, pretty-boy poser, Ben McCallister.

I wish I hadn't. Because when I look at Ben McCallister one last time, he has this expression on his face—it's the particular contortion when fury meets guilt. And I know that look. I see it every day in the mirror.

That night, I crash on the velour couch in my clothes. I wake up Sunday morning with Pete and Repeat sleeping on my chest and face. Either I've claimed their couch, or they've claimed me. I sit up in time to see the last roommate, who's been invisible all weekend, drop a cereal bowl in the sink and disappear out the back door.

"Bye, Harry," Alice calls after him.

So that's Harry. According to Meg, he mostly stayed in his room with his many computers and his jars of fermented kimchi.

Alice goes into the kitchen and returns with a cup of coffee for me, which she announces is free-range and fair-trade and shade-farmed in Malawi, and I nod along as if my coffee needs go beyond hot and caffeinated.

I sit on the couch, watching the cats take playful swipes at each other's faces. One of Repeat's ears gets stuck inside out. I flick it straight for him and he mewls. It's the most helpless sound, and like it or not, there's no way I can take these guys to a shelter, no-kill or otherwise.

After I drink my coffee, I take my phone out onto the porch, where someone has set up a bunch of empty beer bottles in bowling-pin formation. I call Tricia. It's only ten thirty, but miraculously, she answers.

"How's the big city?" she asks.

"Big," I reply. "Look, how do you feel about me bringing home a pair of kittens?"

"How do you feel about living someplace else?"

"It would be temporary. Until I find them a good home."

"Forget it, Cody. I raised you for eighteen years. I'm not taking on any more helpless creatures."

There are many things I resent about that sentiment; not the least is the implication that I'm a helpless creature that she's coddled for years. I'd say I raised myself, but that would be unfair to the Garcias. When I got strep throat, it was Sue who noticed the gook on my tonsils and took me to the pediatrician for antibiotics. When I got my period, it was Sue who bought me pads. Tricia had just waved to the tampons in the medicine cabinet "for when the time comes," not seeming to understand how terrifying the thought of inserting anything *supersize absorbency* might be to a twelve-year-old. As for the fifty hours of driving practice I needed to get my driver's license, Tricia logged all of three of them. Joe did the remaining forty-seven, spending countless Sunday afternoons in the car with me and Meg.

"I might be here a few more days," I say. "Can you cover me at Ms. Mason's on Monday? There's forty bucks in it for you."

"Sure." Tricia jumps at the money. She doesn't ask me why I'm delayed or when I'll be home.

I call the Garcias next. It's a little trickier with them because if I mention the kittens, they'll offer to take them in, even though the way Samson is around cats, it would be a disaster. I tell Sue I need a day or two longer to tie up a few of Meg's loose ends. She sounds relieved, doesn't ask any more questions. Just tells me to take as much time as I need. I'm about to hang up. Then she says:

"And, Cody . . ."

I hate those *And, Codys*. It's like a gun being cocked. Like they're about to tell me they know everything. "Yeah?"

There's a long pause on the phone. My heart starts to pound.

"Thank you," is all Sue says.

x x x

Inside, I ask Alice about the best way to find homes for the kittens. Good homes. "You could put an ad on Craigslist, but I heard sometimes those animals wind up in research labs."

"Not helpful."

"Well, we could put up flyers. Everyone likes pictures of kittens."

I sigh. "Fine. How should we do that?"

"Easiest to take a picture of the cats, maybe email it to yourself, add some text, and print them out. . . ." she begins. "It might be simpler to use Meg's laptop; it has a built-in camera."

The eighteen-hundred-dollar computer her parents got her when she left for college. They're still paying off the credit card bill for that.

I go up to her room and find the computer in one of the boxes. I turn it on. It's password protected, but I put in *Runtmeyer*, and her desktop pops up. I bring the computer downstairs while Alice poses the cats together, which is harder than you'd think, and I understand where the expression "herding kittens" comes from. Finally, I snap a picture. Alice quickly uses the desktop publishing function to make up a flyer, and I take the thing back to Meg's printer to print out a test copy.

I'm about to shut down her computer when I stop. Her email program is right there, right at the toolbar on the bottom, and without even thinking about it, I click it open. Immediately, a bunch of new mail downloads—junk, mostly, crap from anonymous people who don't know she's dead, though there are one or two *Meg, We Miss You* emails and one telling her she's going to rot in hell because suicide is a sin. I delete that one.

I'm curious to know what the last email Meg sent was. Who was it to? Was it the suicide note? As I click over to the sent mail folder, I look around as if someone is watching me. But of course, no one is.

It's not the suicide note. She composed that two days before she died, and, as we now know, set it to deliver automatically the day after she died. After the suicide note, she wrote a handful of emails, including one to the library contesting a fine for an overdue book. She knew she was going to die and she was worried about library fines?

How can a person do that? How can they make a decision like that, write an email like that, and then just carry on? If you can do that, can't you *keep* carrying on?

I check more of the sent mails. There's one to Scottie the week she died. It just says: *Hey, Runtmeyer, I love you. Always.*

Was that her good-bye? Did she send *me* a good-bye that I somehow missed?

I scroll back some more, but it's odd: There's a bunch of

messages from the week before she died, then a big six-week gap of nothing, then it picks up again back in January.

I'm about to shut the whole thing down when I see something Meg sent to a bigbadben@podmail.com a few days before she died. I hesitate for moment. Then I open it.

You don't have to worry about me anymore. ☺

It's a different kind of good-bye, and in spite of the happy face I can feel her heartbreak and rejection and defeat, things I've never associated with Meg Garcia.

I go into her inbox and search for emails from bigbadben. They stretch back to the fall, and the first bunch are mostly quick and witty, one-line bits of banter—at least from him. I can't see her responses here, only his side of the conversation, because his email lopped off her side with every reply. The early emails are after Meg first saw him play, a bunch of *thanks for coming to my show, thanks for being so nice when the band sucks so bad*—bullshit self-deprecation that a six-year-old could see through. There are some notes about upcoming gigs.

Then the tone turns more chummy, then flirty—in one message he dubs her Mad Meg, in another he goes on about her electric shitkickers, which must be the orange snakeskin cowboy boots she picked up at the Goodwill and wore everywhere. There are a couple in which he calls her insane because everyone knows that Keith Moon is hands down the best drummer in the world. There are a few more with this kind of rock-talk that Meg could flirt in for days.

But then there's this abrupt change in tone. *It's cool. We're still friends,* he writes. But I can feel the discomfort even here, three steps and four months removed. I look at her sent mail to see what she wrote to him. I see the early stuff, her side of the banter about Keith Moon, but I can't see what prompted the later emails, because again, there's that chunk of missing sent email. Almost all of January and February is wiped out. Weird.

I click back to Ben's emails to her. Another email says, *Don't worry about it.* Another asks her not to call him that late. Another says, not quite so reassuringly, that yeah, they're still friends. Another email asks if she took his Mudhoney T-shirt and if so, can he have it back because it was his dad's. And then I read one of the last ones he sent. One simple sentence, so brutal it makes me hate Ben McCallister with ice in my veins: *Meg, you have to leave me alone.*

Yeah, she left you alone, all right.

Yesterday, I'd found a large T-shirt, black and white and red, neatly folded. I didn't recognize it, so I'd put it in the giveaway pile. I grab it now. It says MUDHONEY. His precious T-shirt. He couldn't even let her have that.

I go back to the laptop and, with fury in my fingers, send a new email to bigbadben from Meg's account, with the subject line: *Back from the Dead.*

Your precious T-shirt, that is, I write. *There's a limit on miracles and second comings.*

I don't sign it and before I have a chance to overthink it, I've already pressed send. It takes all of thirty seconds for regret to set in, and I remember why I hate email. When you write a letter, like, say, to your father, you can scrawl pages and pages of all the things you think are so important, because you don't know where he lives, and even if you did, there'd be all that time to find an envelope and a stamp and by that point, you would've ripped up the letter. But then one time, you track down an email address and you're near a computer with Internet access so you don't have that nice cushion and you type what you're feeling and press send before you have a chance to talk yourself out of it. And then you wait, and wait, and wait, and nothing comes back, so all those things you thought were so important to say, really, they weren't. They weren't worth saying at all.

x   x   x

Alice and I blanket the part of Tacoma near the college with kitten flyers. Then she gets the smart idea of putting them up around this fancy health food store where the rich people shop. We take the bus, and on the way she tells me the place isn't a Whole Foods, but they might get a Whole Foods here soon, and when I say, "How thrilling," Alice says, "I know," not catching the sarcasm at all, so I look out the window, hoping she'll shut up.

The trip is a bust because the store manager won't let us hang flyers inside, so we hand them out to the well-heeled customers with their recycled bags and they all look at us like we're offering them free crack samples.

It's after five by the time we get back, and even perky Alice is flagging. I'm furious and frustrated. I can't believe it is this hard to find homes for kittens, and the whole thing seems like some kind of sick joke, with Meg getting the last laugh.

The house smells of cooking, a weird, unpleasant odor of spices that don't go together—curry, rosemary, too much garlic. Tree is back, sitting on the couch drinking a beer.

"I thought you were leaving," Tree says coolly.

Alice tacks one of the cat flyers onto the bulletin board by

the door, next to a large flyer for tomorrow's Lifeline vigil. She
explains how I'm trying to find homes for Pete and Repeat.

Tree makes a face. "What, you have something against *kit-*
tens?" I ask her.

She wrinkles her nose. "It's just Pete and Repeat. Those
names. They're so *gay*."

"I'm bisexual, and I don't appreciate your derogatory use of
gay," Alice says, attempting to sound scolding but still somehow
managing to sound chipper.

"Well, sorry. I know they're the dead girl's cats, but the
names are still gay."

When she says this, Tree seems less like a hippie than like
one of the rednecks in our town. It makes me hate her both
more and less.

"What names do you prefer?" I ask.

Without hesitating, she says, "Click and Clack. That's what I
call them in my head."

"And you think Pete and Repeat are bad?" Stoner Richard
asks, appearing with a stained apron and a wooden spoon. "I
think we should call them Lenny and Steve."

"Those aren't cat names," Alice says.

"Why not?" Stoner Richard asks, holding up the spoon, the
contents of which bear the strange odor of the kitchen. "Who
wants a bite?"

"What is it?" Tree asks.

"Everything-in-the-fridge stew."

"You should add the cats," Tree says. "Then she wouldn't
have to find homes for them."

"I thought you were a vegetarian," Alice says acidly.

Stoner Richard invites me to share his horrible concoction. It smells like the spices got into a rumble and everyone lost, though that's not the reason I decline. I'm not used to company. I'm not sure when that happened. I used to have friends—not good ones, but friends—from school, from town. I used to be at the Garcias all the time. *Used to* seems far from where I am now.

I leave the roommates to their meal and go into the kitchen for a drink. I bought a liter of Dr Pepper earlier and stowed it in the fridge, but Stoner Richard, in his zeal to cook, has moved everything, so I have to dig for it. And there, in the back, I find a couple of unopened cans of RC and my stomach drops out because the only person I've ever known to drink that is Meg. I fill an old Sonics cup with ice and RC. When I leave here, I don't want to leave even the smallest part of her behind.

I take my drink to the empty porch. But when I get there, I see the porch isn't empty and I stop so suddenly, the drink sloshes out of the cup and onto my shirt.

He's smoking a cigarette, the cherry of it burning menacingly in the dim, gray twilight.

I don't know what surprises me most: that an email I sent actually had an impact. Or that he looks like he wants to kill me.

I don't give him the chance. I put my drink down on the porch railing and turn around and go upstairs, trying to take them slowly, trying to act calm. He's here for the shirt, so I'll get him the shirt. Throw it in his face and get him the hell out of here.

I hear the sound of crunching gravel and then I hear him on the stairs behind me, and I'm not sure what to do, because if I call out for help then I look weak, but I saw that look in his eyes.

It's like he not only got my email but he got my hatred, too, and now it's cycling back to me.

I go into Meg's room. His T-shirt sits on top of one of the piles where I left it. He's followed me upstairs and is standing in her doorway. I hurl the shirt at him. I want him, every part of him, out of my space. But he just stands there. The shirt bounces off him and falls to the floor.

"What the fuck?" he asks.

"What? You wanted your shirt; there's your shirt."

"What kind of person does that?"

"What did I do? You said you wanted your T-shirt—"

"Oh, cut the crap, Cody," he interrupts. And it's so startling to hear him say my name. Not *Cowgirl Cody* in his stupid flirtatious growl. But my name, plain, naked. "You sent me an email from a dead girl. Are you cruel? Or are you also some kind of crazy?"

"You wanted your T-shirt back," I repeat, but now I'm scared, so it loses some of its conviction.

He glares at me. His eyes are a whole different color here, in the pale light of Meg's room. And then I remember Meg's last email. *You don't have to worry about me anymore.* And the anger comes back.

"Couldn't you let her have a souvenir?" I ask. "Maybe you should do that, with the number of girls you probably screw. Hand out a commemorative T-shirt. But asking for it back? Now that's classy."

"You obviously don't know what you're talking about."

"So enlighten me." There's an edge of desperation in my voice. Because he's right. I don't know what I'm talking about.

Maybe if I'd known, if I'd been more clued in these last few months, we wouldn't be standing here.

He stares at me like I am something putrid. And I can't believe that this is the same smarmy flirt from last night.

"What happened?" I ask. "Did you get bored with her? Is that what happens with you and girls? It's a failure of imagination, because if you had gotten to know her at all, you would never have gotten tired of her. I mean, she was Meg Garcia, and who the hell are you, Ben McCallister, to tell *her* to leave *you* alone?" My voice threatens to crack but I won't let it. There will be time to lose it later. There's always time to lose it later.

Ben's face changes now. Ice crystals form. "How do you know what I told her?"

"I saw your email: *Meg, you have to leave me alone.*" It sounded cruel before. But now, coming from me, it just sounds pitiful.

His face is pure annihilation. "I don't know what's more disgusting: reading a dead girl's email, or writing from a dead girl's email."

"Takes disgusting to know disgusting," I say, now a third grader.

He looks at me, shaking his head. And then he leaves, his precious T-shirt a sad forgotten rag on the floor.

It takes about an hour after Ben leaves for me to calm down. And another hour after that to get the nerve to turn Meg's laptop back on. Ben was right about one thing: I didn't really know what I was talking about. The way he said that suggested *Meg* had done something to deserve his assholishness. I know Meg. And I know guys like Ben. I've seen enough of them go through Tricia over the years.

I open Meg's email program again and go into her sent folder, but all I see are the earlier emails, the ones from November: her side of the flirtation, stuff about which musician wrote the best songs, who was the best drummer, which band was the most overhyped, underhyped. And then, before the holidays, it all abruptly stops. It doesn't take a genius to see what happened: They slept together. Then he tossed Meg aside.

But what's less clear is this hole in Meg's messages. I know we didn't correspond much in the winter, but I'm pretty sure she wrote me some emails. I log onto my webmail program just to be sure I didn't imagine it, and while January is kind of a blank, there are messages from February from her in my inbox. But those messages aren't showing up in her sent folder.

That's weird. Did her computer have some sort of virus that ate several weeks of messages? Or did she move her messages somewhere? I start looking through her other applications, not sure what I'm looking for. I open up her calendar, but it's empty. I check the trash, thinking maybe the deleted files will be there. There's a bunch of stuff there, but most of what I open is gibberish. There's one untitled folder. I try to open it, but the computer says I can't open it in the trash. I drag the folder to the desktop and try again, but this time, I get a message that the file is encrypted. I'm afraid it might have some virus that'll fry her computer, so I drag it back to the trash.

It's only nine thirty and I have not eaten, yet again, and I'm thirsty but don't feel like going back downstairs. So I take off my clothes and lie down in Meg's haunted bed, and right now the sheets smelling like her are kind of what I need. I know that by sleeping here, I'll mingle my smell with hers, lessen hers, but somehow that doesn't matter. That's the way it always was before, anyhow.

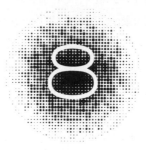

I wake the next morning to a gentle rapping at my door. Bright sunlight is coming through the open shade. I sit up in the bed; my head is full of sand.

There's more knocking.

"Come in." My voice is a croak.

Alice is standing there, another mug of coffee in her hand, harvested by hand by Nicaraguan dwarves, no doubt.

I rub my eyes, accept the coffee with a grunt of gratitude. "What time is it?"

"It's noon."

"Noon? I slept, like, fourteen hours."

"I know." She looks around the room. "Maybe it wasn't Meg. Maybe this room is like that field of poppies in *The Wizard of Oz* and has a soporific effect."

"What do you mean?"

"She slept an awful lot. Like, all the time. If she wasn't hanging out with her 'cool Seattle friends'"—she makes air quotes here—"then she was sleeping."

"Meg likes—liked—to sleep a lot. She ran at such high octane. She needed the sleep to rejuvenate."

Alice looks skeptical. "I never met a person who slept as much as that."

"Also, she had mono in tenth grade," I explain, and as soon as I say it, I remember how awful that year was. Meg was out of school as much as she was in it; whole months she had to do independent study because she was so laid flat.

"Mono?" Alice asks. "Why would that make her tired still?"

"She had a really bad case of it," I reply, remembering how the Garcias wouldn't let me come over and see her, in case I caught it too.

"Sounds more like Epstein-Barr or something." She sits down on the edge of her bed. "I didn't know that about her. I didn't get to know her very well."

"You only moved in a few months ago."

She shrugs. "I know the others. And I don't think they got to know her either. She was a little standoffish."

If Meg loved you, she loved you, and if she didn't . . .The girl didn't suffer fools. "You just have to try to get to know her."

"I *did*," Alice insists.

"You can't have tried that hard. I mean, there couldn't have been a wellspring of love to have put that album cover up on the door."

Alice's Bambi eyes fill with tears. "*We* didn't put that up. She did. And we were told not to take anything down."

Meg put the cover up. I'm sure the suicide experts would call *that* a warning sign, a call for help, but it's hard not to see Meg's twisted sense of humor in it somehow. A final calling card. "Oh," I say. "That actually makes sense."

"It does?" Alice asks. "It seemed so morbid to me. But like I said, I didn't know much about her. I've probably spent more time with you than I did with her," she says wistfully.

"I wish I could say you weren't missing much, but you were."

"Tell me about her. What was she like?"

"What was she like?"

Alice nods.

"She was like . . ." I open my arms to show bigness, the possibilities being endless. I'm not sure if this describes Meg, or how I always felt when I was around her.

Alice looks so beseeching. So I tell her more. I tell her about the time Meg and I got seasonal jobs as telemarketers—the most boring job in the world—and to keep us entertained, Meg did all these different voices for the calls. She wound up doing so well with her voices and selling so much of the crap that she surpassed her daily quota and kept getting sent home early.

I tell her about the time our local library's budget got slashed so badly that it could only open three days a week, which was a major drag for me because when I wasn't at the Garcias', I practically lived at the place. Meg didn't use the library nearly as much as me, but that didn't stop her from going on a mission to stop the closures. She finagled one of those moderately known, now hugely famous, bands she'd become friendly with from her blog to play a Kill Rock Stars, Not Books benefit concert, which brought people from all over the place to our town and raised some twelve thousand dollars, which was great. But because the band was already well known, and Meg was such an attractive poster child, we wound up getting all this national press, and the library was shamed into *extending* its hours.

I tell her about when Scottie, always a picky eater, got so bad that he became anemic. The doctors said he had to eat more iron-rich food, and Sue was beside herself because the kid would not eat healthy, no matter what. But Meg knew Scottie was obsessed with tractors, so she went on eBay and found these tractor-shaped food molds and mashed up potatoes and meat and spinach and put it all in a tractor mold and Scottie gobbled it up.

Then there was the time Tricia and I had the world's worst fight and I ran away to find my dad, even though Tricia claimed he'd moved away years ago. I got as far as Moses Lake before I ran out of money and courage, and just as I was about to start blubbering and lose my shit, Meg and Joe pulled up. They'd been trailing my bus the whole time. But I don't tell Alice about that. Because that's the kind of story you share with a good friend. And I've only ever had one of those.

"So that was Meg," I say, finishing up. "She could do anything. Solve anything for anyone."

Alice pauses, digesting that. "Except for herself."

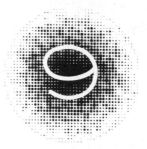

The latest Megan Luisa Garcia Funeral Show is being held at a small promontory down on the Sound. A guitar player and a violinist play that Joan Osborne song "Lumina." Someone reads some Kahlil Gibran. The crowd isn't huge, about twenty people, and everyone's wearing their regular clothes. The guy running the show is from the campus counseling center but, thankfully, he doesn't turn the whole thing into a suicide-prevention public-service announcement, bulleting all the different warning signs that we all so clearly missed. He talks about despair, how it thrives in silence. It's one of the things that drive people like Meg to do what they did and in the aftermath, the despair that she left behind—even for people who may not have known her—has to be honored and felt.

Then he looks out at the assembled group, and even though I've never met him, and even though I'm sitting off to the side next to Alice, and even though it was only begrudgingly that I agreed to go to this thing because I felt bad about accusing Alice of putting up that Poison Idea cover, his eyes stop on me.

"I know a lot of us are struggling to make sense of this. That we didn't know Meg well might make the burden less, but it makes the processing hard. I'm told we have her good friend Cody present, who I imagine is also grappling with this."

I shoot dagger eyes at Alice because clearly she outed me, but she returns my gaze with a level stare.

The guy up front continues: "Cody, I'd like to invite you to share, if you'd like, anything about Meg. Or share what it is that you're going through."

"I'm not going up there," I whisper to Alice through gritted teeth.

She stares at me, all wide-eyed innocence. "What you told me before was so helpful. I thought maybe it would help other people too. And you."

Everyone else is now staring at me. I want to kill Alice, who's nudging me up. "Just tell them about the library, about the food for her brother," she whispers.

But when I get up there, what comes out isn't cute stories about libraries or bands or picky eaters.

"You want me to tell you something about Meg?" I ask. It's a rhetorical question, and my voice is pure sarcasm, but all those innocent lambs bob their heads encouragingly.

"Meg was my best friend, and I thought we were everything to each other. I thought we told each other everything. But it turns out, I didn't know her at all." I taste something hard and metallic. It's an ugly flavor, but I savor it, the way you relish the taste of your own blood when you have a loose tooth. "I didn't know anything about her life here. I didn't know about her classes. I didn't know about her roommates. I didn't know that she'd adopted two sick kittens and nursed them back to health only to leave them homeless. I didn't know that she went to clubs in Seattle and had friends up there and crushes on guys who broke her heart. I was supposedly her best friend and I didn't know any of this because she didn't tell me.

"She didn't tell me that she found life to be so unbearably painful. I mean, I didn't even have a clue." A kind of laugh escapes, and I know that if I'm not very careful, what follows will be something I don't want to hear, that no one wants to hear. "How can you not know that about your best friend? Even if she doesn't tell you, how can you not know? How can you believe someone to be beautiful and amazing and just about the most magical person you've ever known, when it turns out she was in such pain that she had to drink poison that robbed her cells of oxygen until her heart had no choice but to stop beating? So don't ask me about Meg. Because I don't know shit."

Someone gasps. I look out at the crowd, everyone, dappled in sunlight. It's a beautiful day, full of the promise of spring: clear skies, puffy clouds, the sweet scent of early flowers blowing in on the breeze. It's wrong that there should be days like this. That spring should come. Some part of me thought it would stay winter this year.

I see some people are crying. *I* made them cry. I've become toxic. Drink me and die. "I'm sorry," I say before I bolt.

I run off the grassy area, back to the road, heading out of the park, toward the main street. I need to get out of here. Out of Tacoma. Out of Meg's world.

I hear footsteps behind me. It's probably Alice or possibly Stoner Richard, but I have nothing to say to them, so I keep running, but whoever's behind is faster than I am.

I feel a hand on my shoulder. I spin around. His eyes, this

time, look like the color of a sky after sunset, almost violet. I've never seen someone whose eyes change colors, like some mood ring to the soul. If he even has a soul.

We stare at each other for a minute, catching our breath.

"I can tell you things. If you want." His voice has that growl, but there's also a hesitancy.

"I don't want to know *those* things."

He shakes his head. "Not that. But I can tell you things. If you want. About her life here."

"How would you know? If she was just a one-night stand?"

He gestures his head in an away-from-here motion. "Let's go somewhere and talk."

"Why are you even here?"

"Her roommate gave me the flyer," he says, answering how he knew about the service but not why he came.

We stand there. "Come on. Let's just go talk," he says.

"Why? Do you know why she killed herself?"

Recoil. Like the recoil of a gun. It's what he does again. Like he's been physically yanked back. Only this time, it's not anger that's on his face; it's something else. "No," he says.

We walk a ways to a McDonald's. I'm suddenly ravenous, hungry for something that is not vegetarian or organic or healthy but is bred in a daily misery. We both get Quarter Pounder Extra Value Meals and take them to a quiet table next to the empty playground.

We eat in silence for a while. And then Ben starts talking. He tells me about Meg arriving on the indie-band scene, immediately making friends with a lot of the local musicians, which sounds like her. He tells me about how easy it was for her, this eighteen-year-old college student from Bumfuckville, Eastern Washington, swanning in and everyone eating out of her hand, which also sounds like her. At first he was jealous of her, because when he came here from Bend, Oregon, two years ago, he felt like he'd been hazed by the music community before they'd let him play in the sandbox. He tells me about the faux fights they used to have about who was a better drummer: Keith Moon or John Bonham. Who was a better guitar player: Jimi Hendrix or Ry Cooder. Who wrote the catchiest songs in the world: Nirvana or the Rolling Stones. He tells me about Meg adopting the kittens, hearing them crying in a box in a Dumpster near the downtown Tacoma homeless shelter where she worked a few hours a week. She dug them out, brought them to the vet, and spent hundreds of dollars to get them well. He tells me how she hit up some of the more successful musicians in town for donations to pay for the treatments, which, again, sounds exactly like Meg, and how she fed them baby formula with eyedroppers because they were too small to eat cat food. Of all the things he tells me, it's this image, of Meg coaxing tiny orphan kittens to eat, that makes me want to cry.

But I don't. "Why are you telling me all of this?" I ask. Now it's my voice that sounds like a growl.

Ben's pack of cigarettes sits on the table, and in lieu of smoking one, he clicks the lighter on and off, the flame hissing each time. "You seemed like you needed to know." The way he says it sounds like an accusation.

"Why are *you* telling me this?" I repeat.

Ben's eyes are momentarily illuminated by the flame. And once again, I can see there are so many shades of guilt. Ben's, like mine, is tinged with red-hot fury, hotter than the fire he's toying with.

"She talked about you, you know," he says.

"Really? She didn't talk about you." Which is untrue, of course, but I won't give him the satisfaction of knowing she had a moniker for him. Anyhow, turns out that he wasn't the tragic one.

"She told me how at one of your cleaning jobs, some guy tried to grab your ass and you twisted his arm so far behind his back that he yelped and then upped your pay."

Yeah, that happened to me with Mr. Purdue. A ten-dollar-a-week raise. That's how much an unwanted cop of my ass is worth.

"She called you Buffy."

And more than the thing with Mr. Purdue, that's how I know that Meg did tell him about me. Buffy was her nickname for me when she thought I was being particularly kick-ass, à la Buffy Summers, the Vampire Slayer. She called herself Willow, the magical sidekick, but she had it wrong: she was Buffy *and* Willow, strength and magic, all folded into one. I was just basking in her glow.

It feels wrong that he knows this about me, like he has seen my embarrassing baby pictures. Details he has no right to. "She told you a lot for a one-night stand," I say.

He looks pained. What a good faker he is, that Ben McCallister. "We used to be friends."

"I'm not sure *friends* is the word for it."

"No," he insists. "Before it all shot to shit, we were friends."

The emails. The banter. The rock talk. The sudden change.

"So what happened?" I ask, even though I know what happened.

Still, it's shocking to hear him say it, the way he says it: "We fucked."

"You slept together," I correct. Because I know that much. I know that Meg, after what happened to her that other time, would not have done that with someone unless she was into him. "Meg wouldn't just fuck someone."

"Well, I fucked her," Ben repeats. "And when you fuck a friend, it ruins everything." He flicks the lighter on and lets it go dark again. "I knew it would, and I still did it."

Now that's he's being honest, it's both repellent and magnetic, like a terrible car crash you can't help rubbernecking, even though you know it'll give you nightmares later. "Why would you do that, if you knew that it would ruin things?"

He sighs and shakes his head. "You know how it is, when it's in the moment and it's all happening and you don't think about the day after." He looks at me, but the thing is, I don't know. It would probably shock people to learn, but I've never. When you are bred to be white trash, you do what you can to avoid the family trap. Most of the time it seems inevitable anyway. Still, I didn't need put a nail in the coffin by screwing any of the losers in Shitburg.

I don't say anything, just stare at the empty playground.

"We only did it the once, but it was enough. Right after, everything went south."

"When?" I ask.

"I dunno. Around Thanksgiving. Why?"

That makes sense. Her sleeping-with-the-bartender email came before the holidays. But the kittens? Those she found after winter break. And the thing with Mr. Purdue grabbing my ass had happened in February, a few weeks before she died. "But if things went south a while ago, how do you know all this recent stuff, about the cats? About me?"

"I thought you read the emails."

"Only a couple."

He grimaces. "So you didn't see all the stuff she wrote me?"

"No. And a bunch of her mail is missing, between, like, January and the week before she died."

A puzzled look passes over Ben's face. "Do you have a computer here?"

"I can use Meg's. In her room."

He pauses, as if considering. Then he crumples up our empty food wrappers. "Let's go."

x x x

Back in Meg's room, he launches his webmail program. He does a search for her name and a whole screen of emails pop up. He scoots out of the chair and I sit down in it. Repeat comes bounding through the open door to claw at the cardboard boxes.

I start at the beginning, the flirty banter, all the stuff about Keith Moon and the Rolling Stones. I look at Ben.

"Keep going," he says.

And I do. The flirtation grows. The emails get longer. And then they sleep together. It's like a black line drawn in space. Because after, Ben's emails become distant, and Meg's kind of desperate. And then they just get weird. Maybe if they were written to me they wouldn't seem so weird. Except they were to Ben, a guy she slept with once. She wrote him pages and pages of stuff, everything about her life, the cats, me; it reads like very detailed journal entries. The more he tried to push her away, the more she wrote. She wasn't totally clueless. It's clear she knew what she was doing was odd because she ended several notes, some of which were eight or ten pages long, with a need for re-assurance: *We're still friends, right?* Like she's asking for permission to keep telling him all this stuff. I'm embarrassed to be reading this, embarrassed on her behalf, too. Is *this* why she deleted her sent mail?

The emails to Ben go on like this, every few days, for several weeks, and it's impossible to read them all, not just because they're long but because they're giving me a horrible twist in my gut. Within the emails are references to texts and phone calls she made to him. When I ask Ben how often, he doesn't answer. And then I see one of his last emails to her: *Find someone else to talk to,* he told her. Shortly after that email, *You have to leave me alone.* And then I think of her last email to him: *You don't have to worry about me anymore.*

I have to stop. Ben is now looking at me with an expression I don't like. I prefer the cocky strutting asshole from a few nights ago. Because I want to hate Ben McCallister. I don't want him looking at me with soft eyes. I don't want him looking vulnerable, almost needy, like *he* wants reassurance. And I certainly don't want him doing something generous, like offering to take the kittens off my hands, which is what he does.

I just stare at him. Like, *Who are you?*

"I'll leave them with my mom next time I go to Bend. It's pretty much a zoo at her place anyway, so she won't give a shit about two more strays."

"What about until then?" I ask.

"I share a house in Seattle. It's got a backyard, and my house-mates are all vegans, big into animal rights, so they can't say no or they'll risk looking like hypocrites."

"Why would you do that?" I ask. I don't know why I'm challenging him. I need to find a home for the cats; Ben's the only taker. I should shut up.

"I thought I just explained why," he says. The growl back in his voice is a relief.

But by the way he's looking at everything in the room but me, I think he knows that he didn't really explain why. And by the way I'm looking at everything in the room but him, I know that I don't really need him to.

x x x

The next morning, Ben comes by the house for the cats as I'm finishing taping up the last of the boxes. I put Pete and Repeat into their carrier, collect all their toys, and hand them over.

"Where are you headed?" he asks me.

"UPS depot and bus station."

"I can give you a lift."

"That's okay. I'll call a cab."

One of the cats yowls from the carrier. "Don't be stupid," Ben says. "You'll have to pay for two cabs."

I'm half afraid Ben will rescind his offer to take the cats, and that's why he's offering the ride, but he's already loading the duffel bags into the trunk and putting the cats in the back. The car is filthy, full of empty Red Bull cans, smelling of cigarettes. There's a beaded cardigan balled up in the backseat.

The mysterious roommate Harry Kang helps us haul the boxes to the car, and though we have not exchanged two words during my entire stay, he grasps my hand and says, "Please tell Meg's family that my family has been praying for them every day." He looks at me a moment longer. "I'm going to tell them to pray for you, too." And though people have been saying this crap to me all the time since Meg died, Harry's unexpected words bring a lump to my throat.

Pete and Repeat yowl all the way to the UPS place, and Ben waits with them in the car while I ship the boxes. Then Ben drives me to the bus station in time for the one p.m. bus. I'll be home for dinner. Not that there'll be dinner.

The cats continue to screech the whole time, and by the time we get to the bus station, it smells like one of them has peed. By this point I'm convinced he's going to say he changed his mind, that the offer to take them was basically his revenge for my T-shirt email.

But he doesn't. When I open the door in front of the bus station, he says, "Take care, Cody," in a quiet voice.

I suddenly wish I were taking the cats. The thought of returning home alone makes me desolate. As much as I want to put miles between me and Ben McCallister, now that I'm doing just that, I understand what a relief it's been to share this weight with someone.

"Yeah. You too," I tell him. "Have a good life."

It's not what I meant to say. It sounds too flippant. But maybe it's the most you can hope for someone.

The bus breaks down with a flat tire in the mountains, so I miss my connection in Ellensburg and it's after midnight when I get home. I sleep until eight, go clean the Thomas house, and then that night, I lug the two bags over to the Garcias.

I ring the bell, which is something I rarely ever did before, and Scottie answers. When he opens the door, I ask how it's going but I don't need to ask, because I smell butter.

"Cupcakes," he says.

"Delicious," I say, attempting some cheer.

Scottie shakes his head. "I never thought I'd say this, but I'd like some broccoli right about now."

Joe and Sue hesitate when they see me, as if it's not Meg's clothes and books I've brought back, but Meg herself. Then they come forward and are thanking me and Sue is crying silently, and it's just too much to bear. I know they love me. Sue has long said she loves me like a daughter, but it's different now that she doesn't actually have a daughter.

I turn to Scottie. If this is hard on me, it's worse for him. So, as if I'm Santa unpacking gifts, I say: "Shall we see what we've got?"

Except no one wants to see it. So I pull out her laptop, which

I've kept separate in my backpack. I hold it out to Joe and Sue. They look at each other; then they shake their heads. "We discussed it," Joe says, "and we want you to have it."

"Me?" I know how expensive this computer was. "No. I can't."

"Please, we want you to," Sue says.

"What about Scottie?"

"Scottie is ten," Joe says. "We have the family computer. He has plenty of time to have his own laptop."

Sue's face falters, as if she no longer trusts the promise of time. But she pulls it together and says: "And you'll need it for when you go away to college."

I nod, and we all pretend like this is going to happen.

"It's too much," I say.

"Cody, take it," Joe says almost harshly. I understand then that giving me the computer is not really a gift. But maybe my taking it is.

x x x

When it's time to leave, Sue packs up a dozen cupcakes to take home. They're frosted pink and gold, colors that tell a story of sweetness and joy. Even food lies.

Scottie takes Samson out for a walk and joins me half the way home.

"Sorry about the computer, Runtmeyer."

"S'okay. I can play DS."

"You can come over and teach me to play one of your games."

He looks at me seriously. "Okay. But you can't let me win. I feel like people are letting me win because I'm the dead girl's brother."

I nod. "I'm the dead girl's best friend. So it's an even playing field. Which frees me up to totally kick your butt."

It's the first time I see Scottie smile in ages.

× × ×

When I get home, Tricia is there, nuking a Lean Cuisine. "Want one?" she asks. This is the height of mothering for her.

We sit down to Chinese Chicken, and I show her the laptop. She runs her hands over it, impressed, and I wonder if she resents that the Garcias have provided me another thing that she can't. This in addition to all the dinners, the family camping trips, everything that they gave me while Tricia was working at the bar or out with one of her boyfriends.

"I've always wondered how to work one of these," she says.

I shake my head. "I can't believe you still don't know how to use a computer."

She shrugs. "I've got this far. And I know how to text. Raymond showed me."

I don't ask who Raymond is. I don't need to know that he's the latest Guy. Tricia never bothers bringing them around, or introducing me, unless we happen to bump into each other. Which is just as well. They've usually dumped her by the time it takes me to learn a name.

We eat our meals. Tricia doesn't want one of Sue's cupcakes because they're fattening, and I don't want one either, so Tricia digs around for low-fat Fudgsicles with only moderate amounts of freezer burn.

"What was with the cats?" she asks me.

"Huh?"

"You asked if we could have cats. Are you trying to fill up the gap left by Meg with a pet or something?"

I choke on my Fudgsicle. "No." And then I almost tell her because I want to tell someone about Meg's cats, about her whole life there that I knew nothing about. But I'm pretty sure the Garcias didn't know about it either. And this town is small; if I tell Tricia about the cats, she will invariably tell someone, and it'll get back to Joe and Sue. "There were a couple of kittens and they needed homes."

She shakes her head. "You can't give homes to every stray out there."

She says this like people are constantly knocking down our door for a nice, dry, warm place to stay, when, in fact, we are the strays.

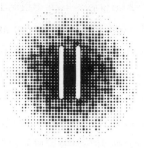

An academic adviser from the community college leaves me a message, saying that they are aware of my "extenuating circumstances" and if I want to come in for a meeting, he will help me find a way to fix my record. Madison, a girl who'd been in most of my classes at school, also calls, leaving another *Are you okay?* message.

I don't return either call. I go back to work, picking up a few more cleaning jobs, six a week now, decent money. Meg's laptop stays on my desk, along with the rest of my schoolbooks, all of them collecting dust. Until one afternoon, the doorbell rings. Scottie is on the porch, with Samson, who's tied up to a rail. "I'm here to take you up on your offer to kick my butt," he says.

"Come on in."

We fire up the computer.

"What are we playing?" I ask.

"I thought we'd start with Soldier of Solitude."

"What's that?"

"Here, I'll show you." He clicks on the web program. "Hmm." He fiddles around some more. "I don't see your network. Maybe we have to reboot the router."

I shake my head. "There's no router, Scottie. No Internet."

He looks at me, then looks like around like he's remembering who I am, who Tricia is. "Oh, that's okay. We can play something on your computer." He pulls the laptop back toward him. "What games do you have?"

"I don't know. It depends if Meg had any games." Scottie and I look at each other and almost smile. Meg hated video games. Thought they sucked out valuable brain cells. And sure enough, there's nothing on the computer except what came preloaded.

"We can play solitaire," I say.

"You can't play solitaire with two people," Scottie says. "That's why it's called *solitaire*."

I feel like I've let him down. I start to close the computer. But then Scottie holds it open. "Is that what she sent the note from?"

Scottie is ten. I am pretty sure it's not healthy for him to be talking about stuff like this. Not with me. I close the computer.

"Cody, nobody tells me anything."

His voice is so plaintive. I remember the good-bye she sent him, also from this computer. "Yes, this is the computer she sent the note from."

"Can I see it?"

"Scottie—"

"I know everyone wants to protect my innocence and stuff, but my sister swallowed poison. It's kinda too late."

I sigh. I have a printout of her suicide note in the box under my bed, but I know that's not what he wants to see. I know he's seen the note, or read it, or heard about it. But he wants to see its origin. I open up the sent mail file. I show him the note. With squinting eyes, he reads it.

"Did you ever think it was weird that she said that the decision was 'my own to make'?"

I shake my head. I hadn't.

"It's just, when we used to get busted for doing something together and she wanted to keep me out of trouble, that's what she'd tell Mom and Dad. 'Scottie had nothing to do with it. It was my own decision.' It was how she'd protect me."

I remember all the times Meg dragged Scottie into one of her schemes and then had to extricate him. She was always taking the fall for him. Most of the time, deservedly so. I still don't quite get what he's saying, so the ten-year-old has to spell it out for me.

"It's almost like she's protecting someone."

After Scottie leaves, I go through Meg's emails yet again. There's all that deleted sent mail, which I haven't been able to understand. Why would she delete only the sent messages but not the inbox? Or did she delete mail from her inbox, too, only I don't know what to look for? Why those six weeks? And what else did she delete? Is there a way to find the old messages? Are they gone for good? I have no idea. I don't know anyone who would know this.

But then I remember Harry Kang, Meg's roommate, who studies computers. I fumble for the scrap of paper Alice wrote her cell phone on, and I call it. She's not there, so I leave a message, asking her to have Harry call me.

The next morning, at seven forty-five, my phone rings, waking me up.

"Hello." My voice is groggy.

"This is Harry Kang," he says.

I sit up in my bed. "Oh, Harry, hi, it's Cody."

"I know. I called you."

"Right. Thank you. Look, I don't know if you can help me

with this, but I have a computer and I'm trying to find deleted emails."

"You're calling me because your computer crashed?"

"It's not my computer. It's Meg's. And I'm trying to recover files that I think she tried to delete."

He pauses now, as if considering. "What kind of files?"

I explain to him about all the missing sent messages and how I'm trying to recover them, and recover any other messages that might've been deleted.

"It may be possible to do that using a data recovery program. But if Meg wanted those files deleted, maybe we should respect her privacy."

"I know. But there was something in her suicide note that makes me think that she might not have acted alone, and then there's a bunch of missing emails. It doesn't feel right."

The line goes quiet for a minute. "You mean someone might've coerced her?"

Can you coerce someone to drink poison? "I don't know what I mean. That's why I want to find those emails. I wonder if they're in this folder I found in her trash. It won't open."

"What happens when you try?"

"Hang on."

I turn on the laptop and drag the file from the trash. I open it and get the encryption message. I tell Harry.

"Try this." He feeds me a bunch of complicated keystrokes. Nothing works. The file remains encrypted.

"Hmm." He gives me another set of commands to try, but still they don't work.

"It seems like a pretty sophisticated encryption," Harry says. "Whoever wrote it knew what they were doing."

"So it's locked for good?"

Harry laughs. "No. Nothing ever is. If I had the computer, I could probably decrypt it for you. You can send it down if you want, but you'll have to hurry because school ends in two weeks."

x x x

I take the computer to the drugstore, which has a shipping outlet at the back. Troy Boggins, who was a year ahead of me in high school, is working behind the counter. "Hey, Cody. Where you been hiding?" he asks.

"I haven't been hiding," I say. "I've been working."

"Oh, yeah," he drawls. "Where you working these days?"

There's nothing to be ashamed of about cleaning houses. It's honest work and I make good money, probably more than Troy. But Troy didn't spend four years of high school going on about how the minute the ink was dry on his diploma, he was getting the hell out of here. Well, I didn't either. Meg did, though like most of her plans, it became my plan too. Then Meg left and I stayed.

When I don't answer, Troy tells me it'll cost forty dollars each way to mail the computer. "Plus more if you want insurance."

Eighty bucks? That's how much a bus ticket costs. The weekend's coming up, and I have cash from the extra shifts. I decide to take the computer to Tacoma myself. I'll get the answers faster that way.

I tell Troy I changed my mind.

"No worries," he says.

I turn to walk away. As I do, Troy says: "Wanna hang out sometime? Go out for a beer?"

Troy Boggins is the kind of guy that, if you added fifteen or twenty years, Tricia would date. He never paid me any attention in high school. His sudden interest should be flattering, but instead it feels ominous. Like without Meg by my side, it's clear what I am. What I've been all along.

x   x   x

When I tell Tricia I'm going back to Tacoma for the weekend, she gives me a funny look. It's not like she'll stop me. I'm eighteen, and even if I weren't, she's never been that kind of mother. "Is there a guy?" she asks.

"What? No! It's for Meg's stuff. Why would you say that?"

She narrows her eyes and sniffs, like she's trying to smell something on me. Then she gives me twenty bucks for the trip.

I text Alice that I'm coming and ask if I can crash, and she responds with a bunch of exclamation points, like we're buddies or something. She says she'll be gone most of Saturday at her internship, but we can hang out Sunday. I tell Harry I'm coming too, and he says he'll look at the computer right away, that he's looking forward to it.

x   x   x

I get in late, but the couch has been made up for me. I crash there. In the morning, Harry and I go into his room, which has, like, five computers in it, all on and humming. We turn on Meg's. He opens her mail program first. "I'm not sure about retrieving the deleted email," he says once he's looked around. "Her mail program is set to use IMAP, so once messages are deleted here, they're also gone from the server."

I nod, as if that makes sense to me.

He clicks on the encrypted file. "She probably meant to throw this away too, but the encryption got corrupted somehow and it prevented the machine from throwing it away."

"What do you mean?"

"You found it in the trash, right?"

I nod again.

"She probably tried to empty it, but watch. . . ." He goes to the menu and selects "Empty Trash."

"Don't!" I yell.

He holds up his hand for me to stop. Some of the things empty, but then an error message reads, "The operation cannot be completed because the item 'Unnamed Folder' is in use."

"I put some dummy folders in the trash so we could see that it'll empty that, but not this. And don't worry, I already copied this folder onto my computer. But my guess is, she meant to toss it, but couldn't."

"Oh."

"Whatever it is, it's something she didn't want people to see. You sure you want to see it?"

I shake my head. I'm not sure at all. "This isn't about what I *want*."

"Okay. I'm doing something this afternoon, but I'll work on it before and when I get home. It's going to take a little bit of doing."

I'm about to apologize, but I see the delight in Harry's eyes, like I've just given him the world's biggest puzzle. So I thank him instead.

He nods. "How are the cats doing?"

"Don't know. That guy Ben took them."

"He lives in Seattle, right?"

I shrug. I think that's what he said.

"If you want to check on the cats, my church group is going up there this afternoon to paint a youth center. We could give you a ride."

"They're kittens, Harry, not babies. And they're probably not even there. He was sending them to his mom." Though the way Ben talked, I didn't get the sense he was the kind of guy who saw his mom every week. "Anyhow, they're not my concern anymore."

He holds his hands up. "Sorry. You seemed pretty into them. Meg was."

"I'm not Meg."

He nods again. "Let me get to work on this."

x x x

The morning drags on. Alice and Stoner Richard aren't home and Harry hasn't left his room, so I sit there, on the front porch, watching the rain come down. In the corner, I see one of the catnip-filled mice the kittens would spend hours attacking. It's like it's staring at me.

"Oh, fine." I grab my phone and text Ben. *How are the cats?*

He texts back immediately: *Out back. Trying to catch rain.* Then he texts a picture of them frolicking in a yard.

Good pastime for Seattle cats.

Beats chasing tail.

You'd know.

Ha! Where are you?

Tacoma.

There's a lag before the next text. Then, *Come visit them? They grow up so fast.*

I'm not entirely sure why my stomach does a little tumble except that the thought of seeing Ben McCallister is both repulsive and the opposite of that. Before I've had a chance to think too much about it, I text back: *Okay.*

Three seconds later: *Need a lift?*

I'm covered.

He sends me his address and tells me to text him when I'm on the road.

✕ ✕ ✕

There's a whole vanload from Harry's church group going to Seattle, and I'm a little shocked to find Stoner Richard crammed into the back.

"Hey, Cody," he says.

"Hey, Richard," I reply. "Didn't take you for a—"

"A Christian?" He laughs. "I'm just in it for the paint fumes. I'm all out of weed."

One of the girls in the middle seat throws a paint roller at him. "Shut up, Richard. You are so full of shit."

Cursing, stoner, do-gooding Christians. Okaayy.

She turns to me. "His father is a minister in Boise. Do you go to church?"

"Only because memorial services are so often held in them."

She and Richard and Harry exchange a look, and even though I don't think she goes to Cascades, it's clear she knows what—and who—I'm talking about.

Someone blasts Sufjan Stevens, and Richard and Harry and the rest of the van sing along all the way to the outskirts of Seattle. I text Ben that I'm nearby.

Repeat just hit the litter box, he texts back. *I'll save it for you.*

I allow a smile at that.

"Careful." This from Stoner Richard. We're pulling onto the off-ramp now, and he is climbing over the back row.

"You're the one surfing in a moving vehicle."

He squeezes next to me. "I know how guys like that are. Saw how he was with Meg. Charming on the outside, but inside, total douche."

And here's the crazy awful horrible thing. For one second, I almost defend Ben. But then I catch myself and I'm appalled, because Richard is right. Ben is a dick. He slept with Meg and then he blew her off, and now that she's dead, he feels bad about it and he's trying to be nice to me to make up for it.

I'm not sure why I'm here, why I'm in Tacoma picking at scabs that need to scar. Or why I'm in Seattle, being dropped off in front of a shabby Craftsman bungalow in Lower Queen Anne. But it's like I'm being pushed along by a momentum stronger than me, because before I have a chance to change my mind, to tell the do-gooders that I'll come with them for the afternoon and paint, Harry is telling me they'll be back around five, and Richard is eyeing me with an expression that I can only describe as paternal, though I'm the last person in the world who would know what that actually looks like, and the van is roaring off.

I stand in front of the fading blue house, beer cans and ciga-rette butts out front. I try to summon some of that anger, that hatred for Ben, to somehow propel me inside.

The door cracks open and out comes a little gray blur. I watch it go by. Pete. Ben was right. He's gotten bigger.

Then the door swings wider, and Ben runs after him in bare feet, his hair wet. "Shit!"

"What?"

"We don't let them out in the front." He dives under a bush and comes back holding Pete by the scruff of his neck. "Too much traffic."

"Oh."

Ben holds out the now-compliant kitten for me to take. So I kiss him on his fuzzy head and he proceeds to claw me right under my ear.

"Ouch!" I yell.

"He gets a little rambunctious."

"I can see that." I hand him back to Ben.

"Let's go inside," he says.

He opens the door to the house. The hardwood floors are scuffed, but there are nice new built-in wooden shelves every-where, full of books, record albums, and flickering novena candles. Ben turns on a light and leans in, and for a second I think he's going to kiss me or something, and my fists tighten. But he pulls back my hair and peers at my neck. "That's pretty nasty," he says.

I touch my finger to the scratch, which is starting to rise into a welt. "It's okay."

"You should rinse it with hydrogen peroxide."

"I'm fine."

He shakes his head. "The cats use the litter box. You could get cat-scratch fever."

"That's not a real thing; it's just a song."

"It is too a real thing. Your glands swell up."

"How do you know so much about cats?"

"We had a bunch of them growing up. My mom didn't believe in spaying or neutering. For pets or humans."

I follow him into a pink 1960s bathroom, humid from his recent shower. He digs around in the medicine cabinet and pulls out a bottle of hydrogen peroxide. He dabs some on a tissue and leans over toward me.

I grab the tissue. "I can manage," I say. The scratch goes white and foamy and stings for a second and then it's fine. And then we're just standing there in the bathroom, all warm and wet and small.

I walk out and Ben follows, giving me the tour: the mismatched furniture in the living room, the menagerie of musical equipment in the basement. He shows me his room, a dark futon and dark walls and an acoustic guitar in the corner and the same nice shelving as in the living room. I don't go beyond the doorway.

The rain has stopped, so he leads me down a long staircase that slopes into the backyard. He gestures around. "This is where they spend most of their time."

"Who?" And then I remember why I'm here. "Oh, the boys."

"Actually, about that . . ." he begins.

"You had them snipped?"

"Meg already did." He stumbles over her name but then

rights himself. "But they're not boys, not both of them. Repeat's a girl. I figured they were brothers."

"They must be littermates, and anyhow, it still works."

"What still works?"

"The joke." Ben looks at me, perplexed, so I explain. "Pete and Repeat went out in a boat. Pete fell out. Who was saved?"

"Rep—" He stops himself. "Oh, I get it." He scratches his head and thinks for a second. "Except she named them wrong, because it's not the girl who's saved."

And there we are. Back to the real reason I'm here. Not to see the kittens. But because of this. Because in some awful way, this binds us now. We stand there in the soggy afternoon. Then he sits down on the steps, lights up a cigarette. He offers me one. I shake my head. "Don't drink. Don't smoke," I say, mimicking the eighties song Meg and I discovered on one of Sue's old mixtapes.

"What do you do?" Ben asks, completing the lyric.

I sit down next to him. "Yeah, that's a good question." I turn to him. "What do *you* do?"

"I do odd construction jobs, woodworking. I play some shows."

"Right. The Scarps."

"Yep. We had a show last night and another tonight."

"Doubleheader."

"You could stay. Catch the show tonight. It's in Belltown."

"I'm staying in Tacoma."

"I could give you a ride back, probably not tonight but tomorrow. You could crash here."

Is he for real? I give him a disgusted look, and he sort of shrugs. "Or not." He sucks on his cigarette. "What are you doing here anyway?"

"Visiting the cats," I say, defensive. "You invited me, remember?" After I texted him. Why the hell did I text him?

"No, I mean on the coast. In Tacoma."

I explain to him about Meg's computer, the deleted files, the encrypted folder, Harry's computer wizardry.

A weird expression crosses his face. "I don't think it's a good idea to read her emails."

"Why, you got something to hide?"

"Even if I did, you already went and read my emails."

"Yeah. That's what got me started on this."

He twirls the cigarette between his fingers. "But those emails were mine. Written to me. It was my right to show you those. I don't think you should dig into private things like that."

"When you die, you're not a person anymore and privacy kind of becomes a moot point."

Ben looks uncomfortable. "What are you looking for, exactly?"

I shake my head. "I'm not sure. But something is suspicious."

"Suspicious how? Like she was, what, murdered?"

"I don't know what I think. But something's weird about it, something's fishy. Starting with the fact that Meg wasn't suicidal. I've been thinking about this. Even if I didn't know what was going on when she moved here, I've known her all her life. And not in all those years did she ever think about this or talk about it. So something else happened. Something to push her over the edge."

"Something to push her over the edge," Ben repeats. He

shakes his head and lights a fresh cigarette with the butt of his
last one. "What, exactly?"

"I'm not sure. But there was this line in her suicide note,
about the decision being hers alone to make. Like who else's
would it be?"

Ben looks tired. He's quiet for a long time. "Maybe she wrote
that to exonerate you."

I hold his gaze for a moment longer than is comfortable.
"Well, she didn't."

x   x   x

It starts to rain again, so Ben and I go back inside. He makes us
burritos with some black bean and tempeh mixture that's in the
fridge and then shows me where he keeps a secret stash of cheese
in a Tupperware container, and grates it on top. By the time we
finish eating, we've spent all of one hour together, and the guys
won't be back until five and the time stretches ahead of us like
a yawn. Ben offers to take me around Seattle, to see the Space
Needle or something, but it's unseasonably cold out and I don't
feel like going anywhere.

"What do you want to do?" he asks.

There's a small TV in the living room. Suddenly, the idea of
doing something normal—no memorial services, no computer
sleuthing, but just hanging out all afternoon in front of the TV,
the kind of thing that hasn't felt right to do since Meg—is so
appealing. "We could watch TV," I suggest.

Ben looks surprised, but then he grabs the remote and
clicks on the set and hands me the changer. We watch a rerun
of *The Daily Show* while the cats snuggle up next to us. Ben's

phone keeps vibrating with texts, chiming with calls. When he goes into the other room to take a couple of the calls, I can hear the low murmur of his side of the conversation—*Something came up, maybe we can hang tomorrow night,* he tells one caller. I overhear a squirmingly long conversation in which he repeatedly explains to some clearly dense girl named Bethany why he can't visit her. He keeps telling her that maybe she can come up to see him. Seriously, Bethany, get a clue. Even I can hear his lack of conviction.

When he comes back to the sofa, I've flipped to MTV, which is having a marathon of *16 and Pregnant*. Ben's never seen it before, so I explain the premise to him. He shakes his head. "That's a little too close to home."

"Yeah, I'll bet," I say.

His phone chirps with another text. "If you'd like some privacy, I can leave," I offer.

"I would like some privacy, actually," Ben says. And I'm about to gather my shit, wait out the next few hours in a café, when he turns off his phone.

We watch the show. After a few episodes, Ben gets into it, yelling at the TV like Meg and I used to. "Good argument for mandatory birth control," he says.

"Have you ever gotten a girl pregnant?" I ask.

Ben's eyes go wide. They're an electric shade of blue now, or maybe it's just the reflected glow of the TV. "That's a personal question."

"I kind of think we're beyond standing on ceremony, don't you?"

He looks at me. "There was a scare once, in high school, but it was a false alarm. Since then I learned my lesson. I always use condoms, unlike these assholes." He points to the TV. "Sometimes I think I should go ahead and get snipped, like Pete and Repeat."

"Like Pete. Repeat's a girl, so she got her ovaries out or something."

"Okay, like Pete."

"Don't you want kids? One day?"

"I know I'm supposed to. But when I picture my future, I don't see it."

"Live fast, die young." Everyone romanticizes that notion, and I hate it. I saw a picture of Meg's body from the police report. There is absolutely nothing romantic about dying young.

"No, it's not like I see myself dead or anything. It's just I don't see myself . . . connected."

"I don't know about that," I say. "You seem pretty *connected*." I gesture to his cell phone.

"I guess."

"You *guess*? Let *me* guess. Did you have a girl over last night?"

His ears go a little pink, which answers the question.

"And will you have a girl over tonight?"

"That depends . . ." he begins.

"On what?"

"If you decide to stay over."

"What the hell, Ben? Are you, like, some kind of addict? Can you not help yourself?"

He holds up his hands in surrender. "Chill, Cody. I meant if you crashed on the couch or something, *you'd* stay over."

"Ben, I will clarify this for you so there are no misunderstandings: I will never sleep with you, or in the vicinity of you."

"I'll cross you off the list."

"A long list, I imagine."

He has the good grace to look embarrassed by this.

We watch the TV for a while longer.

"Can I ask you something else?".

"If I say no, will that stop you?" he answers.

"Why do you do this? I mean, I get why guys want to have sex. I get that guys are all horny all the time. But why a different girl every night?"

"It's not a different girl every night."

"Near enough, I'm guessing."

Ben pulls out a pack of cigarettes, toys with an unlit one. I can see he wants to light up, but I don't think smoking's allowed in the house. After a while he puts the cigarette back in the pack. "You know what you know," he says.

"What's that's mean?"

"It just . . . becoming a man, it's not like it's something that happens instinctively. . . ." He trails off.

"Oh, please. I've never met my father and my mother is hardly a role model, and I don't blame my shit on them. So what's your story, you didn't have a father, Ben? Cry me a river."

He looks at me, his face gone hard, the Ben from the stage, the Ben from Meg's room that first time. "Oh, I *had* a father," he says. "Who do you think I learned it from?"

x x x

At four thirty, Harry texts that they're wrapping up and should be there soon. I start to gather my stuff, and Ben and I go wait out front.

"Am I going to see you again?" he asks.

My breath catches. I'm not sure why.

"Because if I'm not," he continues, "there's something I need to tell you."

"Oh, okay." So this why he wanted me to come up. Not to see the kittens. But to take his confession. "Go ahead then."

He takes a long drag on his cigarette and when he exhales, there's not nearly enough smoke. It's like all that toxic stuff stayed in him.

"She cried. After we slept together. She cried. She'd been okay, and then she was crying."

"Was she drunk?" I ask. "Like, really drunk?"

"You mean did I fuck her when she was passed out? Jesus, Cody, I'm not that big of a shitbag."

"You'd be surprised how many people are."

And I tell him. About Meg's other first time. That party, sophomore year. She'd done a bunch of Jägermeister shots and had been making out with Clint Randhurst. Things went too far too fast. And though she didn't exactly say no, she definitely hadn't said yes. To make matters even worse, Clint must've been the one to give her mono. Because after that was when she got sick.

After Clint, Meg swore that she was never going to do that again unless it was with someone she truly cared about. Which is how I know she cared about Ben, even if maybe she shouldn't have.

"So it wasn't you. You weren't the reason she cried. Or if she did, it was happiness, or relief maybe. She clearly *liked* you. Maybe that's *why* she cried." I tell him this to unburden him—or maybe to unburden me; at Meg's insistence I never told anyone about Clint. But if anything, Ben looks more cut up. He shakes his head, looks down, and doesn't say anything.

When the Do-Gooder Van pulls up, Stoner Richard sees Ben's downcast eyes and looks at me. "What'd he do now?" Richard asks.

"Nothing." I climb in the van.

"If you find anything else on her computer, will you tell me?" Ben asks.

"Okay."

He closes the door behind me and knocks on it two times. And then we drive away.

Harry works on the computer all night. And then the next morning. When I wake up, early, his light is on and I'm not entirely sure he's been to sleep.

"I've almost got it," he says, eyes gleaming with excitement. "This was such an unusual encoding. Did Meg do it herself?"

I shake my head, shrug.

"If she did, then I mourn her loss even more." Now he shakes his head. "We could've had so much fun geeking out together."

I smile politely.

"You never know people, do you?" he asks.

No. You don't.

x x x

Alice wakes up a few hours later and tackles me in a hug like we are best friends.

"Where *were* you yesterday?" she asks.

"No one was here. I went to Seattle with the guys."

"I waited for you and then you didn't come back so I went to the movies. Never mind. You're here now. I'm going to make us French toast!" she declares. "With homemade bread."

I follow her into the kitchen. She goes to slice the loaf of bread but can't get a knife through it. I suggest we go out instead.

We go back to the diner I spent the night in a few weeks ago. Alice doesn't like it because the eggs aren't free-range, but I like it because the breakfast special is two ninety-nine. Alice gabs on about her term, her upcoming finals, summer back in Eugene, which she says, if the weather is nice, is like living in Eden, including the nakedness in some circles. She invites me to come down before she goes to Montana for her summer job. I put on a tight smile. I'm not sure what else to do, because she's acting like we're friends, and we're not friends, we are mutual acquaintances, only the person we're mutually acquainted with is no longer.

"Why'd you go to Seattle yesterday?" she asks after a bit.

"To see the kittens."

"And Ben McCallister?"

"Yeah, he was there too."

Her eyes flicker up. "He's pretty hot, right?"

"I guess so."

"You guess so? He and Meg had a thing, right?"

I think of Ben's tawdry description of it. *I fucked her,* he'd said, so full of distaste, for Meg, for the act, for himself, I wondered why he even bothered. "I wouldn't classify it as 'a thing.'"

"I wouldn't mind a piece of that thing."

Alice seems so sweet, so young, so innocent. What would happen to her after she'd been used and abused by Ben? It's not a pretty picture. "Yes, you would."

When we're finishing up breakfast, Harry texts me. *Cracked it.*

I pay for both breakfasts, and we hustle back to the house. Harry is waiting for us on the porch, Meg's computer in his lap. "Look," he says.

I look.

There's a document open. It has a professional letterhead reading *Hi-Watt Industrial Cleaning Company* and some numbers.

"What's that?"

"It's a business license."

"Why would she have that on her computer?"

"You need a license to buy this." He clicks over to another window. It has a list of lethal chemical agents, where to procure them, how to procure them, expected physical effect, and "success rates." The poison Meg used is listed. It has one of the highest success rates.

I start to feel sick to my stomach.

"There's more," Harry says. He opens another document, this one a sort of checklist, the kind of thing you'd get in a class. But when I peer closer, I see the items in the left-hand column are a sort of syllabus for death. Order poison. Pick day. Write note. Clear email/browser cache. Email note on time-delay delivery.

"Oh God . . ." I begin.

"Cody," Harry says, with an edge of warning in his voice. "There's more."

He opens a simple text document. In an almost breezy tone, it congratulates whoever's reading this on making the *brave and ultimate step toward self-determination*. It goes on to say: *We have no say in our births, and generally little say in our deaths. Suicide is the one exception. It takes a brave soul to choose this path. Suicide can be a sacred rite of passage.* The note continues, listing sickening specific details on the best places and times to do it, how to conceal plans from loved ones. It even offers tips for what to write in the suicide note. Portions of the sample note are Meg's, verbatim.

I lean over the porch banister and throw up into the wild tangle of lavender hydrangea. Alice is crying, and Harry is looking mildly panicked, like he has no idea what to do with either of us.

"Who would do such a thing?" I gasp.

Harry shrugs. "I did a little more digging, Googling some of the advice from the notes, and it turns out there are a lot of 'suicide support groups.'"

"Support groups?" Alice asks, confused.

"To encourage suicide, not prevent it," I say.

Harry nods. "They used to be more active online, but now there are only a few left. Which might explain all the cloak-and-dagger secrecy. This literature seems to come from one group in particular. The Final Solution. Nice name." He shakes his head in mild disgust. "Whoever originated these files clearly didn't want to get found out." Harry smiles, then seems to remember he shouldn't. "The irony is, if she'd kept the files unencrypted and thrown them away, they wouldn't be on her hard drive anymore."

"How do you know for sure it's this Final Solution group?" Alice asks.

"Meg cleared her browser history, but didn't empty her cache." He looks at me, then at the computer. "The Final Solution was in there."

Tricia, the town-crier, has alerted about half of Shitburg that I've gone to Tacoma again, which means that Joe and Sue have found out, only I don't realize that until they call me up and invite me over for dinner, and when I get there, they blindside me with the simple question of why I went back.

"I left in a rush last time and I wanted to make sure I didn't leave anything there."

"Oh, Cody, you didn't have to do that," Sue says. She shakes her head and dumps some boiled-in-a-bag pasta onto my plate; it looks like something Tricia would make. "You're so good to us."

My secret—Meg's secret—feels caustic. I hadn't intended for it to *be* a secret. The entire bus ride home, I'd debated whether or not to tell them—would it make any difference? Would it bring them more grief?—never coming to a decision, but avoiding the Garcias when I got back. And then three days had gone by, and the decision seemed to have made itself.

Sue clears the dishes. She eyes my plate but doesn't mention how little I've eaten. I notice that she just pushed her food around too. "Will you stay?" she asks. "Joe finally went into her room."

Meg's room, which, according to Scottie, no one had really gone into since her death. Scottie said he'd peeked in a few times because it looked the same as always, like Meg was about to come home. I could picture it so clearly: the messy desk full of wires and soldering guns. The corkboard with its collage of old record albums, charcoal drawings, and photos. The graffiti wall, as we called the one opposite the windows that had this ugly floral wallpaper. Until Meg got inspired and tore it down and Sharpied all over the underlying plaster with favorite quotes and lyrics. Sue had been so mad about that, first because it was defacing property and then because members of their church, who'd been over for a potluck, thought that some of Meg's writing was sacrilegious. "You know how people are, Joe," Meg had overheard Sue saying. But Joe had come to Meg's defense. Who cared about those gossips? If the wall was a good outlet for Meg, leave it be. They could paint over it when she moved out. They never did, though. Now I doubt they ever will.

"We found some of your things," Joe says. "And some things of Meg's you might like."

"Another time," I say. "I have to be up early for work."

Is this how it is with lies? The first one comes hard, the second one easier, until they slip off your tongue easier than truths—maybe because they are easier than truths.

I let myself out. But before the door shuts behind me, Scottie is there, leashing Samson.

"Walkies?" he says to me.

"I gotta hurry," I reply.

"That's okay. Samson likes to run, dontcha, boy?"

I take off at a fast clip, and Scottie easily keeps up with me because he's ten and he has legs up to his elbows. Samson bounds along, sniffing for things to pee on.

When we're at the end of the block, he asks me why I went back to Tacoma.

"I told you. I wanted to make sure I didn't leave anything there."

I don't know if it's harder to lie to kids or if they just have better bullshit detectors, but in either case, he gives me this cynical look that hurts my heart. "Why'd you really go?" he asks.

"Scottie, can we not do this?"

"Just tell me why you went. You found something, didn't you?"

Scottie is tall and rangy and has Sue's blond hair, though it's starting to darken. I know he thinks all his innocence has been destroyed, but he's only ten years old. It hasn't. And if it has, he has time to get it back. But not if I tell him. How she posed as a buyer from a cleaning company to order what should've been a heavy-duty upholstery detergent. How she went through all this extra trouble, because that was the Meg way, but also because she apparently was so hell-bent on dying, she needed the chemical with the smallest margin of error. How meticulously she plotted it, in that Meg fashion, like this were another concert she was trying to score a backstage pass to. *First we'll try the publicists and if that doesn't work, we can try the radio station, and failing that, we can always ask some of our band contacts to put in a word for us,* she'd say. Her plans worked. They always worked.

Meg may not have sent Scottie the suicide letter, but she did send him an *I love you* farewell note. I think she wanted to leave him with that. If I tell Scottie what I found, I'll wreck that, maybe wreck him, too. And we've already lost one Garcia this year. I shake my head. "Nothing to find, Scottie, except for lint on the carpet."

And then I leave him there. On the corner. In the dark.

After I decided I wouldn't be going to UW but would be staying at home and attending the local community college, Tricia demanded I get a job. The Dairy Queen was hiring, so I asked for an application. I handed it in to the manager, who turned out to be Tammy Henthoff.

"You're friends with that Garcia girl?" she asked, squinting at my application.

"Meg? Yeah. She's my best friend," I said. "She's in college in Tacoma now, on a full scholarship," I added. I was so proud of her.

"Uh-huh." Tammy was not impressed. Or maybe she was just defensive. Since she'd run off with Matt Parner, people around here hadn't been all that nice to her. She'd lost her job at the car dealership where her husband had worked, and I'd heard that Matt's soon-to-be-ex-wife, Melissa, and all her friends had taken to driving by the DQ and shouting nasty things. Not that Tammy didn't deserve it. But Matt still had his job at the Jiffy Lube and no one drove by there yelling *whore*.

While Tammy was interviewing me, a bunch of high school students came by. The DQ had always been the local hangout, and it was then that I realized that if I got the job, I'd be serving

burgers to people I'd spent the last four years not exactly snub-
bing, but sort of. Meg knew *everyone* here and she had her admirers for sure, but she wasn't close with that many people. She had
her family, the people she met online, and me. In middle school,
teachers started calling us the Pod and it took, and then all sorts
of people referred to us as that. We were known as a twosome.
Even Tammy Henthoff, seven years out of high school, knew
about us. Working here, it would be a daily barrage: *Aren't you
Meg's friend?* And the piggyback question to that: *If so, why are you
still here?*

Right about the same time, the night manager at the restaurant where Tricia works inquired if she knew anyone trust-
worthy who could clean her house, Tricia asked me—almost on
a dare, it seemed; she knew how much I hated cleaning. But you
can be good at things you hate. Pretty soon that one job turned
into two and four and now six.

Just a couple of weeks ago, I got a call about a job as an at-
tendant at Pioneer Park. Sue knew the woman who ran the parks
department, and somehow, in the midst of everything, she put a
word in for me and I got called in for an interview.

It was a good job, decent pay, benefits even. On the day of
the interview with the superintendent, I walked to the park.
And then I saw the rocket ship.

Pioneer Park was where Meg and I learned to ride our bikes.
Where we'd run through the sprinklers and dreamed of the
swimming pool the town sometimes talked about putting in
there (it never happened; nothing here ever does). It was a place
that wasn't her house or my house or school or the DQ, where
we could be alone and talk.

The capsule at the top of the rocket ship was like our magical private clubhouse. Anytime we climbed the rickety stairs and ladder up to the nose cone, we were the only people there, though it was obvious from all the ever-changing graffiti that we weren't the only people to come up here.

Reading the graffiti out loud was one of our favorite things to do. There were hearts of couples long since broken up, and lyrics nobody remembered anymore. New stuff was always being scrawled over the old, though one line, Meg's favorite, remained gouged into the metal: *I Was Here.* She loved that. "What more can you say, right?" she'd ask. She'd written the phrase on her own graffiti wall and kept threatening to get a tattoo of it one day, if she ever got over her fear of needles.

The whole deathtrap probably should've been condemned years ago, but it wasn't. It was the highest point in town, and on clear days you could see for miles. Meg used to say you could see all the way to the future.

I turned around. I never even called the superintendent to cancel.

So I still clean houses. Maybe it's for the best. Toilets are anonymous. They have no stories to tell, no recriminations to fling. They just take crap and flush.

Since coming back from this last trip to Tacoma, I actually find myself looking forward to work. The scrubbing, the endless repetition, the arriving at a manky sink, attacking it with bleach and steel wool and after a time, leaving it gleaming . . . befores/afters in life are never quite so stark.

Today I clean two houses in a row, hauling laundry and ironing pillowcases, and cleaning the squared kitchen tile with a squeegee. The tile isn't really tile; it's linoleum. But that's how Mrs. Chandler likes it done, and who I am to argue?

Over the next few days, when I'm not working, I carry my cleaning zeal over to Tricia's and my tiny house, taking bleach and an old toothbrush and going at the shower grout, which has gone black with mildew. Tricia is so shocked when she sees the tiles go from gray to their previous white-and-blue state, she doesn't even say anything sarcastic.

I keep myself busy in a frenzy until I don't have a gig, and our house is as clean as it's been since we moved in. I sit on my bed and organize my earnings by bill denominations: I've made two hundred and forty bucks this week alone. I have to give Tricia one hundred dollars for my share of bills, but that leaves me with quite a surplus, and nothing to spend it on. Theoretically, I am saving for the move to Seattle. Theoretically, I learned in physics that the universe is expanding at a rate of, like, forty-five miles a second, but it sure as shit doesn't feel that way when you're standing still.

I shove the money into my metal box under the bed. Tricia has been known to pilfer cash if it's lying around. The house is quiet and stuffy, more claustrophobic than normal. I slide on my flip-flops and walk into town. Outside the Dairy Queen, I see a bunch of people I went to school with clustered on the benches under the cottonwood trees, including Troy Boggins. They wave and I wave back but they don't invite me to sit down with them and I don't pretend I want to.

I go to the library instead. Now that Meg is gone and her house is no longer my second home, this is my sanctuary. Plus, it has air-conditioning.

Mrs. Banks is sitting behind the reference desk, and when she sees me, she waves me over. "Cody, where have you been? I was about to send these back." She pulls out a rubber-banded stack of books, more of the Central Europeans. Karel Čapek's *War with the Newts*, Bohumil Hrabal's *Too Loud a Solitude*, a collection of Kafka short stories.

"Thanks," I say. I *am* out of books, but as soon as I enter the cool of the library, I understand that's not why I'm here.

I make my way to the computer terminals. I type *Final Solution* and *suicide* into the search box. It brings up mostly Hitler and neo-Nazi stuff, though there is one page that seems promising, but when I click on it, it won't load. I try the other sites from the search, and they won't either.

"Is there something wrong with the computers?" I ask Mrs. Banks.

"I don't think so. Why?"

"I can't get pages to load."

"Cody," she asks, "are you looking at naughty sites?"

She's teasing, but I flush red anyway. "I'm doing a research project."

"On what?"

"Neo-Nazi groups." Another lie. It just pops right out.

"Ahh, that'll do it. I can lift the filters for you if you like," she says.

"No," I say quickly. Nobody can know about this. And that's when I remember I have my own computer now. And the library has free Wi-Fi. "I mean, I have to leave now. But tomorrow?"

"Anytime, Cody," she says. "I trust you."

x   x   x

The next day, I bring Meg's laptop to the library, and before I get started, Mrs. Banks shows me how to get around the filters. Then I get to work. The Final Solution website isn't so much a website as an entry portal. You have to click on a button claiming that you're over eighteen. When I do, I'm redirected to an index with different topic headings. I open a few messages. A lot of them are spam. A lot more are ranting. I scroll through a few pages and it seems like a waste of time. And then I see a subject heading: *What about My Wife?*

The post is from some guy who claims he wants to kill himself but wonders what it would be like for his wife, whom he loves. *Will it ruin her life?* he writes.

There's a string of replies below. The majority opinion is that his wife will probably be relieved, that she's probably miserable too, and by offing himself he'll put them both out of their misery. *Women are way better at bouncing back from this kind of thing,* one person writes. *She'll probably remarry within a few years and be much better off.*

Who *are* these people? Is *this* who Meg was talking to?

I read the responses again, so casual that you'd think they're offering advice on how to fix a broken carburetor, and as I do, my neck grows hot and something churns in my stomach. I don't know if these people had anything to do with Meg. I don't know if this guy really intended to kill himself, or if he actually did. But I know one thing: You don't just bounce back.

After discovering the Final Solution boards, I spend every moment I can combing through the archives.

Shitburg's not a very wired place, so basically all my research is done at the library, which, even with Meg's intervention, is only open limited hours, most of which overlap with my job. If we had an Internet connection at home, I could get a lot more done, but when I raise the topic with Tricia, even offer to pay, she scoffs. "Why would we get that?"

Once upon a time, I would've gone to the Garcias and used their computer. But I wouldn't feel comfortable doing that anymore, even if I weren't digging into Meg's suicide. So, the library it is.

"How are you liking the Czechs?" Mrs. Banks asks me one afternoon. I'm confused for a second, and then I remember the books I checked out. I haven't cracked a single spine.

"They're interesting," I lie. Normally, I read two or three books a week and have very specific plot or character-related comments for her.

"Would you like me to renew them for you?"

"That would be great. Thank you." I turn back to my computer.

"Still working on that research project?"

"Yeah," I say.

"Anything I can help you with?" She leans in to look at the screen.

"No!" I say a little too loudly as I quickly minimize the window.

Mrs. Banks looks taken aback. "Sorry. You've been so focused, I thought you might need help."

"Thanks. I'm okay. I guess I'm not sure what I'm looking for."

This part is true. Every day more posts are added. There are the ones asking for encouragement or advice on how to tie a noose, and the ones from people with terminally ill spouses or friends who want to help them die with dignity. And then there are the completely random rants about Israel or gas prices or who won *Idol*. There's a whole language that's used, shorthand for different methods, slang, like *catching the bus*, which is the way people here talk about offing themselves.

Mrs. Banks nods knowingly. "I used to be a research librarian. When you're dealing with an unwieldy topic, the trick is to home in on a target. You have to aim for something specific rather than cast a wide net. So, maybe an element of the neo-Nazi movement?"

"Yeah. Thanks."

After she walks away, I ponder what she said. There is a function to search the archives, but when I used that to look for the kind of poison Meg took or the motel she went to or University of the Cascades or anything else specific to her, nothing came up.

But then I go and look at the actual notes and see that everyone has to use some form of user ID. Obviously, Meg wasn't going to use Meg. So I try other things. Runtmeyer. But nothing comes up. Luisa, her middle name. Nothing. I type in the names of her favorite bands. The girl rock stars that she wanted to be. Nothing. I'm about ready to give up when I try *Firefly*.

A whole screen of messages comes up. Some of them contain references to fireflies. And there are at least a dozen usernames that are a variation of *Firefly*. It seems to be a popular name— maybe because fireflies have such brief lives.

And it's while I'm contemplating the link between fireflies and suicidal people that I see it: Firefly1021. 10/21. October 21. Scottie's birthday. With trembling fingers, I go to the oldest one, from earlier this year. The subject line reads *Baby Steps*.

I have been thinking of this for such a long time and I don't know if I'm ready, but I'm ready to admit to thinking about it. Much as I like to think of myself as a Buffy, a kick-ass, fearless person, I don't know if I'm fearless enough to do this. Is anyone?

This must be how archaeologists feel when they unearth hidden civilizations. Or how that guy felt when he found the sunken *Titanic*. When you know something is gone, but you've found it too.

Because, here, this is Meg.

I scan the replies. There are more than a dozen of them. They are so warm, welcoming her to the group, congratulating her on being brave enough to admit her feelings, telling her that her life belongs to her and it's hers to do with as she pleases. And it's the oddest thing, because even though I know what these people are congratulating her for, my first reaction is pride. Because these people met my Meg; they're seeing how amazing she is.

I keep going. A lot of the missives read like they were written by sixth graders, full of typos and grammatical mistakes. But there is one at the bottom from a user called All_BS that stands out.

> Baby steps? Is there such a thing? Lao-Tzu famously said: "A journey of a thousand miles begins with a single step." He also said this: "Life and death are one thread, the same line viewed from different sides." You have taken your first step, not toward death but toward a different way of living your life. That itself is the definition of fearless.

After I read that response to Meg's email, I ran out of the library like the chicken shit that I am, vowing never to go back on those boards. It takes two days to break that vow. And I don't do it out of any kind of bravery. I do it for the same reason I gave in and slept on her sheets back in Tacoma. To be closer to her. Every time I read one of her posts, even though she's writing about death, she feels alive.

Firefly1021
Out of the Frying Pan

Here's the thing that screws with my head. Afterlife. What if there is actually an afterlife, and it's just as bad as the current life? What if I escape the pain of this life only to land somewhere worse? When I imagine death, it's liberation, a release from pain. But my family is Catholic, big believers in hell, and while I don't believe in that version of it, with devils and damnation and all that, what if there's just more of this? What if *that* is what hell is?

Flg_3: Hell is a bullshit Christian construct to keep you in line. Don't buy it. If your in pain, you do what you do to end the pain. Animals bite of there own claws. Humans are more enlitened and have different tools.

Sassafrants: Hell is other people.

Trashtalker: If the afterlife sux, kill yourself again.

All_BS: Do you remember pain from before you were born? Do you remember the torment from before you came into this world? Sometimes a pain is tolerable until it is touched, a tender bruise jostled. So it is with the pain of this life; it is brought about by this mortal coil. "It is not death or pain that is to be dreaded, but the fear of pain or death," wrote Epictetus. Stop fearing. Stop dreading. The pain will go away and you will be freed.

All_BS. The one who called her fearless before. The one who writes in complete sentences and quotes dead philosophers. The one who, in a twisted sort of way, makes *sense*.

I read this latest message again, and a voice inside my head yells: *Stop talking to her. Leave her alone.*

As if this is still happening. As if it's not already too late.

Firefly1021
To Medicate or Not to Medicate?

A friend told me to go to the campus health center to get some meds, so I talked to a nurse there. I didn't tell her everything that was going on, not about what we've been talking about here. But the nurse started going on about the first years away at school and the Northwest Effect and it sounded like standard boilerplate. She gave me some pamphlets and samples and made me an appointment to come back in two weeks, but I think I'll blow it off. I've always said it's better to be hated than it is to be ignored. Maybe on the same lines, it's better to feel this than to feel nothing.

It's one thing to type messages into the ether, but it sounds like she was talking to someone in the real world, too. Someone else other than me. The hot boil of jealousy shames me. It's so pathetic. I'm waging a tug of war, but no one else is holding the other end of the rope.

I skim the responses. Some people warn Meg about SSRIs being a mind-control plot devised by the pharmaceutical industry. Others say that taking them will numb her soul. Others claim that humans have always used mind-altering substances, and antidepressants are merely the latest incarnation.

And then there's this response:

All_BS: There is a difference between using a natural substance like peyote to engage in a consciousness-expanding experience versus allowing a bunch of drones in lab coats to manipulate brain chemistry to such a precise degree that thoughts and feelings are controlled. Have you read *Brave New World*? These new miracle medications are nothing but Soma, a government-produced narcotic to blot out individuality and dissent. Firefly, it is an act of bravery to feel your feelings.

Oh, Meg would've loved that. It's an act of bravery to feel your feelings, even if your feelings are telling you to die.

And again, I wonder: Why didn't she come to *me*? Why wasn't *I* the one she asked for help?

Did I miss something in her emails? I open my webmail, checking to see what messages she might have sent me in January, which is when she posted this one to the boards. But there are no emails between us from January.

It wasn't a fight, exactly. It was too quiet to be a fight. Meg was staying in Tacoma for part of the winter break because of her work-study job, so she was only coming home for the ten days around Christmas and New Year's. I was so excited to see her, but then at the last minute she said she had to go to southern Oregon to visit Joe's family, so she wouldn't even be coming home. Normally, I would've been invited to join them in Oregon. But I wasn't. Well, not until the day before New Year's Eve, when Meg called and begged me to come down. "Rescue me from the holidays," she said, sounding frazzled. "My parents are driving me crazy."

"Really?" I replied. "Because I spent Christmas Day eating an eight-dollar turkey plate at the diner with Tricia, and that was *magical*." Before, we might have laughed about this—as if the patheticness of my life with Tricia belonged to someone else— but it didn't and so it wasn't funny.

"Oh," Meg said. "I'm sorry."

I'd been angling for pity, but now that I had it, it only made me angrier. I told her I had to work, and we hung up. And when New Year's came, we didn't even call each other. We didn't communicate for a while after that. I wasn't sure how to break the ice because we hadn't fought, exactly. When Mr. Purdue grabbed my ass—a piece of news, at last—it gave me the opening, and I emailed her as if nothing had happened.

I scroll back to September, when she left for school. I read Meg's initial emails, the Meg-like rambling descriptions of her housemates, complete with scanned drawings. I remember how I read those messages over and over, even though it physically hurt to do so. I missed her so much, and wished I could've been there, could've gone through with our plans. But I never told her that.

There's a lot that I didn't tell her. And even more that she didn't tell me.

Firefly1021
Guilt

I keep thinking about my family, not so much my parents as my little brother. What would this do to him?

All_BS: James Baldwin wrote that "Freedom is not something that anybody can be given. Freedom is something people take, and people are as free as they want to be." You have to decide if you're willing to grab your freedom, and if in doing so, you might inadvertently set others free. Who knows what path your decision will lead your brother down?

Perhaps freed of your shadow, perhaps freed to be his own person, he will be able to fulfill a potential he might not otherwise reach.

Firefly1021: All_BS, You're bizarrely insightful. I always feel like my brother is limited, by me, by my mother. He'd be a different person if we weren't around. But you can't say such things.

All_BS: Except here we are saying them.

Firefly1021: Here we are. It's why I love this forum. Anything goes. Everything is said. Even the things that are unspeakable.

All_BS: Yes. So many taboos in our culture, starting with death. It's not so in other cultures that see it as part of a seamless cycle: birth, life, death. Similarly, other cultures view suicide as a brave and honorable path to life. The samurai Yamamoto Tsunetomo wrote: "The way of the warrior is death. This means choosing death whenever there is a choice between life and death. It means nothing more than this. It means to see things through, being resolved." I think you have the warrior in you, Firefly.

Firefly1021: Warrior? Not so sure I can handle a sword.

All_BS: It's not about the sword. It's about the spirit. You have to tap in to your strength.

Firefly1021: How? How do I tap into it? How do you do something that brave?

All_BS: You screw your courage to the sticking place.

Firefly1021: Screw your courage to the sticking place. I like that! You always say the most inspiring things. I could talk to you all day.

All_BS: I can't take credit for that. It's Shakespeare. But there is a way for us to communicate more immediately, and privately. Set up a new email account and post the address. I'll email you instructions and we can take it from there.

I taste the sour tang of envy again. I'm not sure if it's because I can sense the closeness between Meg and All_BS. Or if it's because in her litany of people she worried about leaving behind, she mentioned her parents, her brother, but she didn't mention me.

I get a new client. Mrs. Driggs. She takes me through the house and we both act like I've never been here before. It's funny how once you start pretending, you realize how much everyone else is too.

The house isn't big—it's a three-bedroom ranch style—and it already seems pretty clean because she lives there alone. Her husband is gone, dead or divorced or maybe never there. When I was here last, it was just her and her son, Jeremy, and, as everyone in town knows, he is doing three years at Coyote Ridge on drug charges. He got sent away a year ago, but Mrs. Driggs shows me his room, asks me to change the sheets on his bed each week, vacuum the rug.

Jeremy's room looks a lot like it did the one time I came here with Meg in high school: the reggae posters, the psychedelic wall tapestries. Meg had heard that Jeremy had a snake and was fascinated by seeing it eat. So even though he was a senior and Meg and I were freshmen, she got him to invite us over.

The big terrarium with its lush rainforest inside is now gone. As is the snake, Hendrix. What happened to it? Did it die, or did Mrs. Driggs get rid of it when Jeremy was convicted?

When Mrs. Driggs shows me to Jeremy's room, my stomach lurches, just as it had done four years ago when Jeremy had taken that mouse out of a bag and dumped it into Hendrix's cage. I hadn't expected the mouse to be so petlike—so pink and white that it was almost translucent. The way it stood so still, except for its little quivering nose, you could tell it knew what fate was in store for it. The snake, coiled in the corner, didn't move either, didn't let on that it noticed lunch had arrived. For a while, they both just stayed like that. And then Hendrix sprang into action and, in one fluid motion, strangled the mouse. Once it was dead, Hendrix lazily unhinged its jaws and began to swallow it whole. I couldn't watch anymore, so I went to wait in the kitchen. Mrs. Driggs was there, paying the bills. "Dreadful business, isn't it?" she asked. At first I thought she was talking about the bills, but then I realized she meant the snake.

Meg said you could see the lump of the mouse in the snake's body, and when she went back a day later, it was still there, although smaller. She was fascinated by the whole thing and returned a few times to see Hendrix eat. I didn't. Once was enough for me.

x x x

About three weeks after that day together in Seattle, I get a call from Ben.

"You don't write; you don't call," he says in a joking voice. "Don't you care about the kittens?"

"Are they okay?" I ask, worried he's calling to tell me they got smashed by a truck or something.

"They're fine. My housemates are looking after them."

"Why aren't you?" In the background, I hear lots of noise, people, clinking glasses. "Where are you?"

"Missoula," he answers. "Bass player for Fifteen Seconds of Juliet broke her arm so we got asked to be Shug's opening band on a mini-tour. What are you up to?"

What am I up to? I've been cleaning other people's houses and festering at my own, reading and rereading the posts between Meg and All_BS, trying to figure out where to go from here. After that last set of dispatches, their communication dwindles, so it's pretty clear they took their conversation off the boards. Only where? I couldn't find anything on Meg's computer. I found the new email address All_BS instructed her to set up on the boards, but when I emailed it, the message bounced. I asked Harry to look into it. He said the account was activated and disabled within three days, so Meg probably set it up solely for All_BS to instruct her how to contact him directly. "Sounds like they were being careful," he wrote. "And so should you."

Careful. Maybe that explains all the deleted sent emails. Meg covering her tracks, quietly so.

I also can't stop obsessing about this friend who told her to go on meds. Who was it? Some sort of confidante? If so, did Meg also confide about the Final Solution people?

I checked with Alice to see if *she'd* mentioned meds to Meg, but Alice said no, nor had she seen any evidence of Meg taking prescription drugs. Alice asked Stoner Richard, who called me and said that he didn't know anything but that I should try some of Meg's Seattle friends. I'd already thought of Ben, and when Richard had said that, it made me think again that he might be the confidant Meg referred to. But not enough to call him.

"Same old, same old," I tell Ben.

"What are you doing tomorrow night?" he asks.

"Nothing. I don't know. How come?"

"You live near Spokane, right?"

"Near is a relative term out here. About a hundred miles."

"Oh. I thought it was closer."

"Nope. Why?"

"We're playing in Spokane tomorrow night. Last show be-fore we truck back home. I thought you might want to come."

I open the file folder I have, containing printouts of Meg's posts. I've been going over and over them, and I'm no closer to finding out who All_BS is. I suspect he's a guy and that he's older. But that's just a gut feeling. Maybe Ben can connect me with the mystery friend. Maybe he is the mystery friend.

I don't want to see Ben. Or maybe I don't *want* to want to see him. But I need to see him, so I say yes.

x   x   x

Getting to Spokane is expensive and a pain, because the last bus back is pretty early and I don't want to get stuck there for the night. I ask Tricia if I can use her car.

"Can't. Gonna earn me some mad money." She mimes a slot machine and makes a *ca-ching* sound. "Wanna come?"

Tricia loves to gamble, maybe because it's the one area in

her life where she actually has decent luck. When I was younger, she dragged me with her to the Indian casino in Wenatchee a few times.

"No, thanks," I tell her.

I catch a bus to Spokane, figuring I can talk to Ben and skip out on his show if I can't get a lift back tonight. On the ride out, I alternate between nervous and nauseated, but that's pretty standard these days. Spending all this time trying to find Meg and All_BS has put me in a perpetual state of anxiety. I've had trouble eating and sleeping, and I've lost so much weight, Tricia says I look supermodely.

It's a short walk from the downtown station to the taqueria where Ben told me to meet him. It's so hot and dry and dusty, winter having jumped right into summer without ever passing spring this year, which seems fitting. All extremes, no time for gentle transitions.

Ben is already at the near-empty restaurant, in a booth in the back. He jumps up when I come in, and he looks both tired— probably from being on the road—and happy—maybe also from being on the road.

When I get to the edge of the booth, we both just stand there for a second, unsure of what to do. After a slightly awkward pause, I say: "Should we sit?"

He nods. "Yeah, sitting's good."

There's a six-pack on the table. "It's BYO," Ben explains. "Do you want one?"

I take a beer. The waitress sets down a basket of chips and some salsa, and I scoop some up, and find that I can actually eat it. Ben and I drink our beers and small-talk for a bit. He tells me about the tour, about the floors they've slept on, about sharing a toothbrush with the drummer because he lost his. I tell him that's disgusting. That you can buy toothbrushes at any 7-Eleven. But he says it wouldn't make as good a story, and I'm reminded that Ben McCallister is all about the artifice.

We talk about the cats, and he has pictures on his phone, a sort of ridiculous amount of kitten pictures for a guy to have. Our food comes out, and we talk about other bullshit stuff, and after a while it starts to become clear that I'm side-stepping my way around the thing I should be talking about. The reason I'm here.

I take a deep breath. "So, I found some stuff."

Ben looks at me. And those eyes. I have to look away. "What stuff?"

"On Meg's computer. And then from there." I start off by telling him about the documents Harry decrypted. I'd planned to show him the posts Meg wrote to All_BS—I've brought them with me—but I don't get the chance, because he's jumping down my throat.

"I thought you said you were going to tell me if you found anything," he says.

"I'm telling you now."

"Yeah, but only because I called you. What if I hadn't?"

"Sorry. There didn't seem much point."

I don't mean anything by it, but he leans back in the booth, and I can tell he's pissed.

"Cowgirl Cody rides alone, huh?" he says with that growl.

"Didn't used to," I say. I push away my plate. My appetite has vanished again. "That's why I'm doing this."

He's silent for a moment. "I'm sorry. I know."

I press my fingers against my eyes until everything goes black. "So, look. Meg talked about confiding in someone who told her to go to her campus health center and get antidepressants. I thought maybe she was talking about you."

He snorts. "Yeah, right."

"What do you mean, 'Yeah, right'? She sent you all those emails."

"There was nothing about antidepressants in them." He pops open another can of beer. "You read them. They were like stream of consciousness. She wasn't writing to me so much as at me."

"Yeah, I guess. . . ."

"And I told her to piss off, Cody. Remember?" He fiddles with his pack of cigarettes. "It wasn't me. It was probably one of her housemates."

"It wasn't Alice or Richard, and according to them, not any of the people from Cascades. Though maybe it was, I don't know who she knew. But Richard thought it was more likely one of her friends in Seattle."

Ben shrugs. "Could be. Not me, though. But why does any of this matter now?"

Because if she confided in someone about the meds, maybe she also confided about All_BS and the boards. But I don't tell Ben about Final Solution. I'm worried he'll get angry again, even though he doesn't have any right to.

"I need answers," I say, keeping it vague.

"Can't you just ask at the health center?"

I shake my head. "Can't. There's a patient-confidentiality thing."

"Yeah, but the patient's dead." Ben stops, as if this is news to me.

"They still won't tell. I tried."

"Maybe her parents could try."

I shake my head.

"Why not?"

"Because they don't know about this."

"You haven't told them?"

No. I haven't told them about any of this. The secret feels larger than before, almost tumorous. There is no way I can tell the Garcias now. It would devastate them. But I keep thinking that maybe if I find out more about All_BS, enough to do something to actually help, then I can tell them. Then I can face them. I haven't been around their house in a few weeks. Sue keeps leaving me voice mails, asking me for dinner, but the thought of being in a room with them . . .

"I just can't," I say, laying my head on the table.

Ben reaches out to touch my hand, a gesture that is both surprising and surprisingly comforting. "Okay," he says. "We can hit the clubs in Seattle. Find out if she talked to anybody."

"*We?*" The word is a relief.

Ben nods. "We head home tomorrow morning. You ride back with us. We can go around to the clubs. It's Saturday night, so everyone will be out. We'll ask around. We can go through her emails again. We'll find some answers."

x x x

That night at the show, I watch Ben carefully. The band is good—not great, but good. And Ben does his growly, throaty, thrusty trick, and I can see his charisma. I can see the girls in the crowd responding to him, and I forgive Meg a little bit for this. He would've been hard to resist.

At one point, Ben shields his eyes and peers out into the floodlights, just like he did the first time I saw him play. Only this time, I get the distinct impression he really is looking for me.

After the show, we crash at someone's house. I share a room with a very pierced college student named Lorraine, who's pretty nice, even if she won't shut up about the guys in the band. Ben and the rest of the Scarps camp out on the couch or in the basement in sleeping bags. The next morning, we all eat Dumpster-dived bagels and then load up.

"Prepare yourself," Ben says.

"For what?"

"The reek. Eight nights of travel. You'll get a case of jock itch just sitting in the van."

The rest of the band eye me suspiciously. Do they know I'm the dead one-night-stand's friend?

I sit down on a makeshift bench of two-by-fours stacked on top of a couple of amps. Ben sits next to me. We get onto I-90, and the guys bicker about what they should listen to. No one says a word to me. When we stop for gas and the guys go load up on junk food, I ask Ben what the deal is.

"I'm breaking the code."

"What code?"

"No girls in the van."

"Oh."

"But you're not a girl." He looks embarrassed. "Not that kind anyway."

"What kind am I?"

Ben shakes his head. "I'm not sure yet. A previously undiscovered species."

I fall asleep somewhere outside of Moses Lake and wake up with a start, leaning against Ben, my ears popping as we come down the Snoqualmie Pass.

"God, sorry."

"That's okay." He's smiling a little.

"Did I drool?"

"I'll never tell."

He keeps grinning.

"What's so funny?"

"It's just, you broke your promise, about never sleeping in my vicinity."

I jerk away from him. "Technically, I broke it last night, when I slept under the same roof as you. Score yourself a point, Ben. It's the only one you're going to get off me."

His eyes flash, and for a second there's that Ben, the asshole. I'm kind of glad to have him back. But then he scoots a little away, muttering something.

"What was that?"

"You don't have to bite my head off."

"I'm sorry. Did I hurt your feelings?" My voice is laced with sarcasm, and I'm not sure why I'm so pissed off all of a sudden.

Ben scoots farther away, and I'm surprised to realize that maybe I did hurt his feelings.

"Look, I'm sorry . . ." I begin. "I'm tired and kind of keyed up about all this."

"It's okay."

"I don't mean to be a dick."

He smiles again.

"Now what?"

"Most girls wouldn't describe themselves as dicks."

"Would you prefer I call myself a cu—"

"Don't," Ben interrupts. "I fucking hate that word."

"Really? Most guys I know seem to think it's interchangeable for female."

"Yeah. My father is one of those guys. Used to call my mother that. All the time."

"That's gross."

"What's gross is her putting up with it."

For all of Tricia's faults, and they are legion, she mostly leaves her boyfriend drama out of the house. Guys never stay at our place. She goes to theirs. If they call her foul names, at least I never have to hear them.

"Why'd she put up with it? Your mom?" I ask.

Ben shrugs. "She got pregnant with my brother when she was seventeen. Married my dad. Had three more by the time she was twenty-three, so she was kind of stuck with him. Meanwhile he's out and about, carousing. He has two more kids by his girlfriend; it's an open secret. Everyone knows. Including my mom. But she still stayed married to him. They only got a divorce when my dad's girlfriend threatened to take him to court for child support. Cheaper and easier to dump my mom and marry the girlfriend. He knew my mom wasn't the kind to sue."

"That's terrible."

"It gets worse. Mom's finally free of the bastard and we're all older, a little independent. Things seem to be going okay. And what's she do? Goes and gets pregnant again."

"How many are you?"

"My mom had five kids, four with my dad, one with her current douchebag. And my dad has two others that I know of, but I'm pretty sure he has more. He believes birth control is the woman's responsibility."

"You're like the redneck Brady Bunch."

"I know." He laughs. "Only we didn't have a housekeeper like what's her name?"

"Alice," I answer.

"Alice." He smiles. "Ours would have to have a white-trash name, like Tiffani."

"Or Cody."

Ben looks perplexed. I remind him that I clean houses for a living.

His face actually flushes. "Sorry, I forgot. I meant no disrespect."

"Oh, please, it's a little late for that now," I say, though I'm smiling and then he is too.

"So what's your story?" he asks.

"My story? You mean like my family?"

He raises his eyebrow, like he just bared all, and now it's my turn.

"Not much to tell. It's sort of like your story and the opposite of it. It's just me and my mother, Tricia. No dad."

"Did they split up?"

"Never together. She refers to him as the sperm donor, though he wasn't, obviously, because that would've meant Tricia actually intended to have me." Tricia has remained uncharacteristically quiet about my father, and over the years I've suspected it's because he is married. I picture him sometimes, in a nice house, with a nice wife and nice kids, and half the time I resent the hell out of him for it, but the other half of the time, I sort of understand. It's a good life, that. If I were him, I wouldn't want someone like me to fuck that up either.

"Tricia thinks she raised me on her own," I continue, "but really, it was the Garcias who raised me."

"Meg's family?"

"Yeah. They're like a real family. Mom, Dad, two kids." I pause to correct myself but look at Ben and see I don't have to. "Family dinners. Games of Scrabble. That kind of stuff. Sometimes I think if I hadn't met Meg, I never would've known what a normal family was like."

I stop. Because remembering all those times at the Garcias, watching movies on their worn couch, making plays and forcing Scottie to act in them, staying up too late by the dwindling fire on camping trips—all of that fills me with warmth. *But.* Always the *but.*

Ben is watching me, like he's waiting for me to say something else.

"But if that's what happens to normal, what hope is there for the rest of us?" I ask him.

He shakes his head. Like he just doesn't know either.

We get back to Ben's house and he unpacks his stuff, and we both spend a half hour shining a flashlight around the walls and watching Pete and Repeat chase the beam. It's possibly the most fun I've had in months.

Ben makes a list of the clubs that Meg most often hung out in. None of them will get going until around eleven, and they'll stay happening until four in the morning. We pound shots of espresso at his neighborhood café before setting off in his Jetta.

The first club is that one in Fremont I met Ben at. He introduces me to a group of groovy-looking girls in cute dresses and cool shoes—Meg people. They're all about a decade older, but that wouldn't have stopped her. When Ben explains who I am, one of the women embraces me in a spontaneous hug. Then she holds me at arm's length and says: "You'll get through it. I know it seems like you won't, but you will." Without asking anything more, I get that she, too, has been through this, has been left behind, and it makes me feel less alone.

None of these women knows anything about Meg going to the health center; most didn't even know she went to college. If

Meg didn't tell them even this, chances are she didn't tell them about the Final Solution. I don't bring it up.

We go to another club. We're barely past the bouncer when a girl with blonde choppy hair flings herself into Ben's arms. "Where have you been?" she demands. "I've texted you, like, a hundred times."

Ben doesn't hug her back, just sort of taps her uncomfortably on the shoulder, and after a minute, she takes a few steps back, jutting her lip into a fake pout. Then she spots me.

"Hey, Clem," Ben says. He seems tired. "I've been on tour."

"Tour, huh? That's what you're calling it now," she says, still looking at me.

"Hey. I'm Cody."

"Cody's a friend of Meg's," Ben adds. "Did you know Meg Garcia?"

Clem swivels toward Ben now. "Seriously? Are you, like, organizing a sorority for your castoffs? Can we, like, all wear matching outfits?" She rolls her eyes and pouts for real now. Then she makes a disgusted *pff* sound before flouncing off, giving Ben the finger as she goes.

"Sorry about that," Ben says. To his shoes.

"Why should you be sorry?"

"She was . . . It was a while ago . . ." he begins, but I wave my hands to stop him.

"You don't have to explain anything to me."

He starts to open his mouth as if to say more, but then he spots a guy with thick horn-rimmed glasses and the most elaborate pompadour I've ever seen. He's standing with a girl with short bangs and bright red lipstick. "That's Hidecki," Ben says. "He knew Meg pretty well."

Ben introduces us and we talk for a bit, but neither Hidecki nor the girl he's with know anything about Meg or the health center. After a while, I run out of questions, and Hidecki asks about the cats.

"You know about the cats?"

The girl he's with tells me that Hidecki donated a hundred dollars to their rehabilitation fund. "So he feels invested," she says.

"A hundred dollars," I say. "You must like cats."

"I liked *Meg*," he corrects. "She also saved me at least that much money when she fixed my amplifier."

"She fixed your amp?"

He nods. "Swapped the volume pot and showed me how to do it. I was skeptical, but she knew how to handle a soldering gun."

"Yeah. She did," I say. "And the cats are fine. Ben adopted them, actually."

"Ben?" He gives Ben a look I wouldn't exactly describe as friendly.

"Yeah. Even has pictures on his phone. Ben, show him your pictures."

"Another time," Ben says tersely. "We should hit some more clubs."

We go to three more places. I meet all these people who knew Meg. Who miss Meg. But no one knows about the health center. I get some names and email addresses of other people she was friendly with. By four in the morning, we have no direct leads but a bunch of contacts to follow up on. I'm so tired, my legs feel like they might collapse from under me, and the whites of Ben's eyes are redder than Stoner Richard's after a few bowls. I suggest we call it a night.

When we get back to his house, he leads me to his bedroom. I stop in the hallway outside of it, like it's radioactive in there. He looks at me. "You crash in here. I'll sleep on the couch."

"That's okay. I'll take the couch," I reply.

"It's more comfortable here. And quiet."

I wince. "Sorry, Ben, but there's, like, a petri dish of half of Seattle's female population on your sheets."

"It's not like that, Cody."

I scoff. *"Really?"*

"Clem was a while—oh, forget it. I'll just change the sheets for you."

"I'm fine to take the couch."

"Let me change the damn sheets, Cody." I can't blame him for being pissed. It is five in the morning, and he did just come back from an eight-night tour of sleeping on floors and in vans. But even so, he makes the bed, plumping the pillows and pulling down the comforter in one corner so it looks all inviting.

I snuggle into the pillows. The cats scramble to the foot of the bed and tuck in there, their nightly spot, I gather.

I hear Ben brush his teeth, and then I hear the floorboards creaking under his feet. He stops in his doorway, and for a second I'm scared he's going to come in and for a second I'm scared I might want him to. But he just stands there.

"Good night, Cody."

"Good night, Ben."

x x x

I sleep until noon and wake up rested, the achiness I wear like a second skin gone. When I go into the kitchen, Ben's already up, drinking coffee and talking to his housemates, whom he introduces me to. He's eating a bowl of granola and offers me some.

"I can get it," I say. I find a bowl from the drying rack and the granola from the cupboard, and it's weird how I'm making myself at home here.

Ben grins at me, like he recognizes the novelty of this, too, and then chats with his housemates about the tour. They're nice, not the rocker types I'd expected but students and people with jobs. One of the guys grew up in a town about twenty miles from where I live, and we lament the state of eastern Washington, stuck in some kind of time warp, and question why, when you cross the Cascades, heading east, do people start talking with southern accents?

The sun is out and Mount Rainier is lording it over the city, and it's one of those days that make you forget what happens here between October and April. After breakfast Ben and I walk down the steps leading to the yard. Off to one side is a big bunch of lumber, all covered with a tarp.

"What's that?" I ask Ben.

He shrugs. "Just something I do in my multitude of spare time."

I pull up the tarp. Under is the beginnings of some shelves, all clean sloping lines like the ones up in the house. "You made these?" I ask.

He shrugs again.

"They're really good."

"Don't sound so shocked."

"Not shocked. More like mildly surprised."

We sit down on the wooden steps and watch Pete and Repeat chase leaves and tackle each other.

"They do know how to enjoy themselves," he says.

"What? Wrestling?"

"Just being."

"Maybe I should come back as a cat."

He gives me a sidelong glance.

"Or a goldfish. Some dumb animal."

"Hey," he says, mock offended on Pete's and Repeat's behalf.

"Look how easy it is for them. What good is all of our intelligence if it makes us crazy? I mean, other animals don't kill themselves."

He watches the cats, who have turned their attention to yanking on a fallen twig. "We don't know that for sure. Animals might not swallow poison, but maybe they stop eating or separate from the herd, knowing it means they'll be someone's dinner that way."

"Maybe." I point at the cats. "Still, I'd like to be carefree like that again. I'm starting to doubt I ever was. Were you?"

Ben nods. "When I was little. After my dad left, before my mom hooked up and got pregnant with my little sister. Me and my brothers used to go exploring. We'd go swim in the river or build forts in the forest behind where we lived. It was like being Tom Sawyer."

I look at Ben, trying to imagine him young and unburdened.

"Why are you looking at me like that?" he asks. "You don't think I've read *Tom Sawyer*?"

I laugh. It's a strange sound, that.

"I've read *Huck Finn*, too. I am very intellectual."

"I don't know if you're intellectual, but I know you're smart. Meg would've had no patience for you if you weren't. No matter how pretty you are." I feel myself blush a little, and look away.

"You're no stranger to pretty, Cody Reynolds," he replies. "For a dick, that is."

I turn back to look at him, and for a second I forget about everything. And then I remember that I can't forget. "So, I have to tell you something else."

Ben's eyes, they change, like a traffic light going from green to yellow.

"I found other things from Meg. Things she'd posted on this suicide support group."

Ben cocks his head.

"It's not that kind of support group."

His eyes change again, from yellow to red. *Stop.* But I can't stop.

"You should probably just read it. I brought a printout. It's up in your room with my stuff."

I follow him upstairs in total silence, the warmth of the day replaced with a chill, though the sun is still plenty strong. I pull out the big sheaf of papers. "You should start at the beginning."

I watch him read. And it's like watching an avalanche. First a few drifts of blowing snow, and then a wave of it, and then his entire face is collapsing. The sick feeling comes back, magnified a hundred times over by what's playing out all over his face.

When he puts down the last page, he stares up at me, and his expression, it's awful. It's fury and guilt, which I can handle because I'm used to them, but also fear and dread, which set off bombs in my gut. "Fuck!" he says.

"I know, right?" I say. "He had a hand in it. In her dying."

But he doesn't respond. Instead, he goes to his own laptop and brings it to the futon. He opens up his email program and goes to Meg's emails. He scrolls through them until he finds the one he's looking for. It was written two weeks before she died.

"Read," he says in a ruined voice.

He points to midway through the screen.

I haven't been coming to Seattle as much lately, as you've probably noticed, and I have to admit that at first it was because I was feeling kind of low and awkward about what went down between us. I still can't believe I acted the way I did. But it's not like that anymore. Remember, a while back you told me to find someone else to talk to? I have. A whole bunch of someones. Some incredibly intelligent people who have a very contrarian way of looking at things, and you know how that's always appealed to me, going against the grain. I think it's why I've always been drawn to music and to bands and to things like that, but you guys don't have the lock on rebellion. There are so many avenues. There are so many ways to live, to define what living means for you and you alone. We are so narrow in our thinking, and once you understand that, once you decide to not abide by these artificial constraints, anything is possible and you are so liberated. Anyhow, that is what I've been learning from this new community. And they are really helping me. I have no doubt people will be surprised by the direction I take, but that's life in the punk rock world, right? Anyhow, I gotta run. I've got a bus to catch.

I finish reading and look up. Ben is crouched on the corner of the futon. "She was trying to tell me," he says. "About her fucked-up suicide group. She was trying to tell me."

"You couldn't have known from that."

"She was trying to tell me," Ben repeats. "In *all* those emails. She was trying to tell me. And I told her to leave me alone." He slams his fist into the wall. The plaster cracks. And then he does it again, and his knuckles start to bleed.

"Ben. Stop it!" I leap over to his corner of the bed and grab his fists before he can punch the wall a third time. "Stop it! It wasn't your fault. It wasn't your fault. It wasn't your fault."

I repeat the words that I wish someone would say to me, and then suddenly we are kissing. I taste his grief and his need and his tears and my tears.

"*Cody.*" He whispers my name. And it's the tenderness of it that shocks me back to reality.

I leap off the bed. Cover my lips. Tuck in my shirt. "I have to go," I say.

"Cody," he repeats.

"I have to get home *now*. I have to work tomorrow morning."

"Cody," he implores.

But I'm out of the room, the door slamming behind me before he has a chance to say my name again.

Tricia's in a good mood. The weekend I lost big in Seattle, she won big at the Indian casino, so even after paying for the expenses of food, hotel, and gas, she comes home two hundred dollars richer. She fans out the twenties that night at dinner and says we should splurge on something. For Tricia, this usually means something expensive and useless that she sees on the Home Shopping Network, like an ice-cream maker that she'll use twice and then turn into a receptacle for more junk.

"What do you think we should get?" she asks me.

"A year's worth of Internet."

"Why do you keep going on about that?"

I don't say anything.

"There *is* a guy." She smirks at me. "I knew it all along. You'd better not get pregnant!"

If there is one thing Tricia has pounded into me over the years, it's not to make the same mistake she did.

"You've been to Tacoma, what, three times now? And you want an Internet connection so you can go into chat rooms and do what you do. Don't tell me it's not a guy."

After the kiss, Ben tried to get me to calm down, but I grabbed my stuff and started walking toward the bus station, and he was forced to give me a ride. In the car he said, "It's okay, Cody." And I said, "How can you say that? I don't know if she can see us. If she's up there or down there, watching us. But if she is, she's disgusted. You know that, right?"

He shrugged. "Maybe. Who knows?"

"*I* know. And it doesn't matter anyway because *I'm* disgusted."

He didn't say anything else after that. At the station, I asked him to forward me all those long emails Meg had sent him and, after that, never to contact me again.

"It's not a guy," I tell Tricia now.

"If you say so."

In the end, she buys a decorative fire pit.

× × ×

I have read every post I can find written by All_BS. He doesn't post that much. But he posts enough that it's clear he's there, paying attention. And the name? All_BS? What's that all about? Is it short for "All Bullshit"? As in, "These boards are all bullshit"? Or as in, "Life is"?

× × ×

One day, on the way home from the library, I see Sue driving out of the parking lot of the fried chicken fast-food restaurant. My impulse is to duck out of the way.

"Need a ride?" she asks, pulling up alongside me.

I peer into the car. There's no Joe, no Scottie, just a big bag, already seeping with grease. Sue moves the chicken to the back-seat and opens the door for me.

"Where you headed?" she asks, as if there are multiple possible destinations.

"Home," I say, which is true. "Tricia's waiting for me," I add, which is not, but I'm worried she's going to invite me over and I can't face that, especially right now, with the folder full of Final Solution printouts in my hand.

"We haven't seen much of you," Sue says. "I've left you some messages."

"I'm sorry. I've been busy."

"Don't be sorry," she says. "We want you to get on with your life."

"I am," I say. The lies slip off my tongue so easily now, they barely register as untrue.

"Good. Good." She looks at the folder, and I start to sweat. I think she's going to ask about it, but she doesn't. The silence grows and gapes between us, shimmering like the heat on the empty asphalt.

It's not a big town, and within five minutes we are home. I'm relieved to find Tricia's car in the driveway, if only because it backs up my story.

"Maybe come for dinner one night next week," Sue says. She glances toward the bag in the backseat; the deep-fried smell has now settled throughout the car. "If you come, I can make the chili you like. I'm starting to cook again."

"Chili would be great," I say, opening the door. As I shut it, I catch a glimpse of Sue's face in the side mirror, and I understand that we're both of us liars now.

x x x

The next day, I clean Mrs. Driggs's house. It's one of my easiest jobs because it is usually immaculate. I strip her bed, the sheets smelling like old lady, even though Mrs. Driggs can't be more than ten years older than Tricia. I scrub the bathtub, self-clean the oven, Windex the windows. I save Jeremy's room for last. It creeps me out a bit, the ghostliness of it, vacuuming the shag carpet, still bearing the treads from last week's cleaning.

I push the vacuum into the corner where Hendrix's cage once sat. Something clatters in the motor. I switch it off, get down on the floor to inspect what's inside, and find a bobby pin, the kind Mrs. Driggs uses to pull back her bun. So she haunts this empty room, this empty house. She should get a pet or something, maybe some cats. Much better than a snake, although cats would go after mice too. Still, it wouldn't be such a rigged game as it was when Jeremy fed Hendrix—the victim and the victor predetermined. Poor fucking mouse.

I'm sitting there with the bobby pin in my hand when it hits me. How to find All_BS. He's the snake. To get him, I have to be the mouse.

What makes someone appetizing to someone like All_BS? Why did he choose to help Meg and not, say, Sassafrants, or the guy who always asks about rat poison? And how can I get him to think I'm one of those people?

I go back through his posts, looking for a pattern. He responds more to girls than to guys—particularly to smart girls. He doesn't ever reply to the illiterates, or the ranters. He also seems to take an interest in people at the beginning of their journey, the ones who are just starting to think about "catching the bus." And he likes philosophy—his posts are full of quotes— and seems drawn to those whose posts are philosophical too. No wonder he liked Meg.

The first step is obvious. I'll have to post something on the boards. An opening, like Meg's. Something that introduces me to the group, announces my intentions to kill myself, couching those intentions in a question. If I'm too sure, if I'm already shopping for rat poison, I won't seem like a mouse.

It takes me several days to come up with something, and then I get stuck thinking of a username. Everything I want to use is related to Meg, and I don't know how much she told him about herself, so I don't want to give myself away. I glance at the overdue stack of library books and use them as inspiration.

Kafkaesque
Opening Salvo

I've been thinking about catching the bus for a while. I think I'm ready to buy my ticket. I just need some encouragement. I'm worried about my family and not succeeding, and let's be honest, succeeding. I'd welcome intelligent thoughts.

As soon as I post it, I regret it. It sounds fake, nothing like me, and nothing like a suicidal person. I fully expect to be called out as a fraud by everyone on the boards. But the next day, there are several responses. As with Meg, most of them are so nice and encouraging—*Welcome! Congratulations!*—which, in an odd way, is gratifying. Except All_BS isn't among the responders. I might have fooled some of these people. But not the one I'm looking for.

I switch usernames and think of Meg's post about Scottie and try again.

CR0308
Survivor

I have been thinking very seriously about taking my life for several months now, but what's held me back is my mother. It's just her and me, and I worry about what it'll be like for her if I'm gone. Can I live with myself? Will I have to?

This one also smells of bullshit. It's not entirely accurate to say Tricia didn't *want* me, because she did *keep* me. It's more that I don't think Tricia wanted children. What mother makes her two-year-old call her by her first name because she says she's too young to be called Mommy? I know Tricia would probably be pretty bummed if I killed myself, but I also know she's looking forward to having me out of her hair. She tells me this on a regular basis.

I get a bunch of responses, some of them telling me that, yeah, it's a pretty fucked-up thing to do to a single mom. That maybe I should wait for her to remarry or something. Which makes me laugh. Tricia can't *re*marry until she marries, and with her three-month-relationship shelf life, I can't see either of those ever happening.

There's nothing from All_BS. I have this weird feeling that as long as I lie, I won't get a response. Which is kind of a catch-22, because how can I do this without lying?

I pick a new username, something vaguely Meg-related—the Pete and Repeat—but ambiguous enough not to be tied to her. Instead of trying to channel Meg, I try channeling myself.

Repeat
The Truth

I recently lost someone. Someone so integral to me, it's like a part of me is gone. And now I don't know how to be anymore. If there's even a me without her. It's like she was my sun, and then my sun went out. Imagine if the real sun went out. Maybe there'd still be life on Earth, but would you still want to live here? Do I still want to live here?

The next day, there are a bunch of responses, though not one from All_BS. Some of them are weird scientific explanations of how unlikely it is for the sun to actually go out. Others are more understanding of my loss. Others yet suggest that if I were to die, I'd be reunited with the person I lost. They are so certain, as if the Final Solution people have visited death, taken notes, and come back to report. I'm reminded that for so many of these people, this is a kind of entertainment.

But I am starting to understand the appeal of the boards. Yesterday when I hit post, I felt this massive sense of relief. This whole thing might be a charade, but for the first time in a long time, I am telling the truth.

x x x

A few days later I'm at work at the Thomases', trying to figure out how to smoke out All_BS. I'm lost in thought, which is maybe why I don't hear Mindy Thomas walk in while I'm cleaning her bedroom. If I had, I'd have gone and pretended to clean the garage or something.

"Hey, Cody," Mindy calls in a singsong voice. "How's it going?"

"Great!" I say with all the enthusiasm I can manage while holding a feather duster.

Mindy is trailed by her posse, girls all a year younger than me whom I haven't seen much since I graduated. Sharon Devonne waves to me. Sharon was one of Meg's acolytes. She adored her, used to follow her around like Meg was a movie star. Meg pretended to be put out by this, but I knew she thought Sharon was sweet, particularly because she was nice to Scottie. She was his counselor at the Y camp, and he had a huge crush on her.

"Hey, Cody," she says shyly.

"Hi, Sharon. How's senior year going?"

"Almost done."

"Any plans for after graduation?"

"Sleep."

"Yeah, I hear that—"

"You know what?" Mindy interrupts, clapping her hands. "I have the *best* idea. Cody should come to the party. It's next weekend. My parents are going out of town, and it's going to be a rager."

Before I have a chance to make an excuse, Mindy continues: "It'll be so perfect. You can come to the party and do the cleaning up afterwards." Her laughter follows her out of the room.

I stand there, too floored to say anything. Mindy Thomas? We used to take dance class together. She always wore these perfect outfits: leotards, leg warmers, ballet shoes, all matching. Tricia couldn't even afford the class—the teacher, a friend of hers, let me take it for free—so I just threw together what I could: leggings that were ripped, a tank top, mismatched legwarmers that I found at a thrift store. But then one day Mindy came in wearing the same getup as me. I'd thought she was making fun of me, but when I'd told Tricia, she'd laughed. "The little brat is copying you." I had my doubts. One thing I knew for sure: A year ago, Mindy Thomas never would have spoken to me like she just did.

Sharon lingers after the other girls leave. "She's just being a bitch," she whispers. "You should come to the party."

"Thanks, Sharon," I say. I hold up my feather duster to show her it's time to get back to work. She hesitates as if she wants to tell me something else, but then Mindy calls to her and she trots off.

x x x

Later, at the library, I can't stop thinking about Sharon, the way she used to idolize Meg. Meg may have stood out in town, but she definitely had her admirers. She had that thing. People, at least smart people, were drawn to her: people from school, musicians she met online, All_BS—they all found their way to Meg.

How am I supposed to attract All_BS? I don't have what Meg had. People may have called us the Pod, but it wasn't really an accurate description. There was Meg. And me, lassoing myself to her.

I can't do that anymore. To find All_BS, I have to be all me. I take a breath. And I start to type.

Repeat
Repeat

I'm not one of those people who has spent a lot of time thinking about death, or imagining her own death, or dreaming of it, or wanting it. At least I didn't think I was. But so much shit has happened in the last year of my life that I am questioning whether I even have a life, or if what I thought was my life is actually an illusion, or maybe a delusion. Because it doesn't seem like living to me. It seems like persevering, like that's the most I can hope for. I'm not that old, but I'm already so tired. Even getting out of bed each morning seems like an enormous chore. Life seems to be about endurance, not enjoyment, not fulfillment. I don't see the point. If someone told me I could go back and undo my birth, I think I might. I really do.

Is that the same as wanting to die? And if so, what does that mean?

One night I'm sitting at my computer, staring at all of the messages I've posted to the Final Solution boards and all the responses I've received. There are way too many pages to print out now without arousing Mrs. Banks's suspicion, so I've started saving everything to a file on the hard drive.

The door swings open. I snap the computer shut. "Ever hear of knocking?" I ask Tricia.

"When *I'm* living in *your* house, I'll consider knocking," she says.

I'm about to mention that I pay rent and therefore it's my house too, but then I think of the boxful of cash stashed under my bed and decide it's probably wiser if I don't bring money up.

She taps on my computer, which is hot. "I read somewhere that the rise in cancer is linked to how much people stare at their computer screens all day," she says.

"Everything gives you cancer," I reply. "The *sun* gives you cancer."

"I read that computers are really bad. All that radiation. It's not healthy."

"Where'd you read that? In one of the many scientific journals you subscribe to?"

She ignores the dig and sits down on the edge of my bed. "What are *you* reading these days?"

"Me?"

"Yeah, you. You used to always have your nose in a book, and now I only ever see you on that computer."

When I returned the latest batch of books Mrs. Banks had borrowed for me, I pretended like I'd read them all when, in fact, I hadn't finished a single one. I used to read at home at night, but now I can't seem to stop looking at my growing file on Meg, which I've hidden in a dummy folder named *college*. I've still gotten no response from All_BS, and I keep re-reading all the messages, trying to figure out what to do next.

Tricia gestures to the computer. "What's so interesting in there anyway? Is there some other world?"

"It's not another world. It's just ones and zeros—that's all programming is." But that's not true. All_BS is somewhere in there. Meg, too.

Tricia doesn't say anything. She stares at my room, my walls, the pictures tacked up with Scotch tape of me and Meg at shows, me and the Garcias on a camping trip to Mount Saint Helens, Meg and me on graduation day last year, her beaming, me smirking. There are pictures of me and Tricia, too, but they're outnumbered by the Garcias.

"You two always were like day and night," Tricia says, looking at the graduation picture.

"We don't look *that* different. Or didn't." Meg had dark

brown eyes and mine are hazel gray, but that was the biggest distinction. We both had brown hair, and though Meg had Joe's coffee complexion, in summer my olive skin gets so dark that we used to say that I could pass for Joe's daughter. Except I wasn't Joe's daughter, and now this insistence on our resemblance embarrasses me. Was this just another way of trying to lasso myself to Meg?

"I'm not talking about looks," Tricia replies. "Personality. You're nothing like her."

I don't answer.

"Thank God," Tricia adds.

"That's not a very nice thing to say."

Tricia continues to stare at the graduation photo. "She had everything. Those big brains. Fancy college scholarship. She even had that expensive computer you can't seem to get off of." Then she looks back at me. "You just had me. And you're smart, don't get me wrong, but you aren't Meg-smart. You got stuck at the shitty junior college and now, from what I can tell, you don't even have that."

I twist a loose thread from my quilt around my finger until my finger throbs. Thank you, Tricia, for such a precise overview of my inferiority.

"But even with the deck stacked against you, you stuck to your guns," Tricia continues on her tear. "You didn't quit that damn dance class that Tawny Phillips let you join for free, even when you sprained your ankle."

"I couldn't quit. I had the big solo in the dance show, *All That Jazz*," I remind her. I'd forgotten about that. Mindy Thomas had

been so pissed when I'd gotten the coveted role. I'm not sure
Tricia remembers it either. She couldn't come to the show. She
had to work. The Garcias came.

"Right," Tricia continues. "And at school, you hated math,
but you kept with it all the way through goddamn trignastics."

"Trigonometry," I correct.

She waves away the distinction. "You took math all the way
through *that* because you wanted to go to college. My point is,
you never quit on dance, on math, on anything, and maybe you
had more reason to. You had a pile of rocks, and you cleaned
them up pretty and made a necklace. Meg got jewels, and she
hung herself with them."

I know I should defend Meg. This is my best friend. And
Tricia has it wrong. She doesn't know the whole story. And
she's probably jealous of the Garcias for being the family she
never was.

But I don't defend Meg. I may not be Joe's daughter. But right
at this moment, I actually feel like Tricia's.

The next day there is a message from All_BS. It simply says: *Who did you lose?*

It takes me a minute to realize he—by this point I'm almost certain he's a man—is referring to an older post. Which means he's been watching me. I spend an hour thinking about what to write, which story will be most effective, and then I circle back. The true one will.

Repeat: The better half of me.

Within twenty minutes he has responded again.

All_BS: "Nothing is more desirable than to be released from an affliction, but nothing is more frightening than to be divested of a crutch."—James Baldwin

Repeat: What do you mean by this?

The library closes before he has time to respond, leaving me to think about the quote all night. I bring my computer with me to the Chandlers' the next morning, and discover they don't lock their Wi-Fi network. I sneak into the bathroom and check to see if there's a response from All_BS. And there is.

> **All_BS:** Perhaps your better half, as you call it, was nothing more than a crutch. It can be terrifying, after so long using one, to go without. Maybe that adjustment is what you are going through now.

And that's it. Nothing about offing myself, or life being the affliction. Only the suggestion that Meg was my crutch.

The scary thing is, he's right. Meg held me up. And without her, I'm falling down.

> **Repeat:** So you're saying this is temporary, that I shouldn't be thinking about catching the bus because I'm just upset over my loss?

I hear Mrs. Chandler in the next room. I quickly hit post and stash my computer in a corner. The rest of the morning, I worry that I somehow put him off. I practically run to the library that afternoon, relieved to find a response waiting.

> **All_BS:** I'm saying no such thing.

> **Repeat:** Then what are you saying?

He must still be online. Because the reply is instant.

All_BS: What are YOU saying?

I think hard before I answer.

Repeat: I don't know what I'm saying. I don't know what I'm doing. It's why I'm asking you.

All_BS: Yes. That is why you're asking me.

In the middle of June, I get a call from Alice. I haven't spoken to
her since the last time I stayed with her, but when I answer the
phone, she starts burbling away like we chat every day.

"So I checked on the map, and you're in Eastern Washington, right?" she asks after she's caught me up on things I don't
really care about. "Between Spokane and Yakima?"

There are hundreds of miles between Spokane and Yakima.
I love how people consider it flyover. But I don't correct her.
"More or less."

"Cool! I'm working as a counselor at Mountain Bound. I'll be
outside of Missoula, and I'm pretty sure I-90 goes through your
neck of the woods."

"It's not far from here."

"Perfect! It's, like, seven hours from Eugene to Spokane, or
wherever you are. A good one-day drive. And then I can make it
to Missoula the next day."

It takes me a second to understand what she's talking about.
"You want to stay with me?"

"If that's all right," she says.

We almost never have guests. Even Meg only slept here a handful of times. I'm already trying to figure out how to explain Alice to Tricia. Where to put her. Tricia and Raymond still seem to be together, judging by the number of nights she hasn't been home. Maybe she'll stay at his place that night, though if I request that, it's a surefire way to make sure it doesn't happen.

"When are you coming?"

"Day after tomorrow. Give me your address."

And so I don't have a choice. That night, I casually tell Tricia that someone is staying over.

"Your boyfriend?" she accuses.

"There is no boyfriend," I say. Then I think of Ben and then I get mad at myself for thinking of Ben and then I justify thinking of Ben because he was the object of her interrogation the last time this subject came up.

"Then who is it you're talking on the computer with?"

"I'm not talking to anyone. I can't, because we don't have Internet access."

"Ha! But you want it. And now you're blushing. You're hiding something."

This time, she's right. But not about a boyfriend. All_BS and I recently moved our conversation off the message boards and onto an anonymous communication software, and now we "talk" frequently. Our conversations, however, are frustratingly limited by library hours.

They are also frustratingly not about suicide. At least not specifically. We speak in generalities, and sometimes I forget who I'm chatting with. Last week, I mentioned that I had a cold coming on, and he sent a recipe for a tea made of ginger and apple

juice. When it worked, I made a crack about the irony of him
curing my cold. "Nice to know someone cares," I wrote. When
he asked me what I meant by that, I started typing a message
about Tricia, until I realized what I was doing and deleted it.

I had to be more careful, not answer his messages sponta-
neously, or I'd screw up. So now when I'm at the library, I save
his messages to my Meg file and when I'm at home, I write my
responses, sending them the next time I'm online. It's a frustrat-
ing and clunky system, but the delay forces caution.

"The person staying over is Alice," I tell Tricia. "I met her in
Tacoma. She needs a place to crash on her way to Montana."
There. The truth, or a sliver of it. One of the things I've learned
from dealing with All_BS is that if you hew close to the truth, it's
much easier to lie.

"Hasn't she ever heard of a motel?" Tricia asks.

"I'll take the couch; she can have my room."

Tricia sighs. "No. You can take my bed. I'll stay at Raymond's."

I nod, as if the idea never occurred to me.

x x x

The next night, at precisely six o'clock, Alice arrives, tooting her
horn as she comes down the street like she's the marshal of a July
Fourth parade. Some of the neighbors come out to see what the
commotion is, and Alice waves to them, grinning.

"So this is where you live?" she says.

I nod.

"It's not what I expected. It's so . . . small." She stops. "Not
your house. Your house is big. I mean, the town."

My house is a cinder-block cell with two tiny bedrooms. Small would be a step up.

Now she's flustered. "I didn't mean it like that. It's just, you seem so streetwise. I'd have thought you grew up somewhere else."

"Nope. This is me."

We go inside. I show Alice to my room. I've put clean sheets on the bed for her. She flops back onto it, taking in the band flyers on my wall, all the pictures of me and Meg.

"So this is where Meg grew up too?"

I nod again.

"How long did you guys know each other?"

"A long time."

There's a picture of the two of us at a rodeo, maybe from fifth grade. The bucktoothed phase. "Is that you?" Alice asks, leaning in.

I should take all this down. "Yep."

"You must have a lot of history here."

I think of the Dairy Queen. The rocket ship. The Garcias' house. "Not really," I say.

We're silent for a while. Then Alice announces she's taking me out to dinner. "No arguments!"

"All right. Where do you want to go?"

"What are our options?"

"Your usual fast food. A bar and grill where my mother works, but trust me, you don't want to go there. A diner. A couple of Mexican places."

"Is the Mexican any good?"

Joe always said that Sue's cooking was better than his mother's, and much better than any of the places in town. We almost never went to them. "Not particularly."

"I passed a Dairy Queen on the way in. We could go there."

I picture the DQ, Tammy Henthoff, the usual suspects hanging out. "Let's do Mexican," I say.

We head over to Casa Mexicana, full of red booths and velvet paintings of bullfighters. Our waiter is this guy Bill, whom Tricia used to hang out with, which is how it always is in Shitburg. We order our food, and then Alice asks for a strawberry margarita with a shot of tequila. Bill cards her, and she hands over an ID.

"And a virgin for you, Cody?" Bill asks with a smirk.

I hate this town. I can't even order a meal without it feeling loaded. "Just a Dr Pepper."

"Are you twenty-one?" I ask Alice when Bill leaves.

"No, but Priscilla Watkins is." She hands over her fake ID.

I'm impressed. I didn't think Alice had it in her.

As we wait for our drinks, the Thomas family comes in. Mrs. Thomas sort of waves; Mindy, who seems to be arguing with her sister over a hair-straightening iron, ignores me. I shake my head.

"What?" Alice asks.

How do you explain Shitburg to someone who describes her hometown as Eden?

Bill returns with the drinks. As soon as he's gone, I grab Alice's shot and down it. "Order another one."

We keep drinking. Alice grows maudlin. She starts talking

about Meg. Loudly. How she wishes she could've known her better. How glad she is that she knows me. Somewhere it registers that she is saying nice things, but Mindy Thomas is two booths over and I want Alice to shut up.

When the food comes, Alice starts shoveling it into her mouth. "Oh. Yum. This is so good. We have, like, no good Mexican in Eugene!"

"Hmm," I say, forking a mass of cheese off the enchilada. It peels away like skin after a sunburn. I push it to the side and try the rice.

"So, have you talked to Ben McCallister?" Alice asks out of the blue.

It's a dark restaurant, so she can't see my face go red. "No."

"Not at all?"

"Why would I?"

"I dunno. You two seemed like you had a . . . a spark."

A mighty flame followeth a tiny spark. When we first started talking, All_BS quoted that to me—Dante, he said it was. I think he was trying to explain how simple musings could lead to big life-changing ideas. His way of encouraging me, and I had to remind myself not to be reassured by it, because the life-changing idea he was selling me on was life-ending.

"No spark," I say. I push my plate away.

"That's probably good."

"Why?" I hear the challenge in my voice.

"For one, Meg was totally gaga over him."

"I thought you claimed you didn't know her at all."

"I didn't. But she talked about Ben. And invited us to come to his band's gigs. So she must've been."

"Her inviting you to a gig wasn't Meg being into Ben; it was Meg being Meg."

She doesn't say anything for a while, just slurps to the bottom of her drink. "Oh, that reminds me. Did you ever find the person Meg confided in about taking antidepressants?"

"Nope."

"I might know who it is."

"You think?" I don't care anymore, because the point of finding that person was to find All_BS, and I already did that.

"I'm not positive, but I think it's Tree."

"Tree? Right!"

"I think it was," Alice says, sounding wounded.

"You obviously don't know shit about Meg."

"I believe we've established that," Alice says defensively. "I still think it's her."

No. Meg would've hated Tree, and Tree didn't seem that charmed by Meg. "Not her," I mumble. I am suddenly tired, and my limbs no longer feel as if they are totally in my control. I remember, belatedly, why I don't like to be drunk.

"Okay, okay, okay," Alice says, waving her hands. "But she said something that made me think it. I can't remember now. But you should call her."

x   x   x

The next morning, Alice gets ready to leave for her wonderful summer of adventure, and I get ready to clean toilets. I am hungover in a way that has less to do with the tequila I drank than with what it brought out in me. Why wasn't I nicer to Alice? When she has been nothing but sweet to me? When I actually like her? I know I should say something to her, but before I can find the words, she's tooting her horn and disappearing down the street.

I wave until she turns the corner. And as I watch another person drive out of here to some better place, I understand exactly why I wasn't nicer.

x x x

The Purdues are on vacation, so the day after Alice leaves, I have a day off. I head straight to the library, earlier than usual. The comforting hush of the place has been overtaken by the laughter and yelps of little kids. It's story time.

On my way to the tables in the back, I spot Alexis Bray in the story circle, holding hands with her little daughter. I can't remember the girl's name, even though she came with Alexis to almost all of Meg's services, sitting quietly on her mother's lap. At one of the receptions, Alexis asked me if I wanted to go for coffee. I said I'd call her but I never did. I wasn't sure why she wanted to meet in the first place. She was four years ahead of Meg and me, and I didn't know much about her except that she used to go out with Jeremy Driggs, though he wasn't the father of her little girl. Apparently, it was some guy in the Army.

She waves at me now. As does Mrs. Banks, who gestures for me to sit in one of the carrels off to the side, where it's quieter. Although not much. Story time is a pretty raucous affair. The assistant librarian is reading some story about a bunny that keeps telling its mother all the ways it's going to run away, even though, obviously, if the rabbit meant business, it would not be telling its mother. When you're serious, you keep quiet.

One of the little kids shambles away from the circle over to where I'm sitting. His diaper sags halfway down to his knees and there's a big stain of what looks like peas, but could be something grosser, down the front of his *Cars* shirt. I'm disgusted. Kids are like parasites. I suspect Tricia has had the same thought about me. I wonder if Meg did too.

The librarian moves on to a different book, something about disappearing balloons, which sounds even more stupid. Which is maybe why my little foul-diapered friend shows no interest in returning to story time; he just stares at me with soupy eyes.

I try to look away, but it's not easy when someone is staring at you. The effort not to look makes my stomach churn like the agitator of a washing machine. *Churn. Churn. Churn.* I see Alice in the mountains of Montana, surrounded by a bunch of other similarly chirpy people. *Churn. Churn. Churn.* I see Hendrix swallowing that mouse. *Churn. Churn. Churn.* I see Meg at her computer, typing her time-delayed suicide note. *Churn. Churn. Churn.* I see me, at this very library, clicking open her suicide note: *I regret to inform you . . .*

The little kid is still at my side, his grubby, sticky hands inches away from the keyboard. "You *really* don't want to get any closer," I say, giving him my most menacing look, in case the threat in my voice wasn't clear enough.

His chin crumples before he starts to cry. His mom hustles over, apologizing to me, which means she probably doesn't know what I said, but Alexis gives me a weird look, which means she probably does.

So this is who I've become, someone who picks fights with toddlers.

I return my attention to the computer, scrolling through All_BS's words: *the tiny spark, the mighty flame. Screw your courage to the sticking place.* The little kid is now sobbing from the safety of his mother's lap. I feel ashamed, but the shame has forced some clarity upon me: I can keep picking small fights, or brave the big one.

Time to screw my courage. Or go down trying.

In quick succession, I send two messages. The first is to Harry Kang, asking him what kind of information I'd need to track someone down, because all this becoming All_BS's buddy does me no good unless I can find out who he is.

The second is to All_BS:

I'm ready. I want to take the next steps. Will you help me?

As soon as I hit send on the second message, my anger, my angst, my self-pity disappears, leaving only a calm and steely resolve. I wonder if this was how Meg felt.

The little kid has stopped crying and is now staring at me resentfully with his tearstained face. I look back at him and smile.

It doesn't take All_BS long to reply to my message, though he doesn't respond in the way I expected him to: by sending me the same files I believe he sent Meg. Instead, what I get is a message quoting Martin Luther King Jr. *"Faith is taking the first step even when you can't see the whole staircase."* To it he adds: *You've already taken the first step in deciding.* After that comes a link leading to a sort of directory with all these options: pills, poisoning, gunshot, asphyxiation, strangulation, drowning, carbon monoxide, jumping, hanging. When you click on each one, there is a detailed—and I mean *detailed*—list of pros and cons, as well as statistics listing success rates of each method. This is similar to the document I first found encrypted in Meg's trash, but not the same.

Over the next week, more messages come:

"If you realize that all things change, there is nothing you will try to hold on to. If you are not afraid of dying, there is nothing you cannot achieve."—Lao-Tzu.

Do you know what that means? Letting go of the fear? Dying is not about ending something; it's about beginning something. I keep thinking of the moniker you use: Repeat. It's not accidental, I assume. But you realize, repeating is precisely what you're doing. The same thing. It's only when you're willing to do something bold, different, that your life will truly change.

He's proud of me. I can tell. Which makes me proud of myself. I know it shouldn't. But it still does.

I keep waiting for him to ask for specifics. I've spent hours looking at the suicide shopping list, so, without intending to, I sort of planned how I might do it—or rather, I planned myself doing it as Meg did. Getting the fake business license. Ordering the poison. Having it delivered to one of those mailbox places. Writing a will. Packing up my room. Going to the bank to get a fifty-dollar bill for the maid's tip. Composing an email. Setting it for delivery. Checking into a motel.

The information on the sites All_BS referred me to is so thorough that I know how it would feel to take the poison. The burning sensation in my throat, then my stomach; the tingling in my feet that would tell me it was starting to work; then the cramps, followed by coldness as the cyanosis kicked in.

I've imagined it so many times now, first with Meg, then with me, and it's like how it always used to be, when I couldn't tell one of us from the other—when I didn't want to.

So I want him to ask me if I've thought of a method because if he did, I'd be able to tell him, and I think he'd be pleased.

But he doesn't ask.

So I just keep planning.

× × ×

One afternoon I'm getting ready to shower after work. I'm rooting through the medicine cabinet for a new razor when I see one of those massive bottles of Tylenol that Tricia buys from the warehouse store. I know from my research that Tylenol is a terrible, horribly painful, but inexpensive way to do it. I turn off the shower. I go into my room. I pour the white tablets onto my bedspread. How many would I take? How many could I swallow at once? How would I keep from throwing them up?

Staring at the pills, it seems so easy. Like something I could do. Right now. Swallow pills. Jump off a freeway overpass. Find someone's loaded gun. *You don't want to die,* I have to remind myself. *But if you did,* a little voice answers, *imagine how simple it would be....*

The doorbell rings and I'm startled and red-faced with instant shame. I hastily put the pills back in the bottle and shove it into the medicine cabinet. The doorbell rings again.

It's Scottie, holding Samson on a leash and kicking at some dried leaves that have bunched up under the mat. He looks at me in my rumpled, sour-smelling T-shirt.

"Were you sleeping?" he asks.

"No." I haven't been sleeping much lately, which makes me look as if I've always just been woken up. I'm still a little shaken by the Tylenol, so when Scottie asks me if I want to go for a walk with him and Samson, I almost leap out the door.

We set off into the dusky late afternoon. I'm hyper now, a one-woman small-talk machine. I ask Scottie about school, only to have him remind me it's summer break. I ask him what he's doing this summer, and he reminds me that he's at the Y camp. I should know this because it's what he does every summer, as did Meg when she was younger. I used to beg Tricia to sign me up too, but she said she refused to spend money on camp when she was free during the day, so summers meant me counting the hours until the Garcias got home.

Scottie keeps walking and I keep asking inane questions and when I run out of those, I'm about ask if he's got any good knock-knock jokes. He and Meg used to make up the most absurd nonsensical ones—*Knock, knock. Who's there? Lie. Lie who? Lions lie*—and they'd laugh and laugh until someone cried or farted. When I'd shake my head and call them gross, they'd say I lacked their stupid-humor gene, which I knew was them being silly but made me feel bad somehow.

So I don't ask for jokes, and then I run out of small talk. By this point, we've looped through town and Samson has taken two shits, which Scottie has stoically scooped into plastic bags. "Are you looking?" he asks.

"Am I looking?" I repeat.

"For the person. From the note. Who helped her."

I don't know why I'm so surprised that he knows this. He's the one who knew it all along.

My expression must give something away, because he nods slightly, like he understands. "Good," he says.

At the corner of his street, Scottie lets Samson off his leash. "Get him," he says. I think he's talking to the dog, but I realize he's talking to me.

When I get home, I take the Tylenol out of the medicine cabinet, dump the pills down the toilet, and bury the bottle in the garbage. A few days later, when Tricia gets her period and goes crazy trying to find the bottle, I play dumb.

The next time I go to the library, the front door is locked. Which is weird. I know the opening hours by heart. Closed Sunday and Mondays. Open Tuesdays from one to six. I check my phone. Tuesday, three thirty. I give the doors a shake and then, frustrated, a kick.

I come back the next day, when the library should be open all day, but it's the same thing. Mrs. Banks is inside, though. I knock on the door.

"What's going on?" I ask her when she unlocks it.

"There was a small electrical fire over the weekend," she tells me. "We have to rewire, and there's no electricity in the building until then. We've been warning them about the wiring for years." She shakes her head and sighs. "Budget cuts."

"What am I supposed to do?" I cry. The library has become my lifeline, my conduit to All_BS. It's already been four days since we last communicated, and I'm strung out.

Mrs. Banks smiles. "Don't worry. I've thought of that." She goes back inside and returns with a shopping bag full of books. "You can keep them until we reopen. Shouldn't be longer than a week or two. These are off the grid, so to speak," she says with a wink. "So we're on the honor system. But I trust you."

x x x

The next time I have Internet access is Friday at Mrs. Chandler's. But she's there, so there's no sneaking the signal. I'm desperate to hear from All_BS, desperate enough to explain to Mrs. Chandler about the library fire and ask if I can stay after work to check my email using her Wi-Fi connection. Mrs. Chandler looks at me a long time. "You don't have Internet at your house?" she asks. I shake my head, embarrassed. "Of course," she says. "Use it any time."

I'm itchy and anxious when I log on. What if All_BS has lost interest? But then I see the number of unread messages from him. The silence has worked in my favor. Used to hearing from me almost every day, except Sundays and Mondays, All_BS is clearly worried that I haven't responded to his messages in nearly a week. The tone of his messages is one of increasing concern. I can't quite tell if he's worried that I offed myself without telling him—or that I changed my mind.

Tricia always says that guys want you more when they think they can't have you.

I reassure him that it's just Internet access issues. And then I think of Mrs. Chandler's concerned face, and I get an idea.

I don't think I'll have regular access to Internet again for a while, I write, playing up the library's electrical problems. *And I don't know how I'll do this without your help. I already chose my route, but if I don't catch the bus soon, I might miss it. Is there any other way we can communicate? Like on the phone?*

It feels like it takes an hour for his response to arrive, though it only takes five minutes.

That's not wise, he writes back.

I force myself to wait ten minutes before replying. *I don't see any other way,* I write. And then I type my cell phone number. *Call if you can.*

x x x

I hear nothing. And without Internet, we can't have our email communication either. I am disgusted to admit it to myself, but I miss the back and forth. Which really means I miss him.

Work is tedious. No matter how much I scrub and polish, the houses still seem dingy to me. One morning I arrive at the Purdues' and see Mr. Purdue's car in the driveway, and I want to run away, but where is there to go? I steel myself and open the door with the key Mrs. Purdue hides for me under the fake rock.

I'm in the kitchen, digging out the cleaning supplies from under the sink, when Mr. Purdue breezes in. "I took a sick day," he informs me, answering a question I didn't ask.

"Hope you feel better."

"Oh, I'm fine. It's more of a mental health day."

I don't answer as I head to the bathroom. I shut the door, even though that means the fumes will be stronger. I am leaning over the tub with a can of Clorox when I hear the door open behind me. The Purdues have two bathrooms; there is no need for him to use this one. I wait for him to turn around, but he doesn't. He comes closer. He's barefoot and I can hear the sound of his toes cracking against the tile floor.

I stand up and turn around, the Clorox can still in my hand, my finger still on the nozzle. He takes a step toward me. The distance between us is already unnecessarily close, and then he takes another step.

I hold the can to his face and squeeze out a tiny warning shot. "Just give me a reason," I say. "Just one." I mean to be tough, but to my ears it sounds almost pleading.

He backs out of the bathroom, arms up in surrender. By the time I hear the tires squeal out of the driveway, my rage has passed. But unlike the last time he messed with me, I am not at all triumphant or Buffy-like. I already warned him once, but he just paid me ten more bucks and came back for more.

x x x

It's a bleak night. Tricia is out with Raymond, and the neighbors next door are having a party. I still smell of bleach, even after my shower, and it's like it's not the bleach but Mr. Purdue's lechery that won't wash off.

I can't face looking at Final Solution notes, so I try to force myself to do something different. I leaf through a couple of library books, but the words swim on the page. I open Meg's computer for a game of solitaire, but I wind up in her email program again. For the hundredth time I stare at the missing hole of mail, as if the deleted messages might magically materialize and answer all my questions. I back up and read the notes she wrote to Ben. I read what he wrote back

You have to leave me alone. How that had pissed me off. Only it's hard to summon the anger now. Because hadn't I told her the same thing, just without words?

Was she mad at me? For being too close? For pulling away?

For not coming to Oregon over Christmas break? I pull up the email she wrote me after I broke our weeks of silence by telling her about Mr. Purdue's first ass grab. *Ha! That skeevy old bastard. How I wish I could've seen that! I know you'll always be strong; you'll always be my Buffy,* she wrote.

I take out my phone. Ben's texts are still in the log, ending abruptly after I told him to stay away. My finger lingers over the call button. I imagine talking to him, telling him about Mr. Purdue today, telling him *everything* that's been going on the past few weeks.

It's only when I hear the first ring that I realize I've actually hit call. When I hear the second ring, I remember how often his phone rang when we were sitting there watching TV together that day. I picture my call being the one that interrupts his time with some girl now—and with a sudden and abrupt disgust, I see that I've let myself become *that* girl. Before the third ring, I've hung up.

Also in my text log is a message from Alice with Tree's number. *Call her,* Alice exhorted. I haven't, because the whole point of finding the mystery friend was to find All_BS. But right now Tree's caustic bitterness seems to fit the mood.

The world's grumpiest peace-and-love hippie answers. "What?"

"Is this Tree?" I ask, even though I can tell it is.

"Who wants to know?"

"It's Cody." I pause. "Meg's friend."

There's silence on the line, not a friendly one. She's not going to speak. So I continue.

"So, um, I saw Alice a few weeks ago."

"Congratulations."

Good old Tree. At least she's consistent.

"She mentioned that Meg might've confided in you about going on antidepressants or something," I say.

"Confided in me?" There's something between a laugh and a bark. "Why would she do that? We didn't exactly do each other's nails."

It's such a bizarre image that I almost smile. "It didn't seem likely, but Alice mentioned you having said something. She couldn't remember what."

"She never confided in me. But someone should've force-fed her a whole bottle of antidepressants. She so obviously needed them."

The almost-smile dies. "What are you talking about?"

"I've never met anyone who spent so much time in bed. Except for my mom when she's having a depressive episode."

"Your mom?"

"She's bipolar. I don't know if Meg was. I never saw her manic, but I saw her depressed. Trust me, I know what *that* looks like."

I'm about to tell Tree about the mono, how tired Meg had sometimes gotten since then, how if she slept enough for five people, it was because she expended the energy of ten people. *She needs a little time to rejuvenate,* Sue would sometimes say, closing the door, sending me away.

Then Tree says, "Plus, healthy people don't talk that way about suicide."

The hair on the back of my neck rises. *"What?"*

"We had a feminist lit class together, and one night me and her and a few other girls were in a café, studying at a table, and

Meg starts quizzing everyone about how they'd off themselves. We were reading Virginia Woolf, and at first I thought it was because of that. Everyone had their half-baked answers. Guns or pills or jumping off a bridge, but not Meg. She was very specific: 'I'd take poison and I'd do it in a hotel room and I'd leave the maid a big tip.'"

Neither of us says anything. Because of course, that's exactly what Meg did do.

"At which point I told her that she should stop moping and get to the campus health center for some Prozac already."

A friend told me to go to the campus health center to get some meds.

"It *was* you," I whisper into the phone.

I can hear her surprise crackle through the phone. "Me?"

"She said a friend talked her into going to the campus health center, and I've talked to dozens of people, and no one ever mentioned a thing, no one thought to suggest it. Except you."

"We weren't friends."

"Well, *we* were. We were best friends and not only did I not suggest this, I didn't think to."

"Then we both failed her," Tree says. And there's such anger in her voice. And it's then I get it. The animosity. It's Meg. It's the tentacles of her suicide, reaching out, burning people who barely knew her.

"Sorry," Tree mutters under her breath.

"She listened to you. She went to the campus health center and got some meds."

"So what happened?" Tree asks. "Didn't they work?"

"It's my understanding that you have to take them for them to work."

"She didn't take them?"

"Someone talked her out of it."

"Why would they do that? Those drugs saved my mom's life."

I think of all the stuff on the boards, about the drugs numbing your soul. But that wasn't it. It was because someone convinced Meg that her life wasn't worth saving. That death was a better option. It was because, at the very end, when it should've been me whispering in her ear, telling her how amazing she was, how amazing her life was and would be again, it was All_BS doing the whispering.

Tree is right about failing Meg. But it wasn't her that did. It was me. I failed her in life. But I won't fail her in death.

I'm vacuuming at Mrs. Driggs's the next day when my phone vibrates in my pocket. I pull it out and recognize the 206 area code, but the call has already gone to voice mail. A few seconds later it chimes to let me know there's a message waiting.

I stare at my phone in my palm, the vacuum motor whining. Why did he call back? Does he even know it was me who called him? Who knows if he even saved my number, and my outgoing voice mail message is now generic in case All_BS calls.

Whatever he has to say—*who is this?* or something else—I don't want to hear it. I go to delete the voice mail, but I hesitate, and in that moment the phone rings again and I'm relieved and ashamed in equal measures.

"Hey," I say, my heart pounding.

There's a slight pause on the line. "Repeat?" says the voice. The vacuum cleaner is still on, and it takes me a minute to understand that it's not Ben. I flip the phone over to check the caller ID. It's not the 206 number this time. It's blocked. "Repeat," the voice says again, and then I understand I'm not being asked to repeat anything.

"Yes."

"Do you know who this is?"

"I know."

"What's that noise?"

"Oh. I'm at work."

He chuckles. "As am I."

His voice is not what I expected. It's jovial, almost comforting. It's like we already know each other.

The vacuum is still droning. I turn it off. "There. Is that better?"

"Yes." He chuckles again. "If only I could turn off the noise at my work so easily. But I've found a quiet corner. Forgive the delay."

I listen then; in the background, there's an electric clang of something. Cash registers?

"One must choose the risks one takes and mitigate them."

"Yes," I say.

"Speaking of risks and choices, you have chosen?"

"Yes," I say.

"That's very brave," he says.

"I'm scared." It flies out. This absolute truth. All_BS seems to pull it from me. Which is an irony, of sorts.

He continues: "You know what George Patton said? 'All intelligent men are frightened. The more intelligent they are, the more they are frightened.' That holds true for women, too, I'd say."

I don't say anything.

"Have you decided on a method?" he asks.

"Yes, I'm going to—"

"Don't," he cuts me off. "That's a personal decision."

"Oh. Sorry." I'm not just disappointed. I'm devastated. I want to tell him so badly.

"Are all your affairs in order?"

Affairs in order. That's the language one of the sites he referred me to used. It had all the instructions about writing the note, creating a legally binding will.

"Yes," I answer. I feel dazed.

"Remember, the opposite of bravery is not cowardice, but conformity. You are bucking conformity, choosing your own path."

Somewhere it registers that Meg would've loved this sentiment, if he used it on her. She was all about bucking conformity, right up to the very end.

"Now, like all things, it's a matter of following through. Screw your courage—"

"To the sticking place," I finish the sentence without thinking.

There's a pause on the line. Something is being weighed. I've made a mistake.

Then I hear a burst of commotion as the ambient background noise clangs through the phone. Electronic bleeping and the clatter of change. It's the sound of slot machines, lots of them. A sound I recognize from the Indian casinos.

"The door was locked," I hear him bark, his own voice different now.

"Sorry, Smith. Lock's been busted for weeks."

There's the sound of a door slamming, and the noise goes quiet again.

"We should wrap this up," he says in a formal tone. "Best of luck to you."

"Wait," I say. I want him to send me the stuff I found in Meg's trash: the encrypted documents, the checklist, more evidence, more proof to hang him with.

But he's gone.

That night I call Harry Kang.

"Harry? It's Cody."

"Cody . . . Hey . . . ." A car horn blares, and there's a loud cacophony of people talking.

"Where are you?" I ask.

"In Korea, visiting my grandmother. Hold on." I hear his phone shuffle and then the electric ping of a doorbell, and then it's quieter. "There. I'm in a tea shop now. Seoul is nuts. What's up?"

"I might have enough information. Or I've gotten all I'm going to get." All_BS's last words echo in my ears. *Best of luck*. Like it was my high school graduation we were discussing. Or like he knew it was the last time we'd ever speak.

"What do you have?"

"This is what I know for sure. Actually, I don't know any-thing *for sure*. Here's what I have. I'm pretty sure he's on the West Coast somewhere. He always seems to be having dinner when I am or things like that."

"That narrows it down to a few hundred million people."

"I have more. I think he might work at a casino. So, casino on the West Coast. Las Vegas?"

"Which has a population of, what, a million people? If he's even there. He could work anywhere in Nevada," Harry says. "Gambling is legal statewide."

"Or he could work at an Indian casino anywhere," I add.

"Exactly. What else you got?"

"His last name might be Smith. Someone called him that."

"It's helpful to have a name, even if it's the least helpful name in existence." He pauses. "You have anything else?"

"No. Our call got cut short."

"Call? He called you?"

"Yeah."

"Landline or cell?"

"I don't know. It came up as blocked. But he was at work, so I'd guess cell."

"On your cell or landline?"

"Cell. I was at work, and we gave up our landline."

"When?"

"Did we give up our landline?"

"No, Cody. When did he call you?"

"Earlier today."

"Seriously?" Harry's voice perks up.

"Yeah. Why, is that bad?"

"Careless."

"So, bad for him, but good for us?"

"Could be." I can tell, even through the phone, that Harry is smiling. "You'll have to give me complete access to your mobile account."

"Fine."

"And send everything you have on this Smith guy. Usernames. Any accounts you used to communicate. Anything you have on him. Any electronic trail. Email it all to me."

If I have to go stand outside Mrs. Chandler's driveway to pick up a Wi-Fi signal, I'll do it. Though Mrs. Banks said the library is reopening any day. "Done."

"And understand I'll be doing some quasi-legal things."

"For a good cause," I remind him.

"I'll say. I'm going a little crazy at my grandmother's, so it'll be good to have a project. I'll be in touch when I find something."

× × ×

That afternoon I stand outside the Chandlers' empty house, pirating their Wi-Fi signal, and I send Harry everything. The next day, the library reopens. I go in with the laptop and check the anonymous messaging service All_BS and I used, but there's nothing. I check the Final Solution boards, but there's nothing from him there, either. I am pretty certain there will be no more communication from him. But maybe it doesn't matter. Maybe I've gone from being the mouse to being the snake.

× × ×

After three days Harry calls.

"That wasn't easy," he says. He sounds utterly thrilled.

"Did you find him?"

Harry doesn't answer. Instead, he tells me a long and complicated tale about how All_BS used Skype to make some kind of VoIP call, not through a phone, but through a tablet. It's hard to trace a telephone number, but not as hard to track an application's user. "This is how even the best criminals get caught," he tells me. "They are so careful—until they're not."

"So you *did* find him?"

"Like I said. It wasn't easy. The tablet was registered to this guy Allen DeForrest."

"So that's him?"

"I don't think so," Harry says. "When I dug a bit deeper, this DeForrest had a huge online profile. He's all over Facebook and Instagram, lots of pictures and status updates. I figured our guy would be more secretive. But I had this feeling. So I dug up more on DeForrest and discovered where he worked. He's a pit boss at the Continental Casino."

"What's a pit boss?"

"It's like a manager, but you're missing the point, Cody. It's at a *casino*. Your hunch was right! It's not in Las Vegas, but Laughlin, Nevada, which is like a poor man's Vegas."

"But you said you didn't think it was the DeForrest guy."

"Right. I still don't. For one, I thought that your guy, with all his fancy encryption methods, would be more careful than to use his own device. And second, we're looking for a Smith, right? So I hacked into the employee records at the Continental Casino and looked for people with the last name Smith. As you might've guessed, there were a lot of them. But only a couple of B. Smiths."

"B?"

"All_*BS*."

"I thought that meant all bullshit."

"I did too. And it might. But guys like this, who are doing

bad things and keeping it secret, sometimes they still want to brag about it somehow. So I wondered if BS weren't his initials, especially since we already know his last name is Smith." He pauses. "So I checked. There are only three B. Smiths employed by the casino. Bernadette. Becky." He stops. "And Bradford."

The hair on the back of my neck stands up. "Bradford?"

"Bradford Smith. Age fifty-two. Works in the Continental Casino. There's more. I looked up *his* Internet history and found that he pays for the premium broadband package, but, unlike the DeForrest guy, he leaves a very light online footprint. Fits the profile."

"So *that's* him?"

"Might be."

"How do we know for sure?"

"Would you recognize his voice?"

Our one and only phone call. Brief, but indelible. "I think so."

"Good. I got a phone number for his actual cell phone. We can call on a blocked line and conference you in. If we get voice mail, you listen to his outgoing message. If he answers, I'll pose as a telemarketer, and you stay quiet. Either way, you can confirm his voice."

"That's all we have to do?"

"Yep. Hang up, and I'll call you back and patch you in."

"Now? Won't he get suspicious?"

"Who gets suspicious of a telemarketer?"

"Good point."

"Okay. What should we be selling that no one wants to buy?" Harry asks.

"As it happens, I've worked as a telemarketer before. No one wanted supplemental life insurance, and it seems oddly fitting to try to sell it to him." I tell Harry the script.

"Okay. Hang up, and I'll call you back and we'll do this."

When Harry calls back, the line is already ringing. "Shh," he tells me.

The voice that picks up is gruff. "Hello."

"Hello. I'm with Good Faith Insurance Agency," Harry begins in a smooth voice, like he does this all the time. "The reason I'm calling is to let you know that we have drastically lowered our insurance rates in Laughlin. We would love to give you a no-obligation review and quote on your current life insurance policy. If you don't have one set up yet, I'd love to discuss this very wise investment in your future."

"I've already told you, I'm not interested," he says. And hangs up.

We sit there for a moment, in a triangle of silence: Me. Harry Kang. And the disconnected voice of All_BS.

Once again, I'm back at the library for research, but this time, it's easier. I only have to figure out how to get to Laughlin. The hard part is over.

I can't quite believe it. I've been looking for All_BS for weeks, and at times, it has felt like chasing a ghost. But he's here. I have an address. Last night Harry called me once more, this time with all of All_BS's—Bradford Smith's—contact information.

"You are a fucking genius, Harry Kang!" I told him.

"I don't know about effing genius, but I'll take genius," he said. And I could hear the smile in his voice once again.

"Thank you, Harry. Thank you so much."

"No. Thank you," he said quietly. "It was fun. But it also felt good. Like maybe I could do something for Meg." He paused. "Are you going to the police now?"

"I'm not sure. I was thinking I might go there myself first."

Harry went quiet. "Be careful, Cody," he said after a bit. "It seems abstract when you're dealing with people online, but they are still people, and some of them are not nice people, not the kind you ever want to be in a room with."

Sometimes you don't even need to be in the same room for

the damage to be done. "I'll be careful," I promised. "Thank you, again."

"Like I said, I'm glad to do it. And it's not that hard to find someone."

"Really?"

Harry laughed. "Maybe not for me."

And that's when I had the other idea. "Do you think you might be able to track down one more person?"

x x x

The Greyhound to Laughlin takes thirty hours, requires three transfers, and costs three hundred dollars round trip. I have the money, and I can take off the time if I need to. But when I start to contemplate sixty hours alone on the bus, I begin to feel a little sick, the darkness clawing at me. I can't do this alone, with only Bradford and Meg keeping me company.

I list the people I might ask to go with me. There's no one in town. I'd never ask Tricia, and the Garcias are obviously out. The friends from school, never all that close, have fallen away. Who else? Sharon Devonne?

Maybe the Cascades people. Except Alice is still working at Mountain Bound. Harry is in Korea until mid-August. That leaves Stoner Richard. It's not the worst idea in the world. He's home in Boise for the summer, and that's on the way. I could catch a Greyhound to Boise, and we could drive from there.

There is one other person. And as soon as I think of him, I understand that there is no other person. Because he is somehow as linked up in all this as I am.

His voice mail is still on my phone. I never listened to it, but

I haven't deleted it. I listen to it now. All it says is this: "Cody, what do you need from me?"

Words can have so many meanings. That question could be harboring exasperation, annoyance, guilt, surrender.

I listen once more. This time I let myself truly hear that familiar growl of fear and concern and tenderness behind his words.

Cody, what do you need from me?

And so I tell him.

Ben offers to come pick me up at home, but I don't want him to come here. We arrange to meet in Yakima, outside the Greyhound station, at noon on Saturday. Then I call Stoner Richard.

"Cody, long time, no hear. What's the latest and greatest?"

"What are you doing Saturday night?"

"Are you asking me out?" he teases.

"Actually, I'm asking if I can sleep with you," I tease back, before explaining that I'm heading out on a road trip and need a place to crash Saturday night in Boise.

"There's always room at the Zeller homestead. Just be prepared: if you come for a Saturday night, the rev might want you to do things the Jerry way on Sunday."

"Okay," I say, not sure what the Jerry way means, but figuring it's some Jerry Garcia reference. "Also, there's a slight catch."

"Isn't there always?"

"Ben McCallister's going to be with me."

I hear Richard inhale sharply. Either in dismay, or he could be taking a bong hit. "Are you and him, are you guys . . . ?"

"No, no! Nothing like that. I haven't even talked to him in more than a month. He's just helping me out."

"Helping you out? I'll bet he is."

"It's not like that. It's about Meg."

"Oh." Richard's voice goes serious.

"So can you put us up? We're leaving here around noon, so we should get there around six or seven."

"Easily. Speed limit's seventy-five on I-84, but no one goes slower than eighty. You'll make good time."

"So, it's okay for us both to stay?"

"There's always room in Reverend Jerry's manger," Richard jokes. "We're used to having lost souls camped on the floor. For you, we might even scrounge up a couch."

"The floor's fine."

"So long as it's a separate floor from McCallister."

x x x

I wait until Friday night to tell Tricia that I'm going. I've already canceled my Monday and Tuesday cleaning jobs, figuring I'll be back by Tuesday night at the latest. I don't know why I'm nervous about telling her.

She gives me a long look. "Where are you going?"

Tricia doesn't keep me on a leash. But if I tell her, it'll wind up right back with the Garcias, and I don't want them to know anything until I have something solid, something helpful. Also, if I tell her, I'm scared that Tricia, even hands-off Tricia, won't let me go.

"Tacoma," I say.

"Again?"

"Alice invited me down."

"I thought she was in Montana."

I should've learned my lesson from all my dealings with All_BS. The safest way to lie is to shadow the truth.

"She is. She's going home for the weekend," I reply, hoping Tricia doesn't remember that Alice is actually from Eugene.

Tricia eyes me again.

"I'll be back Monday night, Tuesday latest," I add.

"You need me to clean any of your houses?"

I shake my head. Some messes can wait.

x x x

I can't sleep at all Friday night, so Saturday morning I pack a few things—my boxful of cash, which now totals five hundred and sixty dollars, my computer, and my maps—and catch the first bus to Yakima. I arrive at nine thirty and plant myself at a depressing coffee shop near the bus station, spreading my maps in front of me. It's a straight thousand-mile shot from here to Laughlin, cutting a triangle through Oregon and another through Idaho, before shooting down the eastern spine of Nevada.

The waitress keeps refilling my coffee cup and I keep drinking, even though the burnt swill is doing awful things to the acid in my stomach, not to mention my frayed nerves. For the past twenty-four hours, I've done nothing but second-guess the decision to call Ben.

The door to the diner rings. I look up absentmindedly and am surprised to see it's him. It's only ten thirty; he's not due for another hour and a half, and it's a two- to three-hour drive from Seattle, so he must've left at the crack of dawn, or sped like the devil, or both.

My first impulse is to hunch down in my seat, buy myself more time. But I'm about to spend two days cramped in a car with him, so I man up. I clear my throat and say, "Hey, Ben."

His face goes blank for a second, and then his eyes skitter around until he sees me in my booth, the maps splayed out. He looks both nervous and relieved, and once again his face is like a mirror, reflecting my feelings, because that's exactly what's going on with me.

He sits down across from me. "You're early," he says.

"So are you." I slide my coffee over to him. "You want some? She just refilled it. So it's fresh, or fresh to my cup, anyhow."

His fingers curl around the cup of coffee, which is black, no sugar, the same as he likes it, I now remember. I take him in. His eyes are violet this morning, almost bruised; they match the purplish skin under them. "I couldn't sleep," he says.

"Seems to be going around," I say.

He nods. "So what's the plan?"

"Drive to Boise today. We can stay with Stoner Richard—I mean, Richard Zeller. You remember Meg's roommate?"

"I remember."

"He said we could crash at his place. It's his parents'. Unless you want to stay somewhere else." He probably has plenty of places to stop, plenty of rock-and-roll crash pads.

"I'll go where you go."

A simple statement that feels like a blanket.

"You going to tell me what it is we're doing?" he asks.

When I called Ben, I told him I'd found a person linked to Meg's death and needed someone to come with me while I talked to him. I hadn't told him anything else. I figured he didn't need, nor would he want, to know what had happened in these past few weeks when we'd been absent from each other's lives. But now that he's asking, I'm scared to tell. Harry sent me a few cautioning emails, with links to articles about girls meeting guys they'd met online and gruesome things happening. I appreciated his concern but wasn't sure it was applicable. Those were girls with romantic hopes, guys with depraved intentions. That isn't me and Bradford.

But what if Ben doesn't see it that way? What if I tell him and he chickens out? What if he refuses to take me?

When I don't answer right away, Ben asks, "Am I on a need-to-know basis, or something?"

"No. I just . . ." I shake my head. "It's a long drive."

"What does that mean?"

"There's time. I'll tell you. Later. I promise." I pause. "How are the kids?" I ask.

"I brought pictures," he says. And I expect him to show me on his phone, but he pulls out one of those envelopes you get from a photo developer, and slides it across the maps to me. I open it up, and inside are a few snapshots: Pete and Repeat chasing a piece of string, washing each other's faces, curled up sleeping together at the foot of Ben's bed.

"They're so much bigger!"

Ben nods. "Teenagers. Pete brought home a dead mouse. I'm sure it's a gateway thing. It's only a matter of time before they're bringing home all sorts of animals."

"Birds. Rats."

"Then it's possums, then small ponies. I wouldn't put it past those two."

I laugh. It feels like the first time in ages. I hand the photos back.

Ben shakes his head. "They're for you."

"Oh. Thanks. Do you want something to eat? Before we go?"

Ben shakes his head. "I came to kill time while I was waiting for you."

"And here I am."

"Here you are."

The awkward silence that follows doesn't bode well for the next two days.

"Should we get going?" I ask.

"Okay. I should warn you, the cigarette lighter outlet for the iPod is acting up, so the music situation is precarious."

"I'll deal."

"Also, less important to me but maybe not you: the AC's kind of on the blink, which is going to make Nevada desert driving in July rather interesting."

"We'll just stop at gas stations and douse ourselves with water and leave the windows open. It's what Meg and I used to do." And then I stop myself. Everything spools back to Meg. Every piece of my history, it seems.

"Sounds like a plan," Ben says.

We head outside. He unlocks his car. It's remarkably clean compared to the last time I was in it.

"Do you want me to drive first?" I ask. "Or don't you let girls drive your car?"

"I don't make a habit of letting anyone drive my car." He looks sidelong at me. "But you're not a girl anyway."

"Oh, right. Have you categorized my species yet?"

"Not quite." He tosses me the keys. "But you can drive."

x   x   x

As soon as we hit the interstate, I relax. I got my license when I was sixteen, but I so rarely get to actually drive anywhere, I forget how freeing it is to just have open road in front of you, and wind in your hair. With the windows down and the stereo on, it's too loud to talk much, and that's fine. Ben can't ask me about Bradford, can't ask me about the last month, and can't mention the kiss, either.

Outside of Baker City we stop for lunch at a place Ben knows. I'm skeptical about a Chinese restaurant in the middle of redneck eastern Oregon, but Ben says the dumplings are the best he's ever had. It seems like he's been here a lot. The young waitress clearly knows him and keeps finding excuses to come by the table to refill our tea and talk to him until her stern mother comes out from the kitchen and shoos her away.

"Wow. You know everyone on the I-84 corridor?" I ask him.

"Just in the Chinese restaurants. Along I-5, too."

I motion toward the waitress, who is smiling at him. "Is she a fan from when you came through here with one of your bands?"

Ben gives me a look. "I was never here with a band. I ate here with my little sister, Bethany."

That name is familiar. And then I remember that was one of the girls Ben was talking to on the phone when I went to see him in Seattle that first time.

"Bethany is your little sister?"

He nods. "Yeah. She was having a tough time at home. Back then I was couch-surfing in Portland, so I swooped in, all big hero man, to pick her up and take her on a road trip. I was going to take her to Utah. To Zion. I've always wanted to go there." He swigs his tea. "Car broke down here. Piece of shit Pontiac."

"What happened to your road trip? You guys hitch?"

"Nah. Bethany was only eleven." Ben shakes his head. "I had to call my stepfather to come get her, and we hung out here while he drove up. He was so pissed at me that he refused to give me a lift back to Bend. I didn't have anything going in Portland, so I wound up hitching to Seattle. It's how I landed there."

"Oh." It's not exactly the rock-star-chasing-his-dreams story. "Where is she now? Bethany?"

Ben's eyes go flat. "There."

I'm not exactly sure where there is, but by the way he says it, I know it's not a place you'd want to be.

"Let's finish up and get back on the road," he suggests. "You know, Chinese food means we'll be hungry again in an hour."

"Ha. We only have a couple of hours till Boise. And Richard texted to say that they're grilling tonight."

Ben perks up. "Grilling? Like real meat? Nothing tofu?"

I text Richard back to ask if there will be tofu, and he texts me back a puking emoticon. "You're safe," I tell Ben.

We gas up and Ben takes the wheel, and it's only when we get into the car and back on the interstate that I notice Ben didn't smoke after lunch. In fact, he hasn't smoked the whole time we've been on the road.

"If you're not smoking for my benefit, don't worry about it,"

I tell him. But then I notice that the car doesn't smell like an ashtray the way it did before.

Ben smiles kind of bashfully. He lifts up the sleeve of his shirt to show me a flesh-colored patch. "I quit."

"When?"

"A few weeks ago."

"Why?"

"Aside from the fact that cigarettes are deadly and expensive?" he asks.

"Right, aside from that?"

Ben slices the quickest of looks my way before turning his attention back to the road. "I guess I needed a change."

x x x

By six o'clock we are in the outskirts of Boise, the tilting early evening sun making the foothills surrounding the city go red. I pull out the directions that Richard emailed me, and guide Ben through the downtown and out past the military area to a pretty tree-lined street with sprawling ranch houses. We stop in front of one with an overflowing orange bougainvillea bush and a big white van in the driveway. "This is it," I tell Ben.

As we knock on the front door, I kick myself. We should've brought something, some kind of gift or something. That's the kind of thing you're supposed to do. Too late now.

No one answers. We ring the bell. Still nothing. People are home. There's a TV on and there's a sound of voices inside. We knock again. Still no answer. I'm about to text Richard when Ben opens the door and sticks his head inside. "Hello," he calls.

A kid bounds up, a huge grin zigzagging across her face, which is sort of messed up by a cleft palate or one of those things you see in those TV commercials asking for money. "Maybe we have the wrong house," I whisper. But then the kid shouts, "Wichard, your fwiends are hewe," and five seconds later Richard ambles over, scoops the girl up, and ushers us inside.

"This is CeCe," he says, tickling the girl under her arms as she screams in delight. He points around the room to where three more kids are sitting on beanbags and cushions, watching a movie. "That's Jack, Pedro, and Tally."

"Hi," I say.

"Hey," Ben says. "*Toy Story*?"

"Three," Pedro says.

Ben nods knowingly.

"Who are they?" I whisper to Richard as he sets CeCe down.

"Family 2.0," Richard says.

"Huh?"

"They're my brothers and sisters, the second string, though really more like first string. My other brother, Gary, is out back, and my sister Lisa is currently in Uganda working with orphans or something extremely noble."

He slides open the glass door leading out to the patio. Only then does he acknowledge Ben. "Ben," he says cautiously.

"Rich," Ben says back. "Thanks for having us."

"I'm having her. You're just along for the ride."

Out back two men are arguing over the grill, while a woman with cutoff shorts and a cute halter top stands in the kiddie pool, watching them bemusedly.

"You'll let me know when to bring out the corn," she calls.

Then she sees us. "Jerry, Richard's friends are here." She climbs out of the pool and comes to introduce herself. "I'm Sylvia. You must be Cody. And you must be Ben."

"Thank you so much for having us," I say.

"And having us for a barbecue," Ben says, eyeing the grill lustfully.

"We'll only have a barbecue if these mountain goats can stop arguing about what wood to smoke with," Sylvia says.

"Pop," Richard calls.

Richard's dad is very tall, so tall he's stooped, as if he's spent his entire life bending down to listen to other people. "Hello," he says in a quiet voice. "Thank you for joining us tonight."

"I hope we're not imposing."

Sylvia laughs. "As you can see, the term *full house* is relative around here."

"We think Pop is going for twelve kids in all, so he can have his own gang of disciples," Richard's brother Gary says.

"Inherent in the word *disciple* is some sort of discipline, of following one's father, which is a far cry from what goes on here," Richard's dad jokes. He looks at me and Ben. "We're having ribs tonight. The boys and I are disagreeing over hickory or mesquite to smoke with. Perhaps you have an opinion."

"Either's fine . . ." I begin.

"Mesquite," Ben says emphatically.

Richard and his brother fist-bump. "Smartest thing I've ever heard you say," Richard tells Ben.

"Richard!" Sylvia admonishes.

"Mesquite it is," Jerry says, throwing up his hands in good-natured surrender. "We'll eat in about two hours. Richard, why don't you take your road-weary guests inside and offer them something to drink."

Richard raises an eyebrow.

"A cold soda," his father says.

"There's some lemonade, too," Sylvia says.

"The monsters drank it all," Richard says.

"So squeeze some more. We have a ton of lemons."

"When life gives you lemons . . ." Richard begins. Then he looks at me for a second and stops himself. Like he thinks it's wrong to make this joke in front of me. I'm not sure why now, all of a sudden, he should get shy in front of me. So I finish for him.

"Make lemonade."

x x x

Dinner is late and chaotic and delicious. Ten of us crammed around a picnic table under a clear Idaho sky. Ben eats so many ribs that even Richard is impressed, and when Ben explains that he lives in a vegan household, Sylvia throws a few hot dogs on the grill to top him off. I look at this nearly emaciated man and wonder how he can possibly pack it all away. But he does. Two more hot dogs and a pair of ice-cream sandwiches from the Costco box that comes out after dinner. It's past nine when Sylvia and Jerry begin the epic undertaking of bathing and putting to bed all the hyped-up little ones. Gary heads out to meet some friends. Richard throws some logs on a fire pit in the back of the yard and sneaks into the garage for a couple of beers.

Through the window I can see Richard's dad, a picture book open, reading to a bunch of kids in bunk beds. I hear the clatter of Sylvia doing dishes. Over the flickering firelight, I catch Ben's eye, and I swear we are thinking the same thing: *How lucky some people are.*

I'm hit with a sudden wave of aching nostalgia. *I miss this.* But how can miss this when I never truly had it in the first place? It was secondhand through Meg. Like pretty much everything else in my life.

The firelight crackles. Richard finishes his beer and stashes the empty in the bushes. "You want another?" he asks us.

Ben shakes his head. "Better not. We have a big drive tomorrow." He looks at me. I nod.

"So where you going, exactly?" Richard asks Ben.

Ben looks at me, asking the same silent question. I still haven't told him the whole story.

"Laughlin, Nevada."

"I caught that much," Richard replies. He goes to the cooler and grabs another beer for himself and a couple of Dr Peppers for Ben and me. Something in my chest twists, and it's ridiculous because I'm getting emotional because he remembered what soft drink I like. "I guess my question is really why Laughlin?"

I don't say anything. Neither does Ben.

"What? Is it a secret or something?" Richard asks.

Ben looks at me. "Apparently."

"Wait, *you* don't know?" Richard says.

"I'm just along for the ride," Ben fires back.

They glare at each other for a second, and then look at me. Inside, Jerry and the kids are saying prayers, calling out a long list of people to be blessed.

"This is between us," I say, pointing back and forth between me and Richard and Ben.

"A sacred circle," Richard jokes. "Or triangle. A *ménage à silence*."

I give him a look, and then he goes solemn and promises.

"Remember when I came down and Harry was helping me with the computer thing?" I ask.

Richard nods.

"We found an encrypted file on Meg's computer, and it turned out that it was instructions from this suicide support group, a group that supports your decision to end your own life. I did some more digging, and I uncovered her posting to these discussion boards. There was this one guy; he was like her mentor. He encouraged her."

"That's messed up," Richard says.

"Yeah, it is," I say.

"I can't believe Meg fell for it."

"I know," I say. But I lack the conviction on this one. Because now that I know Bradford, I *can* believe it. "So I found this guy, and now I'm going to see him."

"You're *what*?" Ben interjects.

"I'm going to see him," I repeat, but it comes out tepid this time.

"I thought you needed to talk to someone who knew about her death, like the Seattle people," Ben exclaims. He frowns at me like I've violated some treaty.

I take a deep breath to keep my voice level. "I'm talking to the person who *caused* her death."

"Except *she* caused her death," Richard says. "That's the definition of suicide."

Richard and I glare at each other. "Bradford made her do it."

"Which makes going to see him a brilliant idea!" Ben fumes.

"You knew I was looking for him," I shoot back.

"I don't know shit, Cody. Because for the last six weeks, you've refused to talk to me."

"I'm talking to you *now*. I spent the last six weeks trying to smoke this guy out."

"And how'd you do that?" Richard asks, his gaze ping-ponging between Ben and me.

"Harry helped, but mostly it was me. I kind of posed as someone who was suicidal. You know, me appetizing mouse. Him hungry snake."

"Jesus fucking Christ, Cody!" Ben exclaims. "Are you insane?"

"You mean like Meg was?"

That shuts him up.

"How does one do that? Pose as suicidal?" Richard asks. "My only experience is the opposite. Someone suicidal posing as okay."

I could bullshit. I could say I lied, made it all up. But I tell the truth. "I found the part in me that was tired of living," I say quietly. "And I put her out there." I look down, unable to face their shock, or anger, or disgust. "I suppose that does make me insane." I sneak a peek at Ben, but he's staring hard at the fire.

"Nah," Richard says. "Everyone goes there. Everyone has their days. Everyone imagines it. But you know why my pop says that suicide is a sin?" He points his thumb toward the house, where Jerry is now helping Sylvia with the rest of the dishes.

"Because it's murder. Because only God can choose when it's your time to go. Because stealing a life is stealing from God." I parrot all the awful things people said about Meg.

Richard shakes his head. "No. Because it kills hope. That's the sin. Anything that kills hope is a sin."

I chew on that for a while.

"So what do you expect to accomplish? Now that you've found this guy?" Ben asks in a strangely formal tone.

"He has to be liable, somehow, as an accessory, or something."

"So call the cops," Ben says.

"It's not that simple," I say.

"Have you told Meg's family?" he asks.

"You're missing the point," I reply.

"None of this will bring her back," Richard says. "You know that, right?"

Yes, I know that. That's not the point, either, though the point is muddled. But I can't go to the cops or go to Meg's family. I have to do this—do *something*—by myself. For Meg.

And for me.

32

I wake up the next morning to the international coalition of Zeller children leaping onto the couch. I get up, get dressed, and am helping Sylvia with the toaster waffles when Ben pads out, rubbing his eyes.

"Want to get coffee on the road?" I ask him.

"You're leaving already?" Sylvia asks.

I make apologies, say we should get out of their hair, but Sylvia says we're no trouble. "And it's Sunday."

"Services start at ten," Richard says, coming out in a cleanish-looking pair of jeans and a T-shirt with no drug references on it. "Can't you stay? The rev will be bummed otherwise."

I glance at Ben, who hasn't spoken to me since last night. He shrugs the question back to me. I look at Richard and Sylvia and realize it doesn't matter if I brought a gift. This is what matters.

I look down at my cutoff shorts and tank top. "I'd better change."

"You can if you want," Sylvia says. "But we're a come-as-you-are congregation."

We caravan over at nine thirty, Richard driving with me and

Ben, the rest of the family in the van, which has one of those *Coexist* bumper stickers on it.

Outside the church the various Zeller children are scooped up by different congregants, and Sylvia and Jerry go into greeter mode. Richard slips inside with Ben and me.

We take our seats. The pews are a little worn, and it smells slightly of cooking oil. It's the dumpiest of the churches I've been to, and this past year, I've been to a lot. Before that, I hardly went to church at all—Meg's first communion, and the occasional midnight mass. Tricia usually works late Saturday nights, and Sundays are reserved for worshipping the pillow.

The service here is unlike any I've been to. There's no choir. Instead, different people get up and sing and play guitar or piano and anyone can join in. Some of the songs are religious, but others aren't. Ben's all pleased when a bearded guy plays a soulful tune called "I Feel Like Going Home." He leans over and tells me it's by Charlie Rich, one of his favorite artists. It's the first normal thing he's said to me since we argued last night. I take it as a peace offering. "It's beautiful," I tell him.

Jerry sort of stays out of the way for much of the proceedings, allowing a younger guy who leads the youth ministry to run the show. And then, when all the singing is over and announcements have been made, he uncurls himself from his seat where he's been sitting calmly, and in a voice that is quiet but somehow commanding, steps to the pulpit and starts talking.

"A few weeks ago CeCe was sick. She had a fever, was sluggish—that bug that's been going around. I know a lot of us went through it." There is some murmuring and tongue-clucking in the congregation. "Pedro didn't have school that day, so he had to tag along with us to the doctor's. CeCe doesn't like doctors' offices, having been to so many of them. So she was agitated and crying, and the longer we waited, the worse it got. And we were waiting awhile. An hour went by. Then an hour and a half. CeCe kept crying, and then she threw up. Mostly on me." There's sympathetic laughter.

"I'm still not sure if it was because of the virus, or because she had gotten herself so worked up about being at the doctor. Doesn't matter. But this one mother sitting with her own daughter visibly flinched at CeCe's mess. And then she chastised me for exposing all the other children to her.

"On some level, I got it. None of us wants our kids to be sick. But as a father, I was livid. In my head I said many unchristian things about that woman, to that woman. CeCe being sick was the point of our being in the pediatrician's office in the first place, and this was not a Christian way to behave. The nurses were too busy to offer much help aside from giving us some wipes and sanitizer. All the while, CeCe kept crying.

"Eventually, I got her cleaned up and she fell asleep. Pedro found a puzzle, and with a few seconds to spare, I picked up a magazine. It was two years out of date, this being a doctor's office. I opened to a random page. It was an article about forgiveness. Now, this wasn't a religious publication. It was a medical journal, and the article was describing a study that had analyzed all the health benefits of forgiveness. Apparently, it lowers blood pressure, decreases anxiety, minimizes depression.

"I understood then that I'd been sent this article on purpose.

As I read it, I thought of Colossians 3:13: *Bear with each other and forgive whatever grievances you may have against one another. Forgive as the Lord forgave you.*

"And so I forgave everyone in that room: the woman for being so rude, the nurses for being too busy to help, the doctor for keeping us waiting, even CeCe for her histrionics. And then I forgave myself. As soon as I did, my worry over CeCe eased. I felt calm, peaceful, and full of love. And in that moment, I was reminded just why God wants us to forgive. Not simply because it's the key to a better world, but because of what it does for *ourselves*. Forgiveness is God's gift to *us*. Christ forgave us. He forgave our sins. That was his gift. But by allowing us to forgive each other, he opened us up to that divine love. The article had it right. Forgiveness: It's a miracle drug. It's God's miracle drug."

Jerry goes on, quoting more lines from scripture about forgiveness. But at the moment, I'm just not feeling it. Last night I went to bed first, leaving Ben and Richard around the fire. Those two barely tolerate each other, so I figured they'd call it a night soon after. But now, as Richard's father goes on, I can see that's not what happened. Tongues went wagging. So much for a sacred circle.

Jerry continues: "After we saw the doctor, I was settling up at the front desk and I ran into the angry mother again. All the rancor I'd felt was gone. There was no effort to rise above. It just vanished. I told her that I hoped her little girl was feeling better.

"She turned to look at me. I could now recognize how tired she was, like so many of us parents are. 'She'll be fine,' she said.

'The doctor said she's healing well.' I looked at the little girl and saw a small welt, red, still fresh, on her chin. I turned back to the mother and saw something much fresher there: anguish, not nearly so well healed. I wanted to ask her what happened, but Pedro and CeCe were yanking to go, and besides, it wasn't my place. But I suppose she needed to unburden herself, because she told me how a few weeks earlier, she'd been rushing to get out the door in the morning, but her little girl had been dawdling by the flowers. She'd yanked her by the hand and the girl, still busy watching the bees dancing, had slammed into a gate. That's how she'd gotten the cut. 'She'll always carry that scar,' the mother told me in a voice pinched with agony. And then I understood her anger. Just who it was she hadn't forgiven.

"'She will, only if you do,' I told her back. She looked at me, and I knew what I was asking her to do, what God asks us to do—what I'm asking *you* all to do—isn't easy. To let our scars heal. To forgive. And hardest of all, sometimes, is to forgive ourselves. But if we don't, we're squandering one of God's greatest gifts: his miracle cure."

When the sermon ends, Richard turns to me, grinning almost. He seems so proud. Of his father, or himself, for orchestrating this public service announcement. "What'd you think?"

I don't answer. I just push my way out of the pew.

"What's wrong?" Ben asks.

What's wrong is that Richard Zeller and his dad don't know what the hell they're talking about. They don't know about the mornings when anger is the one thing—the only thing—to get you through the day. If they take that from me, I'm wide open: raw and gaping, and then I don't stand a fucking chance.

I go to the lobby, holding back tears of rage. Richard is right behind me.

"Couldn't take the rev anymore?" he jokes, but there's worry in his eyes.

"You told him. You said you wouldn't and you told him. You lied."

"I didn't even see my dad until breakfast, and you were right there."

"Then how'd he know? How'd he have such a perfect sermon waiting?"

Richard glances toward the sanctuary, where the singing has started up again. "For the record, Cody, he works on his sermons for weeks in advance; he doesn't pull them out of his ass. Also for the record, you're not the only one with a chip on her shoulder and some crap to forgive, but if, like the rev says, the magazine opens to the right page—"

"Are you *stoned*?" I interrupt.

This makes him laugh. "I didn't tell the rev about your trip. If you want to know the truth, I had to talk McCallister out of turning around. You've got bigger balls than him, no surprise there." The singing ends. Richard nods toward the pulpit. "Come on back. It's almost over. . . . Please."

I follow Richard back to our row right as Jerry is offering up blessings for the congregation, for the sick and the grieving, for those getting married, expecting babies. Right at the very end, he says: "And may God bless and guide Cody and Ben.

May they find not just what they're looking for, but what they need." I look at Richard again. I'm not entirely sure that he's telling the truth about not saying something to his father. But right now, the betrayal, if there was one, feels less important than the benediction.

Outside the church, Ben tosses me the keys, like he knows that I need to drive. At Twin Falls we cut off the interstate onto Highway 93. Ben starts yawning, his eyes drooping. He camped on the floor of Richard and Gary's room, and he says between Richard's snoring and Gary talking in his sleep, he didn't get much rest.

"Why don't you take a nap?" I suggest.

He shakes his head. "Goes against the code."

"What code?"

"Touring code. Someone always has to stay up with the driver."

"That makes sense if there's a bunch of you, but there's only two of us, and you're tired."

He looks at me, considering.

"Look," I go on. "We can just make up a new code."

He continues to look at me. But then he gives in. He turns his face toward the window and falls asleep, staying that way for the next three hours.

There's something nourishing about seeing him sleep. Maybe it's the sun, or maybe my imagination, but the bluish tinge from underneath his eyes seems to fade a bit. He sleeps until the highway ends and I pull into a gas station to fill up the tank. Inside the station there's a big map with a red circle denoting where we are: the junction of Highway 93 and Interstate 80. To get to Laughlin, we jog east on 80 until we go south on Interstate 15 near Salt Lake City. But if we were to go west, the interstate would take us into California, dipping above Lake Tahoe.

After Harry had gotten back to me with the address, I'd looked at the lake for hours. Though the town where he lived wasn't on the lake, it was near it. The lake looked so pretty, the water so clear and blue.

"How far is Truckee, California, from here?" I ask the guy behind the counter.

He shrugs. But a trucker in a Peterbilt hat tells me it's about three hundred miles.

"Do you know how far it is from Truckee to Laughlin, Nevada? I mean, how far of a detour is it?"

The trucker rubs his beard. "You're probably adding three hundred miles to the trip. It's about five or six hundred miles from Truckee, and about five hundred miles from here. Either way, you got a ways to go."

I thank the trucker, buy $40 worth of gas, a California map, a couple of burritos, and a liter of Dr Pepper. Then I go back to the car, where Ben is digging around for his sunglasses.

"Think we'll make Laughlin tonight?" he asks me.

"We'd be pushing it. We got off to a late start, so we wouldn't get there till midnight." I start to pump the gas.

Ben gets out of the car and starts squegeeing the windows. "We might as well push through. I'm all caught up on my sleep now. How long was I out for?"

"Two hundred and fifty miles."

"So we can make it by tonight. I'll take over."

I stop squeezing. The pump goes silent.

"What?" Ben asks. He glances at the California map in my other hand. "Did you change your mind?"

I shake my head. I didn't. I haven't. I still need to do this. To see it through. But we're close. I mean, we're not *that* close. We're three hundred miles away. And this might not be the right address, or the current one. Harry said he'd moved around a lot. But three hundred miles away is as close as I've been in a long time.

"When do you have to be back by?" I ask.

Ben scrapes a moth off the windshield, then shrugs.

"I might want to take a detour."

"Detour? Where to?"

"Truckee. It's in California, near Reno."

"What's in Truckee?"

If anyone will understand, it will be Ben. "My father."

By ten o'clock, we are climbing high up into the Sierra Nevada mountains, getting stuck behind motor homes and pickup trucks hauling huge motorboats. Ben's been driving for six hours straight. The car needs gas again, and we need to figure out a place to stay, but I want to push forward, to get there.

"We probably should stop sooner rather than later," Ben says.

"But we're not there yet."

"Truckee is right outside of Lake Tahoe. It's summer. Places will be full. We're better off in Reno. Also, if we stay at a casino hotel, it's gonna be cheaper."

"Oh, right." Hotels. Last night I didn't have to think about that.

Downtown Reno is garish. Once we pass through the center, with all the big casinos, their marquees advertising bands that were huge in Tricia's day, it turns depressing: dilapidated motels advertising nickel slots and $3.99 steak breakfasts.

We choose one of the crummy motels. "How much for the room?" Ben asks.

The rheumy-eyed guy behind the counter reminds me of Mr. Purdue. "Sixty dollars. Checkout's at eleven."

"I'll give you eighty bucks for two rooms and we'll be out by nine." I plunk down the twenties on the counter. The guy looks at my chest. Ben frowns. The guy crumples the money in his spidery hands, slides over two keys.

Ben pulls out his wallet and starts to hand me some cash, but I wave it away. "It's on me."

We walk back to the Jetta in silence, its engine still ticking from the long drive today. It has a bigger one tomorrow. I grab my bag and point toward my room at the opposite end of the complex from his. "I'll meet you back at the car at nine."

"Tomorrow's Monday," Ben points out. "Maybe earlier's better. In case he goes to work. You don't want to lose the day."

I hadn't thought of that. I've lost all track of time. We've already been gone two days. "Eight?" I say.

"Seven. Truckee's still a half hour away"

"Okay. Seven."

We stand there, looking at each other. Behind us a pickup truck screeches into the parking lot. "Good night, Cody," Ben says.

"Good night."

Once in the room, I contemplate a bath, but when I see the dingy tub and the ring of dead skin, I shower instead, soaking under the weak stream. I get out, dry myself on napkin towels, and look around the room.

Death is the ultimate rite of passage, and it can be a most sacred ritual. Sometimes, in order to make it personal, you must make it anonymous. This was the advice I found in Meg's decrypted files. Did Bradford himself write that? It sounds like something he might say. I look around the room. This is exactly the kind of place where Meg did it.

I imagine it all, locking the door, putting on the DO NOT DIS-
TURB sign, leaving the note and tip for the maid. Going into the
bathroom to mix the chemistry, fan on so as not to alert other
motel guests with the fumes.

I sit down on the bed. I picture Meg, waiting for the poison to
take effect. Did she lie down right away, or wait for the tingling to
start? Did she throw up? Was she scared? Relieved? Was there
a moment when she knew she'd passed the point of no return?

I lie down on the scratchy bedspread and imagine Meg's last
minutes. The burning, the tingling, the numbness. I hear Bradford's voice whispering encouragement. *We are born alone, we
die alone.* I start to see black spots; I start to feel it happening.
Really happening.

Except that I don't want it to! I shoot upright in the bed. I
put my hand over my heart, which is beating so hard, as if pro-
testing my thoughts. *It is* not *happening,* I tell myself. *You did* not
take poison. You would *not take poison.*

With trembling hands, I grab my phone. Ben picks up right
away. "Are you okay?" he asks.

As soon as he asks it, I am. If not okay, then better. The panic subsides. I'm not Meg catching that final bus, an anonymous
voice whispering in my ear. I'm alive. And I'm not alone.

"Are you okay?" he repeats. And it's a real voice. Solid. If I
needed him to be right here with me, he would be.

"I'm okay," I say.

Ben's quiet on the line, and I just stay there, listening to the
sound of him, comforted by his presence, by the sound of his
breathing. We stay like that for a while, until I'm calm enough to
go to sleep.

I meet Ben at the car at seven with a box of donuts and two coffees.

"What are we, cops?" he asks.

"We are sort of on a stakeout."

Ben holds up a piece of paper. "I got gas. And directions to your dad's place in Truckee."

Dad. Dad's place. It's a foreign concept. Like we're driving to the moon. "Thanks."

He holds out the paper, and for a second I hesitate. Harry had said that my father had lived at six different addresses over the last ten years. It had given me a bad feeling, though I wasn't sure if it was because I was scared I wasn't going to find him, or scared of just what I might find.

I snatch the paper from Ben.

"You want the wheel?" he asks.

I shake my head. Too nervous.

Ben seems to get this because once we're on the road, he goes all chatty, telling me about growing up in a snowboarding mecca like Bend but never having enough money to hit the slopes, so he and his brothers would do crazy things, like outfit their skateboards and ride them down snowy mountains. "My older brother Jamie broke both his elbows one time."

"Ouch."

"Bend's a lot like Truckee. Hippie redneck outdoorsy types."

I nod.

"Here, we're off the highway now. Direct me."

A few minutes later we pull up in front of a dilapidated redwood house. The front yard is littered with crap, a rusting lawn mower, a bunch of kids' plastic toys, a couch with stuffing coming out of it.

"Is this him?"

"This is the address Harry gave me."

"Do you want to go in?"

I look at the grubby front yard. This is not the nice house of the nice man with the nice family I'd painted for myself. Maybe Harry's information is out-of-date.

"Or, we could just wait," Ben says. "See who comes out."

Yes. That. I nod.

We park the car across the street. Ben drinks his coffee and goes through about six donuts. I watch as the house wakes up. Lights go on. Blinds snap up. Finally, after about an hour, the front door yawns open, and a girl comes out. She's younger than me, maybe fourteen, and she seems sullen as she halfheartedly picks up some of the crap off the lawn. A little while later the door opens again and out toddles a little kid in a T-shirt and a diaper. The girl picks up the kid. I watch, confused. Is the girl his daughter? Is the baby his? Or does the baby belong to the girl? Or is it the wrong house?

"You want me to go to the door?" Ben offers.

"As what?"

"I dunno. A traveling salesman?"

"Selling what?"

"Whatever. Cable TV. Makeup. God."

"You need nicer clothes if you're peddling the Almighty."

As we contemplate what to do, a low rumbling grows louder and louder until it's like an explosion, the telltale sound of a Harley-Davidson. It pulls up right next to us, and we both slink down in our seats. The chopper passes and turns into the driveway of the house, where it revs a few times, making the baby scream in fright. The girl picks up the kid and starts yelling at whoever's on the bike. The rider turns off the noisy engine, and pulls off the helmet. A guy. He has his back to us, so I can't see him, but I can see the hatred reflected on the girl's face. The front door bangs open, and a woman with short black hair comes out, a cigarette in one hand, a sippy cup in the other. Stubbing out the cigarette, she picks up the baby and starts arguing with the motorcycle guy.

I watch all of this like it's a movie. The motorcycle guy and the woman keep arguing. She hands him the baby, who starts screaming, so he hands it directly over to the girl. The woman says something, and he slams his hand against the seat of his chopper. Then he turns away, looking right at me, but he doesn't see me. But I see him. I see his hair, the same chestnut color as mine, and his eyes, almond-shaped and hazel-gray, just like mine, and his skin, olive, just like mine.

Just like mine.

There's more shouting. The teen girl sets the baby down and stomps off crying. Then the baby starts wailing. The woman picks it up and carries it inside, slamming the door, and soon he follows, slamming the garage door.

Ben looks at me. Looks back at the house. Looks back at me. Shakes his head.

"What?" I say.

"It's weird."

"What is?"

He glances back at the house, back at me. "He looks like you, but that could be my dad."

I don't say anything.

"Are you okay?" he asks after a bit.

I nod.

"Do you want to go in? Or come back later when they've maybe calmed down?"

When I was little, I liked to imagine my father as a business-man, an airplane pilot, a dentist, someone different. But he's not different at all. He's exactly what I knew he'd be. I shouldn't be surprised. All along Tricia has called him the sperm donor. He was probably some one-night stand I was the accidental product of. There's no fairy-tale reason why he never visited or answered my email or even sent me one lousy birthday card. I'll bet he has no idea when my birthday is. Why would he? That would imply that my existence matters to him.

"Let's go," I tell Ben.

"Are you sure? He's right there."

"Let's go." My words snap. Ben doesn't say anything else. He pulls a U and we go.

Once we're back on the highway, it's like someone has vacuumed the Cody out of me. Ben keeps giving me these worried looks, but I avoid them. I avoid him. I scrunch my sweater into a ball against the window, and eventually, I fall asleep.

When I wake up a few hours later, the cool mountain air of the Sierra Nevadas has been baked away by the hot dry Nevada desert. I can almost forget that the detour ever happened.

My head is hazy from the heat, and there's a metallic taste in my mouth and the crusty remnants of what I suspect is drool on my lips. Ben is watching me, and even though I liked seeing him sleep, being on the opposite end of it, I feel exposed. "Where the hell are we?" I ask.

"Literally the middle of nowhere. We passed a place called Hawthorne a while back, but other than that, nothing. I haven't even seen any cars on the road. On the plus side, you can speed like crazy out here."

I glimpse the dashboard. Ben's going ninety. The empty, straight road stretches ahead of us and shimmers with mirages, little oases of water in the desert that don't really exist. No sooner do we reach one than it disappears into the asphalt and another appears on the horizon.

"At this rate, we should make Vegas by five and Laughlin by seven," Ben says.

"Oh."

"Are you okay?"

"Why do you keep asking me that?" I reach for a now-tepid bottle of Dr Pepper. "This is disgusting."

"When you see a 7-Eleven, holler." He sounds peeved, but then he looks at me and something softens. He opens his mouth to say something, but then seems to think again and stays quiet.

I sigh. "What?"

"It's not you; it's him."

I'm still feeling kind of naked in front of him. So I snap back, "Is that a line you give to girls when you dump them? 'It's not you, it's me.'"

Ben turns toward me, then back toward the road. "I might if it ever got to that point," he says frostily. "I was talking about your dad."

I don't answer. I don't want to talk about my dad, or whatever that man back there was.

"He's a fuckwad," Ben continues. "And it has fuck-all to do with you."

I still don't say anything.

"I mean, maybe I don't know anything about what you're going through, but it's something my mom always told me about my dad. That it wasn't me. It was him. And I never believed her. I always thought she was humoring me. Because it had to be my fault. But seeing that asshole, and you, maybe I'm starting to reconsider."

"What do you mean?" I ask.

Ben's eyes are glued to the road, as if he has to concentrate very hard on the flat, straight highway. "When your dad is an asshole from the get-go—and it doesn't get more from the get-go than denying your existence—it's not because *you* did anything wrong. It's because *he* did." His words spill out in a rush. Then he adds, "And maybe it's none of my business, but I've been wanting to say that to you for, like, the last two hundred and eighty-seven miles."

I look at Ben now. And again I wonder how it is that we can feel so many of the same things and be so utterly different.

"You thought it was your fault, with your dad?" I ask him.

Ben doesn't say anything, just nods.

"Why?"

He sighs. "I was a sensitive kid. A crybaby. Always running to Mommy. He hated that. Told me to toughen up. So I tried. I tried to man up. Be like him." He grimaces. "But he still couldn't stand the sight of me."

I don't know what to say. So I just tell Ben that I'm sorry.

He lets go of the wheel for a second, raises his hands in the air, like, *What you gonna do?*

I have to resist the urge to touch Ben on the cheek. I can't imagine what that must have been like, having a dad whose idea of manhood was how Ben described it. Spending your life emulating that and trying to escape it all at once. I think of Tricia. About her being gone so much, and about her endless string of three-month flings. About refusing to put me in touch with my father. About how she basically abdicated her job, let the Garcias take over parenting me. I've always resented her for this, but now I'm wondering if maybe I should be thanking her.

x   x   x

Traffic picks up around Vegas and then, suddenly, we're in a huge city and it's disorienting and strange, and then an hour later, we're back in the middle of nowhere, and then an hour after that, we're in Laughlin.

Laughlin is like a strange hybrid: part nowhere desert town, but plunked down in the center of it are all these high-rise hotels jutting out from the banks of the Colorado River. We drive through the depressing strip of downtown to a more modest stretch of motel–casinos, stopping at the Wagon Wheel Sleep 'n' Slots, which is advertising rooms for forty-five dollars a night.

We pull in and ring the bell, and a friendly woman with her hair in braids asks if she can help us.

"Do you have two rooms?" Ben asks.

The cash is depleting faster than I'd thought. I think about last night's motel-room-induced panic attack, Ben's comforting voice on the other end of the phone. What he told me earlier today in the car. "One room, two beds," I say.

I pay for the room and we go unpack the car. It was so clean and tidy when we left, but now it's littered with trip detritus. I attempt to tidy some of it while Ben carries both of our bags up to the room.

When I get upstairs, he's shuffling through a bunch of papers.

"They have takeout menus. Do you want to go out and grab something to eat? Or order a pizza?"

I remember our afternoon a few months back: burritos, TV, the couch.

"Let's do pizza."

"Pepperoni? Sausage? Both?"

I laugh. "One or the other."

Ben picks up the menu, and a half hour later pizza, garlic knots, and vats of Pepsi and Dr Pepper show up at the door. We spread it all out on a towel on one of the beds and sit cross-legged, having a picnic.

"God, it's good to be out of the car," I say.

"Yeah. Sometimes after a tour, my ass vibrates for days."

"Too bad it's not one of those motels with the vibrating beds; you could keep the magic going."

"I've never actually seen one of those," Ben says.

"No, me neither. I actually haven't stayed in that many motels." The truth is, I can count on one hand the number of nights I've stayed in a hotel or motel. Tricia wasn't one for vacations. Most of the trips I've taken have been with the Garcias, and we usually went camping or stayed with their relatives.

"So not many opportunities to share a motel room with a guy before?" Ben asks lightly as he pays an inordinate amount of attention to his pizza crust.

"None."

"So you've never shared a room before?" Ben asks. "With a guy?" He seems strangely shy.

"I've never shared *anything* with a guy before."

Ben looks up from his crust and stares me in the face, like he's trying to determine exactly what I'm saying. I hold his stare, letting my look answer the question. His eyes, a soft blue, like the empty swimming pool outside, widen in surprise.

"Not anything?"

"Nope."

"Not even . . . a pizza?"

"Oh, I've eaten pizza with guys before. But I've never *shared* one. There's a big difference."

"There is?"

I nod.

"So what about now?"

"What *about* now?"

He looks at me.

"What's it look like?" I ask.

His brow crumples, a squall of confusion, as if he's not sure we're talking about pizza anymore. He glances at the corpse of the pie. "It looks like you had two slices and I had four and you don't like pepperoni as much as I do."

I nod, acknowledging the greasy pile of pepperoni I've picked off.

"And that this is all happening in a motel room that we're both sitting in," he continues.

I nod again. For a moment I'm reminded of the pledge I made never to sleep under the same roof as him. Maybe he is too. Obviously, tonight I'm breaking that, though the truth is, I broke it in spirit a while ago. And none of it seems to matter anymore.

"So what does that mean?" he asks. He's trying to sound casual, but he looks eager, and very young.

"It means that I'm sharing with you." That's all I'm willing to give him, though in truth, it seems like a lot. Then something I said yesterday when I was trying to convince him to nap in the car comes back to me: *We can make up a new code.*

I think that's what we might be doing here.

I wake up the next morning in a darkened room, shafts of bright morning sunshine slanting through the blackout shades. The clock reads ten thirty. I passed out around midnight.

Ben is still asleep in the other bed, and he looks sweet, all curled up around one of the pillows. I take a minute to stretch, letting my muscles ease out of the crampedness of twenty-four hours in the car.

"Hey," Ben calls, his voice sticky with sleep. "What time is it?"

"Ten thirty."

"Are you ready for today?"

The pizza box is still on the dresser. It seems crazy that last night—in another room that Bradford might recommend, right in his backyard—I was able to forget why I'd come here. But now there's no forgetting. No denying. I am hot and cold and sick to my stomach. I'm not ready. I'll never be ready.

"Ready," I tell him.

He stares at me a long minute. Watches me as he peels off his nicotine patch and puts on another one. "You don't have to do this," he says. "I'll be just as happy if we turn around right now."

It's a nice thing to say. But we already aborted one mission.

That one didn't matter. This one does. I shake my head.

He puts on a shirt. "What's your plan of attack?"

"I thought we'd stake out his house all day, like we did . . ." I don't finish. Ben gets it.

"But you said he worked at one of the casinos," Ben replies. "They don't have regular shifts. He could work the graveyard."

I hadn't thought of that. "It might be a long stakeout."

Ben looks at me for a minute. "What's the name of the place he works at?"

"The Continental." We drove past it yesterday. It made me shiver in the afternoon heat to think of being that close to him. If he had such a strong effect on me over the computer, with all those miles and false identities between us, what is he going to do to me in person?

Ben opens the phone book and leafs through the pages.

"What are you doing?" I ask, but before he answers, he's dialing. When someone answers, he starts talking in a kind of a hick accent: "My buddy Brad Smith works there. I don't mean to hassle him, but I went and locked myself out of my house and he's got my spare keys. Can you tell me what time he's on today so I can come grab 'em?"

There's a brief pause as he's put on hold. He looks at me and winks. The voice comes back on the phone. "Oh. Right. Course. You know what time he gets off? I can swing on by and grab my spare set off him." More silence. "Five? Great. I'll have to manage till then. Thanks. I will. You too."

Ben hangs up. "His shift is over at five."

"Five," I repeat.

"So assuming he goes straight home, five thirty or six."

"Aren't you a good detective." I smile at him.

Ben doesn't smile back. He's all business now. "I say we get to his place early to sniff it out, and then you do your thing."

"My thing?"

"You have a thing, right?"

"Of course I have a thing." I've spent the long hours of the drive working out exactly what I'll say to him. Like lines in a play. More pretend. Pretend to be Meg. Pretend to be suicidal. Pretend to be strong enough to do this.

"Okay, so that gives us"—he looks at the clock—"six hours."

I nod. Six hours.

"What do you want to do in the meantime?"

Throw up. Run. Hide. "I don't know. What is there to do here?"

"We could sit by the pool, but I stuck my hand in it last night and it was warm as piss."

"Too bad I left my bathing suit at home."

"We could hit one of those all-you-can-manage dollar-ninety-nine buffets."

"I'll bet you can manage a lot."

"And I'd kill for an iced coffee. It's, like, a thousand degrees. You'd think they'd ice something other than the beer. We can grab breakfast at a casino, and then gamble."

"I'm gambling enough on this trip; plus, I have no extra money. What I really want is to zone out. Like, at a movie or something."

"Okay. Buffet and movie. It's a date." He stops himself, even blushes a little. "Not a date, but, you know."

"Yeah, Ben," I say. "I know."

× × ×

We don't find iced coffee, but we do find a buffet, at which Ben eats an absurdly huge amount of eggs, bacon, sausage, and various other meat products, as if trying to store up for the vegan life back home. I manage to get down half a waffle. After, we find a Cineplex in town, and watch one of those ridiculous movies about machines that turn human. It's part three or four in a series we haven't seen before, but it doesn't matter. We groan at the terrible plot and share a tub of popcorn, and there are whole minutes when I forget what I'm doing today. By the time the film lets out, it's almost three o'clock.

I go back to the motel to change. I'm not sure why, but I've brought one of my nicer outfits, which happens to be a skirt-and-top ensemble I wore to one of Meg's many memorial services. Ben and I pay for another night at the Wagon Wheel, deciding, rather than leaving tonight, to get up at the butt-crack of dawn and power through the drive home, doing it in shifts, rock-and-roll-tour style.

At the front desk we get directions to Bradford's apartment complex. It's not that far from here, about a half mile away.

"Let's walk," I say. We have time, and I'm too nervous to sit around waiting, so we walk along the dusty streets until we find a sun-bleached stucco building surrounded by dead grass, with a cracked cement pool.

But we're early. It's only just five. "We probably shouldn't hang out right here," I say. So we walk back a ways toward a liquor store a few blocks away.

"What time do you want us to go in?" Ben asks.

"I should go at five thirty."

"And what time should *I* go?"

"I kind of think I need to do this alone."

Ben's eyes narrow. "I kind of think you don't."

"I appreciate that, but I need to talk to him myself."

"So you want me to lurk in the bushes?" He doesn't seem pleased with this option.

"Bradford is cagey. If he so much as suspects that anyone is with me, there's no way he'll talk to me." It isn't that I'm not frightened of Bradford; I am. But it needs to be just me in there. "I want you to wait for me here."

"Here?" Ben is incredulous.

"Here." I am pleading.

"So I was just the ride, is that it?"

"You know that's not true."

"Then why *am* I here?"

Because I need you. That's the truth. And it's almost as frightening as what awaits me down the road. But that's not what I tell Ben. "Because you're wrapped up in this too."

Recoil.

"So that's what this is about?" His voice is hard, flat, angry, like the day he came for the T-shirt. "In that case, there's no fucking way I'm letting you go see this guy. I already have Meg's death on my conscience. I'm not adding yours to the pile."

"He's not going to kill me."

"Why not? He killed Meg. Isn't that what you've been saying all along?"

"Yeah, but not like that. He's not going to pull a knife on me or anything."

"How the hell do you know that? How do you know he doesn't

have an arsenal of shotguns? How do you know the suicide shit isn't some side project? How do you know he doesn't have a dozen bodies buried in the backyard?"

Because Bradford Smith uses a different type of weapon, and leaves you to do the dirty work yourself. "I just know," I say quietly.

"You know what, Cody? You don't know shit."

I don't know shit? I look at Ben and it's like: *Who the hell are you? I know where you came from too. We crawl in the same muck, Ben McCallister.* I'm angry now. But that's good. Angry is better than scared.

"Wait for me here," I say.

"No way. You want to be like your friend and walk right into a trap? I'm telling you: don't. I'm telling you, this guy is dangerous, and going to see him is a fucked-up idea. I never warned Meg, but I'm warning you. That's the difference between you and me: I *learn* from my mistakes."

"Ben, the difference between you and me would fill up a book." I'm not sure how these words can feel so good and so false at the same time.

Ben gives me one last look, shakes his head, and then he walks away.

x x x

There's no time to contemplate Ben's desertion, which I think I've been expecting all along. It's just me and Bradford. As it needs to be.

He lives in Unit J in a completely nondescript complex. White door. Levolor shades in the window. I can't see inside. At the unit next door, a couple is out on the patio, drinking beer. They don't so much as look at me, but it's reassuring, knowing they're there.

I ring the bell.

The man who answers has white hair and a beard. He's wearing a pair of shorts and an oversize Hawaiian-print shirt that hangs over his gut. He's grasping a large sweating glass in his hand, full to the top, the ice not yet melted. I'm not sure whether I'm relieved or disappointed. Because this can't be him. This guy looks like a sloppy Santa Claus.

But then he says, "Can I help you?" And the voice: soft, guarded, familiar.

It takes me a second to find my own voice. "I'm looking for Bradford Smith."

I can see something—suspicion, strategy—pinging across his face. "What's your business here?"

What's my business here? I had a story to tell him, a way to worm myself inside. But it vanishes from my head, and I can't think of what to say except to blurt out the truth. He's always had that effect on me, this person I've been lying to.

"You're my business."

He squints. "I'm sorry, but do we know each other?"

My heart is thudding so hard and fast, I swear he must be able to see it through my blouse. "My name is Cody." I pause. "But you probably know me better as Repeat."

He doesn't answer.

"Do I need to *repeat* myself?"

"No," he says calmly. "I understood. You oughtn't be here."

He starts to close the door. And all I can think is: *I invited you to help me die, and you're shutting the door in my face.* It fires up my anger. Good. I need it now.

I wedge my foot in the doorway. "Oh, no, I *should* be here. Because I also know someone named Meg Garcia. You might know her as Firefly. Did you know her real name was Meg? That she had a best friend named Cody? A mother? A father? A brother?" The speech I rehearsed during the long drive is coming back to me.

Now that I've shown my hand, I half expect him to slam the door on me, but instead he steps outside. One of the beer-drinking neighbors throws an empty beer bottle into a garbage can; it clanks and shatters. Bradford appraises his neighbors, lips pursed. He looks at me and opens the door behind him. "Perhaps you'd better come inside."

For half a second I think of Ben, the arsenal of guns, the buried bodies. But then I go in anyway.

It is spartan, and neater than any of the houses I clean— *after* I clean them. My legs are shaking, and if I sit, he'll see my knees knocking, but if I stand, they might buckle. I split the difference and lean against the plaid couch.

"You knew her?" he asks.

The look on his face is peculiar. It's not sinister at all. It's almost eager. And that's when I realize that he doesn't know the gory details—and he *wants* to. I don't say anything. I refuse him that satisfaction.

"So she did it," he says. Of course he knows this now. My coming here gave it away. I gave him the satisfaction anyway.

"Because of you. You killed her."

"How could I have killed her?" he asks. "I never met her. I didn't even know her name until just now."

"Maybe you didn't actually do it with your hands, but you did it. . . . You did it the cowardly way. What was it you said? 'The opposite of bravery is not cowardice but conformity.'" I make air quote marks with my fingers. I have this part planned too. "I'd say the opposite of bravery is you!"

I sound so brave myself when I say it. No sign of the chicken-shit I truly am, about to collapse on my jelly legs.

His mouth twists, like he just tasted something a little off. But then he composes himself again, and his smile is two clicks away from benevolent. I hear a high-pitched whine in my ear as sweat breaks out on parts of my body that don't normally sweat.

He's looking at me now, running his thumb across his fingers. His nails are neat and trimmed, much better kept than mine, which are ragged from scrubbing sinks and toilets.

"You lost the better part of you," he says. "That's what you wrote. It was her. Meg. Your 'better half.' And you're trying to redeem yourself, because she left you out of the decision."

He has my number. He always has. Even when we were corresponding over a message board, he saw through me. All at once, the folly of my plan, of "catching" him, drains out of me, and so does the remaining strength in my legs. I sink onto the couch. "Fuck you," I say, because whatever script I came up with is useless now.

Bradford goes on in this almost gentle voice. "Except maybe you don't mean she was your better half. Maybe she was your *other* half." He takes a sip of his drink. "Sometimes we meet people and are so symbiotic with them, it's as if we are one person, with one mind, one destiny."

He's talking to me the way he would on the boards, circular, so it takes a minute to understand what he's suggesting.

"You're saying I want to die, like Meg?"

"I'm just repeating your words."

"No! You're putting your words into my mouth. You *want* me to die. Like you wanted Meg to die."

"How did I 'want' Meg to die?" he asks, now making air quotes himself.

"Let's see: you told her how to get poison. How to write a suicide note. How to keep it from family. How to alert the police. How to erase incriminating emails. You told her not to go on antidepressants. You told her not to keep living."

"I told no one any of this."

"You told her *all* of that! You told *me* that!"

He stares at me. "Cody. It was Cody, wasn't it? What *exactly* did I tell you?"

My mind spins as I try to recall the specifics, but I can't think of anything except for a collection of stupid quotes.

"Now it's coming back to me. . . . The sunless planet. That was also you?" he asks.

Yes. That was me.

He sits down, settling in, like he's about to watch one of his favorite movies.

"I thought that was an interesting way to put it. Would you want to go on living if the sun went out? But, Cody, do you ac-tually know what would happen if the sun died?"

"*No.*" It comes out a squeak. Like a mouse.

"Within a week, the temperature on Earth would drop to below zero. Within a year, it would fall to minus one hundred. Ice sheets would cover the oceans. Crops, needless to say, would fail. Livestock would die. People who didn't die of the cold would soon die of starvation. A sunless planet, which is what you called yourself, wasn't it? It's *already* a dead planet. Even if you're still going through the motions."

I'm a planet without its sun. I'm already cold and dead. That's what he's saying. So I should just make it official.

Except, why then is there this heat traveling its way up my body, like a circuit? Heat. The opposite of cold. The opposite of dead.

There's a click at the door. And then a kid—zits, backpack, frown—walks in. My first thought is that Bradford lures people here, and this is another one of All_BS's victims. Only this time, this time I'm here too, and I can save him. It's not too late.

But then Bradford says, "What are you doing here?"

And the kid says, "Mom says you got the days mixed up again. She was pissed about it." He sees me then, gives me a questioning look.

"Go to your room, and we'll discuss it in a second," he says gruffly.

"Can I use your computer?"

Bradford nods curtly. The kid disappears down a hall. As I watch him go, I can't help but notice how drab this place is. The wood table with a stack of napkins in the middle. The generic prints hanging on the wall. There's a chipped bookcase; it's not full of philosophical tomes but supermarket paperbacks, the kind found in Tricia's break room. There's one big book, a reference book called *Bartlett's Familiar Quotations*, lying sidewise, so I can see all the sticky notes jammed into it. *This* is where he gets quotes from?

I hear the chime of the computer, and it's like my brain clicks on.

Crappy condo, shitty job, depressing town. Bradford's life is a lot like mine. Except that every night, he fires up his computer and plays God.

"You should go now," Bradford says. The calm, taunting tone has vanished. His voice is icy again, like it was on the phone when someone barged in on him.

From down the hall, his son—who must be what, thirteen, fourteen, not so much younger than me?—calls out, asking for a sandwich.

Bradford's voice is tight as he promises a turkey and Swiss. He looks at me: "You should go now," he repeats.

"What would you do if someone did to him what you did to Meg?" I ask. And for a second I picture it. His own turkey-sandwich-eating son, dead. Bradford grieving as the Garcias have grieved.

Bradford stands up, and I know he has seen the scenario I just conjured. As he walks toward me, the vein in his neck bulging, I should be scared. Except I'm not.

Because I don't want his son to die. It wouldn't even anything out. It would just be one more dead kid. And somehow, this is the thought that gives me the strength to stand up, to walk past him, and to leave.

x x x

I keep it together as I walk out the door, down the gravel path, past the drinking neighbors, who are blasting classic rock now. I am okay until I look back at the condo and picture the man who made Meg die—a monster, a father—preparing a turkey sandwich for his son.

The sob that rises up comes from deep within me, as if it's been festering there for days, or weeks, or months, or maybe so much longer. I can't hold it back, and I can't be near him when it comes. That's where the danger is.

So I run.

I run down the dusty streets, churning up sand that flies into my nose. Someone is coming toward me. At first I think it's a mirage; there've been so many of those lately. Except he doesn't disappear the closer I get. Instead, when he sees me crying, he too starts to run.

"What happened?" he repeats over and over, his eyes alive not just with worry, but with fear. "Did he hurt you?"

Even if I could get the words out, I wouldn't know what to say. He was a monster and he was a person. He killed her and she killed her. I found Bradford but I didn't find anything. I'm choking on sand and dust and phlegm and grief. Ben keeps asking if he did something, and I want to reassure him, he didn't; he didn't hurt me or touch me or do any of those things. What finally comes sputtering out is this:

"He has a son."

I try to explain. A teenage son. A son he protects, loves, even as he convinced Meg to die, tried to do the same to me. Only I can't get out the words. But Ben was with me yesterday in

Truckee. Which is maybe why it makes sense to him. Or maybe it's that we've always made sense to each other.

"Oh, fuck, Cody," he says. And then he opens his arms automatically, like hugging is something he does. And I step into them automatically, like being hugged is something I do. As he holds me, I cry. I cry for Meg, who is forever gone from me. I cry for the Garcias, who may be too. I cry for the father I never had, and the mother I did. I cry for Stoner Richard and the family he grew up with. I cry for Ben and the family he didn't grow up with. And I cry for me.

After I calm down, we walk over to one of the paths along the river. It's evening now, but the powerboats and Jet Skis are still zooming around. The mighty Colorado seems less like a major river than a paved aqueduct. Like everything about this trip, it's not what I hoped for. I tell Ben I can't believe that *this* is the grand Colorado River.

"Follow me," he says. And I do, down a boat ramp, to the edge of the water. "I used to have a big map over my bed." He kneels down next to the water. "The Colorado River starts in the Rocky Mountains and cuts through the Grand Canyon and goes all the way to the Gulf of Mexico. It might not seem like much here"—he leans over and scoops a handful of water—"but when you hold the water, you're kind of holding a piece of the Rockies, of the Grand Canyon."

He turns to me with his still-cupped hands, and I open mine as he lets go of his, and the river water, which has come from places unknown, with stories untold, flows from him to me.

"You always know the thing to say to make it better," I say, so quietly I think my words have gotten drowned out by the Jet Skis.

But he hears. "You didn't think so when you first met me."

No. He's wrong. Because though I hated him, there has always been something about Ben McCallister that made it better. Maybe that's *why* I hated him. Because it's not supposed to be better. And certainly not with him.

"I'm sorry," I say.

He reaches over and takes my wrists, and I clasp his, my own hands still wet with the mysterious river.

I don't let go and neither does he, and the river water stays between us all the way back to our motel, where, inside our overheated room, we start to kiss. This one is as hungry as the one at his house months ago, but it's different, too. As if we are opening ourselves to something. We kiss. My shirt falls to the floor, then Ben's does, too. The feel of his bare skin against mine is astonishing. I want more. I tug off his jeans. I unzip my skirt.

Ben stops kissing me. "Are you sure?" he asks. His eyes have changed again, to that inky blue of a newborn's.

I am sure.

We make our way to the bed in a tangle of limbs. He is warm against me, hard, but restrained, too.

"Do you have a condom?" I ask.

He leans over, pulls a shiny foil wrapper out of his wallet. "Are you sure?" he asks again.

I pull him to me.

When it happens, I start to cry. "Should I stop?" Ben asks.

I don't want him to stop. Though it is painful—more than I expected it to be—I'm not crying because of how much I *hurt*. I'm crying because of how much I *feel*.

After, Ben falls asleep, locking me in the cavern of his arms. It's like eighty degrees in the room—that poor air conditioner coughing in the window is no match for the desert's brutal heat—and Ben himself radiates warmth like a furnace. But I don't move, even though I'm hot and sticky with sweat. I don't want to move, and eventually I fall asleep. I wake up a bunch of times in the night, and every time I do, Ben's arms are still locked around me.

And then I wake up in the morning, and they're not, and I'm cold, even though the room, which never cooled down in the night, is starting to get hot again. I sit up. There's no sign of Ben, though his stuff is in a neat pile in the corner.

I slip into the shower. There's an achiness between my legs, my virginity freshly gone. Meg loved that I seemed tough and sexy, and was a virgin. And now I'm not. If she were here, I could tell her about it.

The shower goes icy, though it has nothing to do with the water temperature. Because I realize I couldn't tell her. Because I did it with *him*. With Ben. And he was hers first, even if it was just once.

I fucked her. That's what he said.

But I'm different. He and I, we became friends first.

The rest of that conversation hurls back to me. *Before it all shot to shit, we were friends.* And then: *When you fuck a friend, it ruins everything.*

No. This is different. "I am different." I say it out loud in the shower. And then I almost laugh. Because how many other girls have fed themselves this line about Ben McCallister to make themselves feel better in the shower the morning after?

Faces flash before me: my father's. The look of hatred for him on that teen girl's face. Bradford's look of fury when I said the thing about his son. The various shades of loathing I've seen on Ben's face, which have no doubt been reflected on mine.

I think of one of the first emails I read from him. The one that got this whole thing started.

You have to leave me alone.

Through the cardboard walls, I hear the sound of the door opening and closing. I turn off the taps, now embarrassed to be in the bathroom with all my clothes out in the room. I wrap myself in as many towels as I can find, and tiptoe to my bag.

"Hey," Ben says. Out of the corner of my eye, I can see he's not looking at me, either.

"Hey," I say back, eyes lasering in on my heap of clothes.

He starts to say something, but I interrupt. "Hang on. Let me get dressed."

"Yeah, okay."

In the bathroom, I throw on my dirty-even-for-me cutoffs and a T-shirt, and spend some time toweling off and trying not to think of how, out there, Ben would not look at me.

I take a deep breath and open the door. Ben's busy mixing up some kind of drink. Without looking up, he starts talking superfast. "I was on a mission to find iced coffee. Apparently there are Starbucks here, but they're all in the casinos, and I didn't feel like dealing. But nowhere else had iced, not even the actual coffee shop. So in the end I got some fresh-ish hot coffee and my own ice, and I think that'll work."

He's talking a mile a minute, babbling about iced coffee with the kind of caffeinated specificity I've only ever heard from Alice. And he still isn't looking at me.

"I got half and half," he goes on. "For some reason I like my cold coffee with milk. It reminds me of ice cream or something that way."

Stop talking about coffee! I want to scream. But I don't. I just nod.

"Do you want to hit one of those buffets, power up before we hit the road, or should we put some distance between us?"

Yesterday Ben said that the difference between him and me was that he learned from his mistakes. He was right. And I'm an idiot.

"I vote for distance," I say.

His eyes flicker up for a second and then they skitter away, like I gave the right answer. "That's cool. Whatever you want."

I want you. I want to lie back down on the bed and have his arms lock around me. But I know that's not how it works. When you fuck the bartender, the free drinks dry up. I learned this from Tricia. I learned it from Meg. I learned it from Ben himself. It's not like he didn't tell me exactly what he was.

"In fact, I need to get home," I tell Ben.

"That's where we're headed." He folds a shirt.

"Like, now."

He stares at the bedspread on the mostly made bed we didn't sleep in last night. "Car needs gas and probably oil," Ben says. His voice is harder, that hint of a growl returning. "If you're in such a hurry, you could take care of that while I pack up."

"Sounds like a plan," I say. His arms, the comfort of them, feel so far away now. "Meet you at the car?"

Ben tosses me the keys and I catch them, and he's about to say something but then doesn't, so I scoop up my crap and haul it outside. I'm gassing up, when my phone rings and I reach for it. Ben. This is so stupid. We're both being stupid.

"Cody! Where the hell are you? You were supposed to be home two days ago."

It's not him. It's Tricia. As soon as I hear her voice, my throat closes.

"What's wrong?" she asks.

"*Mom?*" I say.

"Cody, where are you?" I hear the fear in her voice. Because I never, ever call her Mom.

"I need to come home."

"Are you hurt?"

"No. But I need to come home. Right now."

"Where are you?"

"Laughlin."

"Where the hell is that?"

"Nevada. Please . . . I want to come home." I'm about to lose it.

"Okay, honey, don't cry. I can figure this out. Laughlin, Nevada. Cody, hang tight. I'm gonna work this out. Leave your phone on."

I have no idea how Tricia is going to figure this out. She's as broke as me. And she doesn't know how to use a computer and she probably doesn't even know where Nevada is, let alone Laughlin. But I feel better somehow.

x x x

Ben's waiting downstairs in front of our room when I get back. I dig my sunglasses out and put them over my red eyes. I pop the trunk and he loads everything in. "I'll drive," I say.

It's maybe not the best idea. I'm shaky, but at least if I'm driving, I'll have something to focus on.

"Okay," Ben mumbles.

"Tell me when you would like to stop and eat," I say formally. He just nods.

In the car, he focuses on the music, but the iPod adapter has died, so there's only radio, and it's all crap. He finally lands on a Guns N' Roses song, "Sweet Child o' Mine." I used to like the song, but now, like everything, it's digging a crater into my stomach.

"My mom loved this song," he says.

I nod.

"Listen, Cody." It sounds exactly like the Garcias and their *And, Cody*'s.

Before I can answer, my phone rings. I reach for it and it falls onto the floor. I swerve.

"Watch it!" Ben shouts.

"Answer it!" I shout back.

He scrambles for the phone. "Hello," he says. He turns to me. "It's your mom."

"Tricia," I say, taking the phone.

"You shouldn't drive and talk at the same time," Ben scolds.

I roll my eyes at him, but I pull on to the shoulder.

"Where are you now?" Tricia doesn't ask me who answered or why I'm not in Tacoma like I said I would be. It's never been her way to worry about the details.

"I don't know. About twenty miles outside of Laughlin. On Highway 95."

"Have you passed Las Vegas yet?"

"No. It's not for another forty miles or so."

I hear her sigh with relief. "Good. There's a one-thirty non-stop flight on Southwest from Vegas to Spokane. Think you can make it?"

"I think so."

I hear Tricia say something and in the background, lots of voices. "Okay, we'll book you on that. If you miss it, there's another after, but it connects through Portland, so you'd have to change planes." I listen to her talk, like she's some kind of travel agent, like we do this all the time, when in fact I've never been on an airplane before.

"Call me once you're on the plane so I'll know when to pick you up. They don't let you go to the gate anymore, apparently, so I'll meet you down at baggage claim."

"Okay," I say. Like any of this makes sense to me.

"I'll text you the flight information," she says, and I'm at once grateful to Raymond for introducing her to this technology.

"And I'll see you this afternoon. I'll get you home."

"Thank you," I say.

"What are moms for?"

I hang up and look at Ben, who's looking at me, confused, though I can tell he heard both sides of the conversation.

"What's going on?"

"I'm gonna get out in Vegas, fly the rest of the way home."

"Why?"

"It'll be easier, faster for you; you won't have to go out of your way." The route from here to Seattle passes right through my part of eastern Washington, and now he'll have to drive those thousand miles alone. But I *am* making it easier for him. That part is true.

We spend the next hour in silence. We get to the Las Vegas airport around noon. I pull in to the loading zone, where the cars are parked two abreast. Behind us, there's beeping, mad rushing, like cowboys, moving the cattle along. I grab my things and Ben gets out of the passenger side, watching me.

I turn to him. He's standing there, leaning up against the car. I know I have to say something. To thank him. To release him. Maybe releasing him *is* the way to thank him. But before I say anything, he asks, "What are you *doing*, Cody?"

It hurts. It all hurts so much. But this is wrong. In so many ways. So I say to him what I said all those months back, though there's nothing flip about it. It's maybe the most you can wish for anyone.

"Have a good life," I say. And then I slam the door shut behind me.

Tricia picks me up at baggage claim just like she promised, and marches me to the car. As soon as my seat belt is snapped, she orders: "Talk."

Strangely, it's not the part with Ben I'm worried about. Telling Tricia I ran off to Nevada with some guy I tossed my virginity to—that part comes out easy. She doesn't look delighted about it, but once she's certain that we used protection and used it properly and is suitably reassured that no pregnancy will result, she lets that part go.

"But why were you in Laughlin?" she asks me.

This is the thing I'm scared to tell her. And not for the reason I've been telling myself, which is that she'll blab it all over town, though she might.

Tricia went with me to most of Meg's memorial services. She wore her hotsy black dress and got dewy-eyed at all the appropriate parts. But we have hardly spoken about Meg dying. About Meg choosing to die. There was only that one conversation in my bedroom a few weeks ago. It's been pretty clear she doesn't want to talk about it, or hear about it. For all her talk of

Meg and me being different, I think she worries that we aren't.

When I finally tell her about Bradford and the Final Solution boards, she doesn't seem completely surprised. "Mrs. Banks said something intense was going on with you and that computer."

"Mrs. Banks? When did you talk to her?"

"Who do you think helped me book your ticket?"

So Tricia's already been talking about me in town. But it doesn't feel bad. Not at all, actually. It's like I have allies.

"How was your first flight, by the way?" Tricia asks.

I'd spent the duration of it staring at the parched landscape below, tracing the path Ben and I took on the drive down, trying not to think about him on his solo return trip.

"Fine."

We pull on to I-90, and I start to tell her about Bradford. About making myself bait. I tell her how persuasive he was, how he started an echo chamber in my head. I tell her about everything, except the detour to Truckee. I'm not sure why. Maybe I'm trying to spare her, but I don't think so. I've lost a lot recently, and a father—well, you can't lose what you never had.

I keep waiting for her to get furious, but instead, when I tell her some of the things Bradford wrote to me, she looks terrified. "And you went and confronted him?" she asks.

I nod.

"I can't believe I . . ." She trails off. "I'm just glad you're okay."

"Me too." I say. "I'm sorry. It was stupid."

"Yeah, I'll say." She reaches over to stroke my cheek. "It was also brave."

I manage a smile. "Maybe."

She guns the engine and pushes us into the fast lane. Then, after a while, she says, "You have to tell the Garcias. You know that, right?"

And the gloom and guilt fall as fast as a winter sunset. "It'll break their hearts."

"Their hearts are already broken," Tricia says. "But maybe it'll help mend yours, and right now, we'd all settle for that."

x   x   x

When we get back in town, Tricia drives past our house, and even though I'm exhausted and about to dissolve into a million pieces, I let her take me where she's taking me.

"I gotta get to work," she says, pulling into the Garcias' driveway. "I'll see you later."

"Thank you," I say. I hug her across the stick shift. Then I grab my file on Meg, Bradford, and Final Solution, and head toward the front door.

Scottie opens up.

"Hey, Runtmeyer," I say softly.

"Hi, Cody," he says, and he seems embarrassed, or maybe he's pleased, by the return of this nickname. "It's Cody," he calls into the house.

Sue comes out, wiping her hands on an apron. "Cody! You finally came for dinner. Can I make you a plate?"

"Maybe later. I need to talk to you about something."

Her expression falters. "Come in," she says. "Joe," she calls. "Cody's here. Scottie, go play upstairs."

Scottie gives me a look, and I shrug.

Joe and Sue go into the darkened dining room, which has a

fancy wood table that we used to eat family dinners around. Now it is piled with papers and other signs of disuse. "What is it, Cody?" Joe asks.

"There's some things I need to tell you, about Meg. About her death."

They both nod, reach for each other's hands.

"I know she killed herself. I'm not saying she didn't. But you need to know that she was involved with this group . . ." I begin. "It calls itself a suicide support group, but it's the kind of support that encourages people to kill themselves, and I think that's why she did it."

I watch their faces, awaiting their horror, but they are kind, expectant, waiting for me to continue. And it hits me: this is old news.

"You know?"

"We know," Sue says quietly. "It was in the police report."

"It was?"

Sue nods. "They said it explained how she got that poison. It's common with those groups."

"The Final Solution." Joe practically spits the words. "That's what the Nazis called the Holocaust. Meg knew that. I can't believe she'd fall into a group that used that as its name."

"Joe." Sue puts her hand on his arm.

"So the police found the encrypted files? They know about Bradford?" I'm confused. Bradford didn't seem to know anything about Meg's death.

Now Joe and Sue look confused, too. "What files?"

"On Meg's computer. In her trash."

"I don't know about that," Sue says. "They just said they

found evidence that Meg was involved with this group from her Internet searches."

"Who's Bradford?" Joe asks.

"Bradford Smith," I say.

They look at me blankly.

"He's the one, from the boards. Wait, I thought you said the police knew about this."

"They told us she was involved with these sickos who preyed upon vulnerable people like Meg, encouraging them to commit suicide," Joe says.

"But you don't know about Bradford?" They shake their heads. "Bradford Smith? On the boards, known as All_BS?" Still no recognition. "He's the one who helped her, pushed her. He was like her death mentor. He coaxed her, offered her advice."

Sue nods. "Right. That's how these groups work."

"But it wasn't the group. It was him."

"How do you know about this, Cody?" Joe asks.

I back up and explain. The encrypted file, which led me to the Final Solution boards, which led me to Firefly1021, which led me to All_BS. "I spent weeks on the boards, trying to smoke him out. It took a while, but I did it, and then I guess I got him to believe I was like Meg, and I sort of fooled him into calling me. He was careful about it, calling via Skype on a tablet, but I was able to trace the call and from there figure out where he worked and then where he lived."

They're still staring at me. "You did all that yourself?" Sue asks.

"Not exactly. Harry Kang, Meg's former roommate, he did all the technical stuff, and another person drove me to Laughlin to see Bradford—"

"You went to see this man?" Joe interrupts.

"That's what I'm trying to tell you. I just now got back."

"Cody!" Sue admonishes in the same tone she'd scold Meg and me for staying out too late or driving too fast. "That was *very* dangerous."

Joe and Sue are watching me now with worried parental expressions. And though I've missed this, so much, I don't want them looking at me like that. I don't want to be their child. I want to be their avenging angel!

"Don't you see? This guy did it! She wouldn't be dead if it weren't for him."

"He told her to kill herself?" Joe asks. "He helped her do it?"

"Yes! And he tried to help me, too! Look."

I flip open my files to show them the notes, the messages. But as I read what he wrote to Meg and me, what I see is a bunch of other people's quotes. Links to other pages. Everything at arm's distance. He didn't tell Meg to use poison. He didn't buy it for her. He didn't offer me any specific advice beyond cold remedies. He never once outright said to me: *You should kill yourself.*

I told no one anything, I hear him say. He'd almost taunted me when he asked me what specific advice he'd given. I remember wanting him to ask me about my chosen method so badly, but he never did.

But that doesn't change anything. He's still responsible. "It was him," I insist. "Meg wouldn't have killed herself if not for him. *He's* the reason."

Joe and Sue exchange a glance, and then they look at me. And then Sue tells me exactly what Tree told me a few weeks ago, only I didn't hear it. How long have I not been hearing it?

"Meg suffered from depression, Cody," Sue tells me. "She had her first clinical episode in tenth grade. She had another last year."

Tenth grade, the year in bed. "The mono?"

Sue nods, then shakes her head. "It wasn't mono."

"Why?" I ask. "Why didn't she tell me?"

Sue taps her chest. "I've struggled with this for such a long time, not only depression but the stigma of it in a small town, and I didn't want her saddled with that at age fifteen." She pauses. "If I'm honest, what I really didn't want was for her to be saddled with a disease she got from me. So we kept it quiet."

Joe looks down at the table. "We thought we were doing the best thing at the time."

"We got her on antidepressants, of course," Sue says. "And she improved. So much so that she wanted to go off them after she graduated high school. We tried to talk her out of it. I know depression, and it's not something that visits once and disappears."

Sue's moods. The house's smells. *Depression. That's what it's like?*

"We knew things weren't right as soon as she got down there," Joe says. "She was sleeping all the time, missing classes."

"We tried to get her help, to get her on track," Sue says. "We were thinking of making her take a term off. We talked about it—fought about it, more like—all through winter break."

"That's why we couldn't invite you to join us," Joe says.

Winter break. *My family is driving me crazy.*

"We had decided to force the issue if she wouldn't take steps. To bring her home if we needed to, even if it meant losing her scholarship. But then in the New Year, she seemed to get better. Only she wasn't. She was planning her escape."

"I didn't know," I say.

"None of us did," Sue says, starting to cry now.

She was my best friend. If I'd been there, for the winter break, or for the school year, I would've known. About her depression, how bad she was feeling. It might be different. She might be here.

"I didn't know," I repeat, only this time it comes out as a piercing howl. And then my grief bursts like an aneurysm, the blood everywhere.

Joe and Sue watch me hemorrhage, and as they do, it's like they finally understand.

Joe reaches out to grab my hand as Sue says the words I've been yearning to hear: "Oh, baby, no, no, no. Not you. It's not *your* fault."

"I was going to move to Seattle," I say between sobs. "We were going to have this great life together, but . . ." I don't know how to finish. I didn't have the money. I got scared. I got stuck. So she went. And I stayed.

"No!" Joe says. "That's not it. You were the world to her. You were her rock back here."

"But that *is* it. Don't you see?" I cry. "When she went away, I was mad. At me mostly, but I took it out on her. I wasn't there for her. If I had been, she would've come to me instead of him."

"No, Cody," Sue says. "She wouldn't have."

There's a devastating finality in Sue's voice. *She wouldn't have.* Meg would've kept it a secret, as she always did.

Joe clears his throat, his way of holding back tears. "I get why you went after this guy, Cody. Because if this Bradford did it, then someone else murdered her. Someone other than her.

Then maybe we could grieve her with clean, simple broken hearts."

I look up at Joe. Oh, God. I miss her so much. But I am so angry with her. And if I can't forgive her, how can I forgive myself?

"But if Meg weren't sick in the first place, she wouldn't have been in that man's crosshairs," Sue says, looking imploringly at Joe. "He wouldn't have had any power over her. Look at Cody. She went on those boards, she tangled with that man. We just read the messages." Sue turns to me now. "And you're still here."

No! They don't understand. How he burrows into the mind, plays games, hits all your weak spots. He could've brought me down too.

But then I look around. I'm sitting at the dining room table I've eaten so many meals around over the years. Meg is gone. The last few months have been hell. But Sue's right. I'm still here.

The file is open, the pages splayed. Everything I went through to get this—the rabbit hole I went down with Bradford? I'd thought it was a mark of his strength. But maybe it was a test of mine.

I'm still here.

I put the pages back in the folder and slide it over to Joe. "I think I need to stop with this," I say. "You guys do what you think is best."

He takes the file from me. "We'll show it to the police first thing in the morning."

There's a moment of silence. Then Sue says, "And, Cody," but it doesn't scare me like before. "Thank you," she finishes.

Then she and Joe are up, out of their seats, holding me so

tight, and we are all crying. We stay like that for a long time until Sue says, "You're a bag of bones. Please, Cody. Let me feed you."

I lean back in the upholstered chair. I'm not hungry, but I say okay. Sue heads toward the kitchen. Joe stays with me.

"You should've told us," he says, tapping the file.

"You should've told me, too," I say.

He nods.

"And Scottie. You should tell him. He already knows. I mean, he doesn't know the specifics, but he suspects someone helped Meg. He's the one who clued me in."

Joe strokes his chin in wonderment. "Nothing gets past kids. No matter how much you try to protect them." He sighs. "We've started talking to families of other suicide victims. Putting it out in the open. It's the only thing that seems to help." He grasps my hand so tight, the metal of his wedding band leaves an imprint. "I'll talk to Scottie," he promises.

Sue comes back in from the kitchen. She puts down a heaping plate in front of me, some kind of stew.

I take a bite.

"It's homemade," Sue tells me. Then she smiles. It may be the weakest smile I've ever seen, but it's there.

I take another bite. It turns out that I'm hungry after all.

I fall asleep that night at nine o'clock, still in my clothes, and when I wake up at five the next morning, Tricia is asleep at the kitchen table. I touch her lightly on the wrist.

"Did you just get home?" I ask.

She shrugs, all bleary-eyed and fuzzy.

"Were you waiting up for me?"

She shrugs again. "Sort of."

"You can go to bed now. I'm fine."

"You are?" She yawns. "How'd it go with Joe and Sue?"

"Good. I'll tell you about it later, when you're semiconscious."

"Semiconscious," she repeats. But then she gets serious. "But you're okay?"

I nod. "I am okay." I've been saying that for a long time, but now I understand that it's true.

"We'll go to breakfast in a few hours. Diner?" she says.

"Sounds like a plan."

Tricia trudges to bed. I unpack my bag and put all my filthy stuff in a pile. I'm going to have to take a trip to the Laundromat today, or maybe I can ask Mrs. Chandler if I can do a load at her place when I'm there next. People have been pretty generous when I've asked for help. I put on a pot of coffee and go out to the front porch while the coffee brews.

Dawn is breaking. The hills are pink with the first blushes of morning light, though a layer of mist still covers the ground. There's almost no one out on the street at this hour, no cars, save for the paperboy's pickup truck.

In the distance, I hear another car, the tick of its engine familiar, though it's not the Garcias' Explorer, and Tricia's ancient Camry is parked in the driveway. It blurs down the next block, and I do a double take. No. It's not possible.

But then it loops around and comes back down the next block, going slowly, like it's lost. I stand up from the porch and walk toward the street. The car stops suddenly. Then it just sits there in the middle of the street, engine idling, before reversing up the block and turning onto my street, stopping right next to the curb where I'm standing.

He looks like hell. A day's worth of beard on his face and who knows how many months of sleeplessness purpling his eyes. Maybe he got this bad on the trip and I didn't notice because it happened by degrees, but the Ben who steps out of that car is almost unrecognizable from that pretty, snarling boy I saw onstage a few months ago.

"What are you doing here?" I ask him.

"What do you think I'm doing here?" And he sounds so wrecked, it kills me. "Have a good life?"

"*How* are you here? It's, like, a twenty-four-hour drive." I calculate how long it's been since I left him in Vegas yesterday: a little more than seventeen hours.

"It's twenty-four hours if you stop."

That explains it. Driving all night alone can age you a year in a day.

"How did you know where to find me?"

He rubs his eyes with the heel of his hands. "Meg told me where she lived. It's a pretty small town." He pauses. "I've always known where to find you, Cody."

"Oh."

He looks so exhausted. I want to take him into my house, lay him down on my bed, pull up the sheets, and touch his eyelids before they flutter to sleep.

"Why'd you run off like that?"

I don't know what to tell him. I got happy. I got scared. I got overwhelmed. I put my hands over my heart, hoping that explains it.

We stand there for a moment. "I saw Meg's parents," I say at last. "I told them about Bradford. Apparently, the police had already told them about Meg's involvement with the Final Solution people."

Ben's drooping eyes widen in surprise.

"They also told me that Meg was depressed. She'd had a bad episode in tenth grade that I didn't recognize even though I was right there and even though I was her best friend. And she had another after she moved to Tacoma. Before she met you." I look at him. His eyes, like the skin under them, seem bruised. "So, apparently, it's not your fault. Or mine." I try to say this last part flippantly, but my voice hitches.

"I never thought it was your fault," Ben says softly. "But I figured out that it wasn't mine, either."

"But you said that her death was on your conscience."

"It is. It always will be. But I don't think I ranked enough to have caused it. And besides . . ." he trails off.

"What?"

"I keep thinking, if it were my fault, it wouldn't have brought you into my life."

My eyes fill with tears.

"I'm in love with you, Cody. And I know that this is all complicated and confused in a wholly fucked-up way. Meg's death was a tragedy and the worst kind of waste, but I don't want to lose you because of the fucked-up way I found you."

And now I'm weeping. "Fucking Ben McCallister. You make me cry more than almost any person I've ever met," I say. But I step toward him.

"I shed a few tears myself last night." He steps toward me.

"I'll bet. A thousand miles is a long way with no iPod."

"Yeah. The music was what was missing." He takes another step toward me. "I shouldn't have let you go. I should've said something yesterday, but it was intense for me, too, and you scared me, Cody. You scare me a lot."

"That's because you're a city dick," I reply. "City dicks are always scared."

"So I've been told."

"Well, you scare me, too," I say.

I open my arms for him. And as it always is when I let myself be with Ben McCallister, scared is the opposite of what I feel.

We stand there, holding each other in the waking morning. He brushes a lock of hair out of my eyes, kisses me on the temple.

"I'm pretty fragile right now," I warn him. "Everything's sort of coming down all at once."

He nods. For him, too.

"And this could be tricky. 'Complicated and confused in a wholly fucked-up way,' as you put it."

"I know," he says. "We'll just have to ride it out, cowgirl."

"Ride it out," I repeat. I lean my head against him. His whole body heaves.

"Do you want to come inside?" I ask. "Sleep for a while?"

He shakes his head. "Maybe later."

The sun is up, and the early morning mist has burned off. I reach for his hand. "Come on."

"Where are we going?"

"For a walk. I want to show you around. There's a crazy rocket ship at the park where the view goes on forever."

I interlace my fingers with his, and we take off walking. Toward my past. Into my future.

Epilogue

The year after Meg died, we laid her to rest.

We have one more service. There are no candles at this one, no "Amazing Grace," not even a religious officiate. But there will be Meg. Joe and Sue had her cremated, and now her ashes will be scattered in the various places she loved. They struck a deal with the Catholic cemetery to give her a grave there, so long as there wasn't a body.

Today we're going to let some of her go in the hills of Pioneer Park. Her friends from town will be here, along with several of the Seattle people, and, of course, the friends from Cascades.

Alice picked me up in the dorm and drove up with me last night, and Tricia welcomed me home as if I'd been gone two years rather than two months. Since I've been at school, she's texted me practically every day. (Raymond is history, but his texting legacy remains.) But she seems glad I did it, took the leap and applied for (begged for) mid-term admission at the University of Washington. "I won't be eligible for any scholarships, and probably not even many grants. I'll have to take out loans," I told her.

"We'll both take out loans," she said. "There're worse things to have hanging over you than debt."

x x x

Alice fusses over what to wear, regretting now that she didn't bring anything black, no matter how much I reassure her that it's not that kind of service. We've all worn enough black. Even Tricia scored a new dress off a sale rack; it's turquoise.

"What are you wearing?" she asks me.

"Probably jeans."

"You can't wear jeans!"

"Why not?"

Alice has no answer for that. "When is everyone else getting here?"

"Richard got in last night. Ben left early this morning. He's meeting us at the park. He said Harry's catching a ride with him."

"I never see Harry anymore. He has an internship with Microsoft so he's never on campus."

"I know. We talked last week." Harry had called to tell me that amid all the scrutiny, the Final Solution boards shut down. That was the one concrete thing I managed to accomplish from all this. The police had questioned Bradford Smith, subpoenaed his computer, even. I liked to picture his look of indignation, crumbling into fear, when the cops knocked on his door, when they walked away with his files. He must've known that it was me behind this, the sunless planet who turned out to have some light left in her after all.

But there were no charges filed. Bradford had been too careful, hadn't broken any laws. He'd used other people's words, links to anonymous websites. Not enough tracked back to him.

Before the boards got shut down, I occasionally went on them and checked for All_BS, but I didn't find him. He could've changed his username, or changed to a different group, but somehow I don't think so. For now, at least, I believe I've silenced him.

Joe and Sue met with attorneys who said that I might have gathered enough evidence for a civil suit. They're discussing it, but Sue says she doesn't have the stomach for the fight. It won't bring Meg back, and right now, she says, we need not vengeance but forgiveness. I've thought a lot about Jerry's sermon lately. I think Sue may be right. Though Bradford Smith isn't the one any of us needs to forgive.

Tricia comes to my door, all dolled up in the new dress that she'll freeze in and in heels that will get muddy on the trails. She looks pretty. She glances at Alice, she looks at me, she looks at the picture of Meg, the one of her and me as kids at the rodeo that I've left up on my wall. "Let's do this thing," she says.

× × ×

We climb the trails of Pioneer Park into the small clearing in the woods. In the distance, I hear Samson barking. Rounding the corner, I spot Joe and Sue talking to people they've met in their suicide survivor group. The Seattle musicians are tuning their instruments. Scottie is playing Hacky Sack with Richard and Harry. Sharon Devonne and some other people Meg knew from school are talking to Mrs. Banks and her husband. Alexis and her fiancé, Ryan, now back from Afghanistan, each hold a hand of their little girl, Felicity. I'm a little surprised to see Tammy Henthoff here, standing alone. She catches my eye and we nod.

Ben is off to the side, looking down the hill. I follow his gaze to the rocket ship, and at the same time, we turn to look at each other. I don't quite know how so much gets communicated in one look, but it does. *Complicated and confused in a wholly fucked-up way* is a good way to describe it. But maybe that's just how love is.

Ready? he mouths.

I nod. I am ready. Soon the musicians will gather and play the Bishop Allen song about fireflies and forgiveness and I will eulogize my friend and we will scatter a bit of her to the wind. And then we will go down the hill, past the rocket ship, to the cemetery, to her grave, where a marker will say:

Megan Luisa Garcia

I WAS HERE

Author's Note

Many years ago I wrote an article about suicide in which I interviewed friends and family members of young women who had taken their lives. That was when I "met" Suzy Gonzales, though I didn't really meet her because she had already been dead for a few years. Listening to friends and relatives talk about Suzy, I kept forgetting I was reporting a piece on suicide. The portrait they painted was of a bright, creative, charismatic, nonconformist nineteen-year-old—the kind of girl I might have interviewed because she was publishing her debut novel, or releasing her first album, or directing a cool indie movie. On the surface, she didn't strike me—or the people I interviewed—as someone who would kill herself.

Except for this one detail: Like every other young woman I'd profiled in that article, Suzy suffered from depression. When she started to have suicidal thoughts, she reached out for support, going to her university's health center, but ultimately placing her trust with a suicide "support" group, which both applauded her impulse to end her life and gave her advice on how to do it.

I never really stopped thinking about Suzy, about the article I might've written about her—the book she might've written, the band she might've fronted, the movie she might've directed—had she gotten proper treatment for the condition that had put her in such pain that ending her life seemed like the only way to relieve it.

More than a decade later, Suzy was the spark of inspiration for the fictional character of Meg. And from Meg came Cody, *I Was Here*'s heroine. Cody is a young woman decimated by her best friend's death, left raw and grieving, full of sadness and anger and regret and questions that will never be answered. Cody and Meg are fictional, but it doesn't stop me from wondering: if Meg knew what her suicide would do to her best friend, to her family, would she have done it? Or from wondering if in the depths of her depression, Meg could even fathom such a ripple effect.

According to the American Foundation for Suicide Prevention, studies have consistently suggested that the overwhelming majority of people who take their own lives—90 percent or more—had a mental disorder at the time of their deaths. Among people who die by suicide, the most common disorder is depression, though bipolar disorder and substance abuse are also risk factors. Often, these illnesses are undiagnosed or untreated at the time of death.

Note that I'm calling them *illnesses*. The same way that pneumonia is an illness. But with mental disorders, it gets thorny, because "it's in your head." Except it's not. Researchers have shown a link between a risk of suicide and changes in brain chemicals called neurotransmitters, like serotonin. This physiological condition causes a mental (and physical) reaction that can make you feel truly dreadful, and, like pneumonia, if left untreated, in extreme cases, can be fatal.

Thankfully, there are treatments, usually a mix of mood-stabilizing medications and therapy. Refusing treatment for depression or a mood disorder is akin to getting a pneumonia diagnosis and refusing to take antibiotics and go on bed rest. And doing what Meg and Suzy did? That would be like getting a pneumonia diagnosis and then going online for help that advises you to smoke a pack of cigarettes a day while running in the rain. Would you ever follow that kind of advice?

Not every person who suffers from depression will be suicidal. The vast majority won't. And not everyone who has a thought about what it would be like to die is suicidal. When Richard says, "Everyone goes there," I think he is right. I think everyone has days or weeks so lousy, they fantasize about simply not existing. This is different from having suicidal thoughts taking over your head, having the thoughts become plans, the plans become attempts. (For a list of specific warning signs and risk factors, go here: http://www.afsp.org/understanding-suicide/warning-signs-and-risk-factors.)

Like Cody, like Richard, I have gone there. I've had my days. But I've never seriously considered suicide. Which isn't to say my life hasn't been touched by it. Someone very close to me attempted suicide long ago. He got help, and went on to live a long and happy life. If suicide is a sliding door of might-have-beens, in Suzy and Meg's case, I see the ghosts of their lives unlived, and in this other case, I see the flipside: a happy, full life that might never have been.

Life can be hard and beautiful and messy, but hopefully, it will be long. If it is, you will see that it's unpredictable, and that the dark periods come, but they abate—sometimes with a lot of support—and the tunnel widens, allowing the sun back in. If you're in the dark, it might feel like you will always be in there. Fumbling. Alone. But you won't—and you're not. There are people out there to help you find the light. Here's how to find *them*.

If you are in pain and needing help, the first step is to tell someone. Parents, older siblings, aunts, uncles—find any adult whom you trust: a minister, a school counselor, a doctor, a nurse, a family friend. This is a *first* step, not a final one. It's not enough to confide in someone. Once you tell someone, he or she can help you find the professional help and support you need.

If you cannot reach out to a responsible adult, or are unsure what to do next for yourself or a loved one, the National Foundation for Suicide Prevention has a crisis hotline for immediate support: 800-273-TALK.

The American Foundation for Suicide Prevention's website (http://www.afsp.org) has a wealth of information, from risk factors and warning signs to important resources for survivors of suicide, including information on finding a support group.

LGBT youth account for a disproportionate number of suicides. If you are gay, lesbian, trans, bi, or queer, and are thinking of ending your own life, contact the Trevor Project (www.thetrevorproject.org). Their 24/7 hotline number is 866-488-7386.

To learn more about Suzy Gonzales, go to http://www.suzyslaw.com.

Acknowledgments

This is the place where writers tend to thank all the people who helped get a book made. But there's a difference between thanking—a show of gratitude—and acknowledging—a recognition of a contribution. So this time, I'm going to try to stick to the true spirit of the word and acknowledge those responsible for bringing *I Was Here* to life.

I acknowledge Michael Bourret, whose advocacy, support, candor, and friendship makes me brave—and makes me want to be braver.

I acknowledge the entire team at Penguin Young Readers Group. This is our fifth book, and seventh year, together. At this point it feels like a marriage, albeit one with many sister wives (and even a few husbands): Erin Berger, Nancy Brennan, Danielle Calotta, Kristin Gilson, Anna Jarzab, Eileen Kreit, Jen Loja, Elyse Marshall, Janet Pascal, Emily Romero, Leila Sales, Kaitlin Severini, Alex Ulyett, Don Weisberg, and last but certainly not least, my publisher, editor, and friend, the wonderful Ken Wright.

I acknowledge Tamara Glenny, Marjorie Ingall, Stephanie Perkins, and Maggie Stiefvater, for reading drafts at critical times, and offering wise, thoughtful, and expansive feedback.

I acknowledge my Brooklyn Lady Writer™ friends, with whom I work, drink (coffee mostly), plot, and dream: Libba Bray, E. Lockhart, and Robin Wasserman. Tip of the hat to Sandy London, even though he's not a lady, and to Rainbow Rowell, Nova Ren Suma, and Margaret Stohl even though they're not Brooklyn.

I acknowledge my Brooklyn non-writer friends who help me keep it together: Ann Marie, Brian and Mary Clarke, Kathy Kline, Isabel Kyriacou, and Cameron and Jackie Wilson.

I acknowledge Jonathan Steuer for helping me to sound mildly proficient in computer geekery.

I acknowledge Justin Rice, Christian Rudder, and Corin Tucker for first inspiring me with their music, and then again with their generosity.

I acknowledge Lauren Abramo, Deb Shapiro, and Dana Spector for getting my work to a wider audience.

I acknowledge Tori Hill for being a magical elf in the night who gets things done.

I acknowledge the greater YA community—authors, librarians, booksellers. To quote the great Lorde: "We're on each other's team."

I acknowledge Mike and Mary Gonzales for their grace and generosity.

I acknowledge Suzy Gonzales, the spark of this book. I would've preferred to know her, not the character I invented because of her. Suzy's parents tell me that in life she always tried to help people. In death, too, perhaps.

I acknowledge all of the women and men who have struggled with depression or mood disorders or mental illness and suicide, and have found a way to cope, and better yet, to thrive.

I acknowledge all the men and women who have struggled with depression or mood disorders or other mental illness and suicide, who have not found a way to cope, and who have succumbed.

I acknowledge the American Foundation for Suicide Prevention (www.afsp.org) for tipping the scales in favor of the thriving, and for helping us to understand this complicated condition better.

I acknowledge my parents, siblings, in-laws, nieces, and nephew for all their myriad forms of support.

I acknowledge Willa and Denbele for their ferocity and their love.

I acknowledge Nick, for being here, with me.